# Sticks and Stones

*Sadie Gordon Richmond*

*Also by this author:*

*Front Page News*
*Sins of Silence*
*Shadow Lines*
*One in a Million*

*For Penny*

## Camden Town, 17 March

It wasn't until the bell rang for last orders that Justin realised for how long he had been sitting at the bar staring through his pint. Glancing needlessly at the clock above the bar as he reached for the glass in front of him, he debated quickly ordering another versus going straight home to drink the half bottle of absinthe on the mantelpiece. The fear of waking up with gaps in his memory had always deterred him from drinking to get drunk, so the noxious-tasting remnant of the previous year's housewarming party had, thus far, remained untouched. On this occasion, worrying about what he might not remember come morning seemed almost incidental compared with his desperation to obliterate, albeit temporarily, an existing memory.

Realising Floyd would probably be back at the flat by now, he abandoned all thoughts of returning home and tipped his now empty glass in the direction of the barmaid, who moved to pour another. With a sigh, he replaced the glass on the bar, thinking back over the past six hours. He hadn't been able to pinpoint where or how the row with Floyd had started, although he wasn't sure that mattered; the problem, as far as he was concerned, lay with his ordinarily placid friend's monumental overreaction. Floyd, meanwhile, would presumably contend that the problem was Justin's. And it was his word everyone was likely to believe.

Counting out a handful of loose change, Justin toyed with the idea of spending the night at Vinnie's flat in Holloway, but quickly rejected the idea. There had been a time when he had idolised his elder brother, but these days Vinnie was more interested in getting high than anything else, and visiting him would serve only to heighten Justin's anxiety. It would probably also culminate in another argument, as had most of their meetings since Justin had learned Vinnie was taking heroin. He drew a deep breath, closing his eyes and trying to gather his thoughts.

'Justin!' A cheerful voice exclaimed behind him. He jumped violently, and whipped around to find a familiar face grinning at him.

'Jeez, Val, you almost gave me a heart attack!'

'Sorry,' Valentine offered, perching on the stool beside Justin's and leaning purposefully over the bar. 'How are you doing? I've not seen you in eons! I – five lagers please –' he gave the barmaid a winning smile before returning his attention to Justin. 'What've you been up to?'

'Studio.'

'Ah,' Valentine raised his eyebrows knowingly. 'How's the album coming along?'

'Not great. Floyd and I keep falling out.'

Valentine's eyebrows rose again, this time in surprise. 'I didn't think Floyd ever fell out with anyone. What's the problem?'

'I don't know,' Justin shook his head slightly. 'He's been really weird recently. I don't know what's up with him. We're barely even talking at the moment.'

'And how about you? Are you all right?'

'Why does everybody *always* assume it must be me that has the problem?' Justin asked, miserably. 'I am so *sick* of being treated like a fucking headcase!'

Valentine raised his hands in mock surrender. 'Sorry – sorry, I didn't mean –'

'I know what you meant.'

Valentine sighed. 'Come on, mate, cheer up. Can I get you another beer before the bar shuts?'

Justin hesitated, then nodded, watching the barmaid lining the pints up on the bar in front of them. Valentine conveyed his wish to add another to the order with a hand gesture before pulling his wallet from his pocket.

'Who are you here with, then?' Justin asked, as Valentine drew out a handful of cards and shuffled through them.

'Your brother for one. Plus Matt, Quary and A.J.'

'Vinnie's here?'

'Yeah.'

Justin didn't reply, immediately regretting his decision to stay for another drink.

'What's up? I thought you'd be pleased to see him. He said he's not seen you in weeks.'

'Oh yeah, It's great being reminded my brother's a smackhead,' Justin snapped, sarcastically.

'He's still your brother,' Valentine observed, passing a credit card across the bar.

'And I don't want to watch him kill himself!'

'Now you know how he feels.'

Justin stared at Valentine. 'That is *not* fair!'

'I'm sorry, I know it's not,' Valentine reached for one of the pints in front of them. 'I'm sorry, Justin, that was out of order.'

'I just want him to stop.'

'Yeah, I know, but you can't make that decision for him.'

Justin didn't immediately respond. 'I don't know where to turn anymore,' he admitted, eventually. 'Vinnie only cares about getting high, I barely even see Suki with the hours she and I are working, Floyd seems to be on another fucking planet –' he trailed off, his voice wavering. 'I'm actually dreading going home.'

Valentine regarded him thoughtfully for a moment before saying, 'Look, why don't you come and have a drink with us, and then if you still don't want to go home you can come back with Quary and me. We've a fridge full of beer, we can pick up some chips or pizza on the way back, and you're welcome to crash in the back room. How's that sound?'

Justin managed a weak smile. 'Ok. Thanks.'

'No problem.'

He moved to stand. 'I'll be with you in two minutes.'

'We'll be in the corner by the fruit machine.'

Justin nodded before making his way around the crowd of drinkers at the bar and heading through the door that led to the men's toilets. He descended the stairs and pushed open the door at the bottom. The two men inside jumped apart guiltily, then relaxed upon seeing him, and, a split second later, Justin understood the reason for their reaction. A.J. had a bundle of crumpled bank notes in his hand and Vinnie was in the process of stuffing a small packet of beige powder into his pocket. Justin looked accusingly at his brother, who averted his gaze, dropping his hand to his side. Justin turned his eyes on A.J.

'You fucking lowlife!' He breathed. The reality of the situation sinking in, he launched himself at A.J., slamming his fist into the other man's jaw. A.J. staggered backwards and Justin delivered another punch before Vinnie grabbed hold of him and pulled him away.

'You're despicable!' Justin yelled, struggling as Vinnie dragged him towards the door. 'What sort of lowlife *scum* sells smack to their *mates*?'

'Jesus, Justin, do you want the whole *pub* to know?' Vinnie hissed, viciously twisting Justin's right arm behind his back until he cried out in pain.

'Go back to the adventure playground, Justin,' A.J. spat, advancing towards them. 'Nobody gives a shit what you think! You're a fucked-up waste of space, and the only reason anyone tolerates you is because you're Vinnie's brother!'

'And you're a social parasite!' Justin threw back. 'Someone needs to serve you up a big fucking share of the misery you're feeding off!'

'Yeah?' A.J. responded, derisively. 'Is that a threat? Are you going to take me on?' He plucked Justin's glasses from his face, dropped them to the floor and crushed each lens in turn with his heel. 'You can't even turn a fucking *cooker* on! Don't try to play games you don't understand!' Seizing hold of Justin's arm, he wrenched him free of Vinnie's grip. Justin had no chance to get his balance, and, with nothing to hold onto, no way to stop himself crashing to the floor. His head struck the edge of the sink on the way down, and as the pain filtered through the immediate shock of impact, A.J. kicked him in the stomach. Justin gasped, beginning to cough, and before he even had a chance to move A.J. kicked him again.

'Stop it!' Vinnie exclaimed, leaping to his brother's defence. 'Someone's going to come down here in a minute, and then we're all going to be in deep shit!'

This gave A.J. pause, and he stepped backwards. Bending down, he grabbed hold of Justin's long hair, forcing him to meet his eyes. 'You fuck with me, I will *end* you. Understand?'

'Yes,' Justin managed, wishing his voice didn't sound so strained.

'What was that?'

'Yes!'

'Now I don't want to see you for a *very long time*, so once you've finished snivelling, you can fuck off home! It's past your bedtime anyway!' A.J. released his hold on Justin's hair, slamming his head into the floor as he did so, then turned and left the room, flinging the door shut behind himself. Justin closed his eyes, his head pounding.

'Justin, come on,' Vinnie bent to help him up.

'Fuck you!' Justin yelled, kicking out in protest.

'Justin –'

'Get the fuck out! I *hate* you for what you're doing! You don't care about me! All you care about is your next fucking hit!'

Vinnie hesitated, then the door swung open. Valentine appeared in the doorway, stopping short when he saw Justin sprawled on the floor.

'What the hell is going on?' He demanded, looking accusingly at Vinnie.

Vinnie held out his hands. 'How the fuck would I know? It's not my fault my brother's a nutjob, is it?' He pushed past Valentine and started back up the stairs. Valentine crouched beside Justin.

'What happened, mate?' He asked, taking Justin's arm to help him as he struggled to sit up.

'Why's he doing this to me?' Justin managed, desperately.

'I really don't think it has anything to do with you,' Valentine replied, patiently. 'You can't –'

'Don't look at me like that!'

'Like what?'

'Like all this is in my head!'

A couple of seconds passed before Valentine responded. 'Why don't we get off home?' He suggested, eventually, straightening up and reaching to pull Justin to his feet. As Justin stood up, a wave of dizziness hit him and he staggered sideways, falling against the tiled wall. Valentine grasped hold of him to keep him upright.

'Are you all right?'

'Too many beers,' Justin lied.

'Did you have a fight with Vinnie?'

He nodded.

'Oh mate –' Valentine rested a hand on his shoulder. 'Look, it's over now. Let's get out of here. We'll leave the others and get a cab back to mine. All right?'

Justin nodded again, drawing a careful deep breath. Turning to follow Valentine back up the stairs, he raked a hand through his hair, trying to make sense of the jumbled thoughts running around his head. Amid the turmoil, he felt sure of one thing: Valentine was wrong. This was far from over.

## Soho, 19 May

Saturday night at Garlic and Shots reminded Suki of a toy she had owned as a child: a puzzle featuring a picture of a cartoon cat, superimposed on the tiles of a grid. These could be moved about, one at a time, with each slotting into the space left by that moved before it. With the tiles disarranged, the aim of the game had been to return them to their rightful places and so reconstruct the picture. Retrospectively, Suki wondered whether the cat might actually have been a tiger, but it had been more than a decade since she had last seen the puzzle, and, in the hazy memory that remained, the creature's face was frustratingly elusive.

Busy nights in the basement bar left Suki feeling like a human tile in a living version of the puzzle. The place was scarcely bigger than the front room of her mother's suburban semi, and it seemed as if every time a person moved everybody else was displaced in order to compensate. Suki found it infuriating. She liked Garlic's. The atmosphere was good, the bar served doubles at discount and she was almost guaranteed to know *somebody* there – but she hated the crush. And, although summer was still some weeks away, the temperature and humidity below stairs were already almost unbearable.

Several minutes of having her toes trampled, ribs elbowed and drink spilled passed with no sign of Sally, and Suki supposed she might have decamped to the terrace in search of something approaching fresh air. Having fought her way up the stairs and down the narrow corridor that led to the back door, however, she might as well have stepped out of a steam room and into a sauna. The air outside felt less damp, but the heat was even more intense, thanks to the two gas-powered braziers that loomed over the metal tables like miniature beacons. Wondering what had possessed anybody to switch them on, Suki cast her eyes quickly over the crowd before turning back the way she had come. Downing what remained of her drink, she threaded her way between the shabby tables and chairs of what the management rather optimistically called a *restaurant*, and stepped out onto Frith Street.

Sally had presumably taken her usual route via the Crobar, and not made it any further. In days gone by, Suki would have done the same, but since Fin had discovered it was one of her regular haunts he had taken to routinely turning up there after work. Quite aside from the embarrassing fact he was always dressed wholly inappropriately for the rock bar – how he'd ever found employment in a goth venue was a mystery to her – the last thing she needed on a Saturday night was a lonely ex-boyfriend trailing around after her like a stray puppy. Suki turned left into Bateman Street. She would see Sally at the club.

Besides its obvious number and variety of bars and clubs, one of the best things about London's West End, Suki thought as she walked up Dean Street, was all the pedestrian alleyways running between and behind the patchwork of pre- and post-war buildings that only a fraction of the people walking the capital's streets seemed to know about. The worst thing was knowing she shouldn't walk down them alone at night, but doing so anyway. A whistle and an unoriginal, 'Great legs' from a scruffily dressed young man in a flat cap changed her mind. The *worst* thing about Soho was the losers you had to deal with on your way from *a* to *b*.

What was it that made men think it was acceptable to hit on girls in the street? And why did so many people believe the girls it happened to must have been *asking for it* by walking around in miniskirts and low-cut tops? If you were pretty you still got harassed wearing trousers and a polo neck. Even as she thought this, a rugby-type in a dinner suit who was loitering by the NatWest cash point on the other side of the road called out, 'Hey, what are you doing all alone? You're lovely! Can I come with you?'

Suki raised her eyes heavenwards, turning into St Anne's Court. She knew she should stick to the roads, and she knew Justin would be dismayed if he learned she was still taking shortcuts, but really, who was going to tell him?

As she passed the closed but still dimly lit restaurants, she felt her heart jump. Just ahead of her were three people, two of whom were involved in some sort of altercation, and none of whom looked like individuals she wanted to walk past. Something about the way the man and woman to one side of the passageway were struggling and shouting gave her the impression the argument was either about drugs or drug-induced – maybe even both – and she hesitated, her mind racing through her options. The third member of the group, a tall, dark-haired man in a long black coat, caught her eye and gave her a strange half-smile. 'You got a light, sweetheart?'

Suki shook her head, feeling panicked. She sensed her chances of travelling the final few yards to Wardour Street safely were small, but she was too far from Dean Street to turn back. It seemed she had little choice but to look confident, keep walking, and pray to the God she'd never believed in.

The hand that landed on her shoulder ought to have made her scream, but all she managed was a gasp. She felt faint, and, out of options, stumbled forwards towards the fighting couple and their threatening companion. Unexpectedly, he moved aside as she neared, and moments later, feeling dizzy and disorientated, Suki emerged onto Wardour Street.

'You all right hun?' A voice asked as the hand on her shoulder gently turned her around.

Suki nodded automatically, a second or two passing before she realised she recognised the face looking down at her. 'Yes. Thanks.'

'What the hell were you thinking walking through there alone?'

'I dunno – I didn't – I –' she trailed off with a weak shrug.

'Ok, come on, let's get you a drink. Where are you headed?'

'St Moritz. Justin's DJing there tonight.'

Alec's eyebrows rose. 'He kept that one quiet.'

'It was a last-minute thing – he's filling in as a favour to Reed.'

'Ah.'

'Please don't tell him – about –' Suki stopped. 'He'd go spare, and he has enough to worry about right now.'

'Just promise me you won't do that again.'

'Never.'

'Ok,' Alec nodded, turning to walk in the direction of the St Moritz club. 'Are you guys going to the Cheap Appeal gig tomorrow?'

'Yes. We're thinking of –' Suki broke off, suddenly realising aloud, 'You're not at Polaroid.'

'Well spotted.'

There are some questions you really *really* don't want to ask, but can't get away with *not* asking. This was one such question.

'How come?'

Suki held her breath waiting for the answer. For Justin, DJ work was a novelty, but for Alec it was a career. Polaroid was an alternative rock night that he ran on Saturday nights at a club in Camden, and, although he worked with other people at other venues during the week, Polaroid was his baby. He was always very reluctant to hire an extra DJ and take the night off, and, since nothing special appeared to be happening that night, Suki suspected there was another reason for his presence in Soho.

'Do you and Justin walk around Camden with your eyes shut?' Alec exclaimed. 'The fucking venue burned down on Wednesday night! It was on the news and everything!'

'Burned down?' Suki echoed. 'God. Did anyone get hurt?'

'No, no,' Alec shook his head. 'It was after closing. Only the manager and his girlfriend were still in there, and they were in the office, so they climbed out the window.'

'That was lucky. If the place had been full it would've been chaos.'

'Luck had nothing to do with it. The fire wasn't an accident.'

'Are you sure?'

'The police seem to be,' Alec replied, raising his eyebrows for emphasis. 'So I'm gonna have to find a new venue. If you hear of anything, let me know.'

Suki nodded, feeling shaken. She wondered how Justin would take the news. Even now, after a house move and months of reassurance, there were still days when he asked whether she could smell gas twenty times an hour, and she suspected paranoid fears about fire would be next on the list. One little word was almost guaranteed to unsettle him for weeks. *Arson*.

Why any band should want to play on a Sunday night, Meredith had no idea. Venues wanting to pack in the punters seven days a week she could understand, but she couldn't see much in it for the musicians. For starters, they were more than likely feeling worse for wear after the preceding Saturday night. On top of that, so were a good many of their fans, which, combined with the fact the majority were facing the unappealing prospect of returning to work the following morning, was bound to dampen the atmosphere. All in all, it generally made for a subdued and unmemorable occasion, and at some point Meredith almost invariably had the feeling she ought to be at home watching a TV drama and tucking into a frozen pizza.

But she wasn't going to miss a Cheap Appeal gig, and neither, it seemed, was anybody else. Like many of the pubs and clubs in and around Camden, the Barfly doubled as a live venue, and, despite the fact it was a Sunday, had been heaving by nine o'clock. Currently, Meredith, her boyfriend and two of her friends were squeezed around a tiny table just inside the door, waiting for the sound of drums from upstairs to alert them to the band's arrival on stage.

'What is it about this time of year?' Collette asked, gesturing towards the crowd. 'The minute the sun comes out, fat people seem to think it's suddenly ok to wear hideously unflattering clothes.'

Following her gaze, Meredith's eyes alighted on an obese twenty-something woman clad in a skimpy pink camisole, with straps narrower than those of her bra, and a denim miniskirt. Her ample stomach overhung the skirt's waistband, and the uneven contours of her dimpled thighs were plainly visible.

'People that size should have to buy two tickets,' Collette added nastily, reaching for her drink.

'You bitch!' Laura exclaimed, laughingly.

'Come on, this venue's busy enough as it is! It's bad enough we have to inhale two hundred other people's sweat without running the risk of being pressed up against the clammy flab of a beached whale!' Collette shuddered theatrically. 'Who the hell makes miniskirts that size anyway?'

'Not Nightshade, that's for sure,' Laura replied. 'I swear they think all goths are anorexic. I was in there earlier, and everything they sell seems to come in different variations of small!'

'Yeah, it's weird,' Collette agreed, returning her glass to the table. 'The old shop in Soho was smaller, but the clothes were bigger. What's with that?'

'Goth went and got trendy, didn't it?' Neil sneered, draining his pint glass. As if *he'd* been there when it started or something. Silently, Meredith cursed him. Why did he always have to behave like such a *loser* in front of her friends?

'You see, that's the thing I've never got about you lot,' Collette responded, with thinly veiled contempt. 'I've never seen a group of people trying so hard to look different and all looking so completely the fucking same!'

'Maybe that's why they only make the clothes in one size!' Laura giggled.

'If only. Last time I had the misfortune to end up at a goth night there was a woman there the size of a house in a corset so tight her breasts sloped upwards! It was positively frightening! I'm sorry, but people shouldn't be allowed to wear whatever they feel comfortable in if it makes the rest of us *uncomfortable*!'

Meredith felt more than a little uncomfortable herself, and hoped the venue's dim lighting was sufficient to hide the colour rising in her cheeks. Collete's remarks had transported her back six years to a world of grey kilts, white blouses, hockey on Tuesday afternoons and sneaky lunch-time trips to the high street for magazines and Diet Coke. To melting pens in Bunsen burners, passing notes and scrawling graffiti on flip-top desks. And to a windowless cloakroom and words she wanted, more than anything, to forget.

*I'd love to see you in a cocktail dress. If you met a blind man you might even pull. Blow jobs are only three calories, you know. And at least you wouldn't have the dilemma of spit or swallow – it'd be a natural reflex.*

Casting her eyes around the room in an attempt to divert her thoughts from the vicious words of a teenage bully, the sight of an old friend did nothing to lift her spirits. Suki was standing near the bar with Justin's arm wrapped around her waist, his thumb hooked loosely into the waistband of her black miniskirt. Even in the simple black halterneck she had teamed with it she looked stunning. But then, she always had done. She had been blessed with a size ten figure and yet no need for a padded bra, vivid turquoise eyes and long, straight strawberry blonde hair that didn't go frizzy in the rain. And as if that wasn't enough, she had the soft prettiness and grace that meant that even in a baggy t-shirt and with her hair scraped back into a ponytail she could turn heads.

Meredith had always envied her, but in the past her friend's beauty had afforded them both opportunities Meredith would never otherwise have had the chance to enjoy. Guest list places, backstage parties, free merchandise and free drinks. There had been gigs at the Borderline, the Garage, the Underworld and the Forum. Gigs in Brighton, Reading and Kingston that left them running to catch the last train home. Nights at the Dublin Castle, watching the people who were there to be seen, not to see the band. Quiet evenings sitting in the Dev on the off-chance guys like Matt and Vinnie might drop in. Guys who slept with Meredith because she was there and she was willing, and who were intrigued by Suki because she didn't spread her legs like the groupies they'd grown so accustomed to.

As if sensing her gaze, Suki turned. Her eyes met with Meredith's, but she didn't smile. She wouldn't be seen with Meredith now: her boyfriend was an underground star, and the same people she and Meredith had once watched from afar were now her friends. They didn't make excuses to cut her conversations short, nor give her the cursory polite smile that Meredith had come to know so well. Suki turned away again as Justin leaned to whisper something in her ear. She laughed and nodded, and Meredith wondered bitterly whether they were laughing at her. Ten years of friendship sold out in the pursuit of the *beautiful people*.

Or at least, so it had once seemed to Meredith. Lately, she had increasingly found herself questioning whether it really had been Suki's relationship with Justin that had shattered the friendship, or whether his presence had simply put untenable pressure on hairline cracks that had long existed just beneath the surface of her consciousness. Seeing Suki so unencumbered by the millstone that ought to have been theirs to share threw Meredith's sorrow into sharper relief. Suki didn't deserve happiness any more than she did. And, much as Meredith wanted to believe karma would one day catch up with her former friend, deep down she knew life didn't boil down to such simple cause and effect.

At that moment, Suki raised a hand to tuck her hair behind her ear, and Meredith caught her breath. Suki was wearing an engagement ring.

## Two

Detective Sergeant Daniel Freeman reached for the manual sandwiched between two box files, jumping in response to the loud buzz that sounded as his mobile phone vibrated against the desk's surface. Holding up his left hand to indicate that he wouldn't be a moment, he reached for it and checked the screen, only to feel the same disappointment that every other message had brought in the past twenty-five minutes. Actually, to be precise, it had been twenty-seven minutes since he'd hit send. Twenty-seven minutes he'd been waiting for her reply.

'Anything interesting?' CID's newest recruit enquired, sounding less than interested himself.

'No.' Daniel forced a smile. 'Sorry, where were we?'

Noel all but rolled his eyes. 'You were about to look something up, but you hadn't quite gotten round to telling me what.'

'Right. Yes.' Daniel nodded, reaching once again for the manual. Setting it on his knees, he flicked through the table of contents, desperately trying to focus his mind on the task in hand. He had almost succeeded when Noel's voice interrupted him.

'Mmm,' he grunted, appreciatively, his eyes fixed at a point above Daniel's computer monitor. 'Getting out of bed in the morning just got a whole lot easier.'

Daniel turned his head in the direction of his colleague's gaze. Beyond the line of dividers separating the open-plan office from the corridor that bypassed it, his colleague Rebecca Palmer was engaged in a conversation with Leighton Campbell, a forensic pathologist with whom they regularly worked. She was laughing at whatever he was saying, and Daniel felt jealousy bite.

Daniel had considered Rebecca a friend as well as a colleague long before Leighton's arrival at the pathology unit, and had felt flattered that she seemed to consider him something of a confidante. When his relationship with his long-term girlfriend, Jessica, had unravelled, she had been a willing listener, and, although she was romantically involved elsewhere, he had quickly come to realise he would have liked to take their relationship further. As Rebecca's friendship with Leighton had grown, however, Daniel had had her undivided attention less and less often.

An incorrigible flirt, Leighton had a way of carrying off cheeky remarks without causing offence, and a curious allure that seemed to draw women to automatically reciprocate. Even as Daniel thought this, Rebecca reached up to tuck a portion of her hazelnut bob behind her ear, resting her other hand on Leighton's upper arm. Leighton said something else, and Rebecca laughed again, turning to go.

'Ah,' Daniel nodded, looking back to Noel. 'Totally out of your league, I'm afraid.'

'Don't underestimate me. What's her name?'

'DS Palmer, to you,' Daniel responded, tossing a file into Noel's lap.

'And how did you keep her a secret from me last week?'

'She's been working over in Guilford.'

'Really?' Noel replied, distractedly, his focus still on Rebecca. Moments later, she entered the office and headed towards them, her soft blue angora jumper clinging to her petite hourglass figure, the colour almost a match for her eyes. Her elfin features were still caught up in the smile resulting from the exchange with Leighton, and, realising that watching her for a second longer might constitute staring, Daniel smiled himself and greeted her with, 'Becks, how was Hampshire?'

'Surrey, Dan,' Rebecca corrected, reaching the desk next to his and looking around herself in puzzlement.

'Sorry, we borrowed your chair,' Daniel apologised, indicating the one Noel was occupying. His colleague immediately began to rise, but Rebecca shook her head and waved him back down.

'It's ok, I'm not staying,' she said, turning her eyes questioningly on Daniel, no doubt waiting for him to introduce their new colleague.

'Sorry. This is DC Noel Osborne, he joined us last week,' he glanced at his companion, adding, 'This is DS Rebecca Palmer.'

'Nice to meet you,' Noel smiled, standing and holding out a hand.

Rebecca shook it. 'How are you settling in?'

'The place is growing on me,' he answered, raising his eyebrows pertinently and tipping his head to one side.

'Really?' Rebecca responded, coolly.

'Are you in town this week?' Daniel enquired.

'So it would seem.'

'I sent you a message before. I thought maybe if you weren't busy we could fit a drink in sometime.'

Rebecca nodded, glancing at her watch. 'Sure. I can't stick around right now – I told Forrester I'd meet him at the car in five, and that was at least ten minutes ago. I just came to grab my things.' She turned to retrieve her mobile phone and purse from beneath a report that lay open on her desk, tossed them into her handbag and pulled her jacket from its precarious position on a stack of filing trays.

'Maybe see you later, then.'

'Unless the world comes to an abrupt end,' Rebecca smiled, turning and heading back towards the corridor.

'I get it,' Noel observed in a lazy drawl, moments after Rebecca had disappeared in the direction of the lifts. '*You* want her, don't you?'

Daniel frowned. 'She's a good friend, that's all.'

'Oh really?'

'Besides, she's engaged.'

'That's not irreversible.'

'Becky is very careful to keep her work life and personal life separate.'

'So was my last girlfriend,' Noel grinned.

Daniel shook his head slightly in disbelief. 'You haven't a hope, mate,' he remarked, reaching for his coffee. 'Have you heard of Astatine?'

'The band?'

'No, the chemical element,' Daniel returned, sarcastically. 'What d'you *think*?'

'I rarely go a day without hearing about them. My kid sister has a crush on their alcoholic fuck-up of a lead singer.'

'Ah. Well Becky's going to marry him.'

'You are kidding me?' Noel exclaimed. 'What's a girl like that doing with such a twat?'

Despite having similar sentiments, Daniel took some delight in the expression on Noel's face, and smiled to himself as he returned his attention to the file in his lap. At least now he knew why she hadn't replied to his message.

## Three

Sally was slouching on her bed in front of MTV with her laptop resting across her thighs, trawling through a vast selection of band photographs and wishing she'd made more of an effort to edit them before now. It was incredible how many pictures you had to take to get just one or two decent shots of a live performance, and she felt thankful that in the digital age she didn't have the additional cost of wasted films to contend with. Her finances were tight enough as it was, and she was beginning to despair of ever being able to afford the Mac computer with Retina display she regularly flirted with in the Apple Store. On several occasions Suki had asked why she didn't just hit her brother up for the cash – he was a generous guy, he could easily afford it. His generosity was precisely what stopped her. Sally knew he'd agree to a loan in a heartbeat. She also knew he'd never accept any repayment.

The telephone made her jump, and she reached to answer it, glad to have a temporary distraction. 'Ha-lo?'

'Hey Sal.'

'Suks. What's up?' Sally rearranged herself so that she was sitting cross-legged and wondered why she had bothered to ask. There was one reason, and one reason only, that her flat mate ever called her at home.

'Nothing much. What you up to?'

Sally felt exasperated. Did Suki really think a couple of minutes' small talk was all it took to disguise the fact she'd called to dissect her latest row with her boyfriend?

'I'm putting a new portfolio together.'

'For your interview?'

'Uh-huh.'

'When is it again?'

'Tomorrow.'

'That came round quick.'

'Uh-huh,' Sally clicked open one of the photographs she had relegated to the *maybe* folder and regarded it critically. She supposed she might as well get it over with. 'So. What are you doing?'

'Waiting for Just to come back.'

'What happened?'

'Oh I dunno – he had another fight with Floyd before I got here and he's been going on about it all evening,' Suki sighed. 'He keeps saying over and over that there's something wrong with Floyd and asking me what he should do about it.' She paused. 'I know it's not his fault, but how can anyone fail so completely to learn from experience? How many times does he have to blame everything on the people around him before he realises *he* is the one with the problem?'

'You know Justin and logic don't get on,' Sally responded, coolly. 'He has a mental illness, Suks. If he had a broken leg you wouldn't expect him to walk, would you?'

'I know, but this has happened, like, a *million* times before, and it's as if he has absolutely no memory of it! You try to explain how irrational what he's saying is and he loses it!'

Sally felt inclined to point out how many times she and Suki had had *this* same conversation. What bugged her more than anything was that Suki appeared to have absolutely no qualms over the fact she was bitching about Justin to someone who was, first and foremost, *his* friend.

Sally and Justin had grown up on the same dismal council estate in Harlesden. Hung around the now condemned concrete playground with the rusty climbing frame and faded hopscotch squares until their parents deemed them old enough to be let out of sight alone. Shared their first cigarette, and later their first beer – both stolen from her elder brother – behind the derelict bus station opposite the school. He had been her first boyfriend. She had witnessed his initial slow, terrifying descent into psychosis. His mother's increasing anxiety as doctors repeatedly dismissed his behaviour as *he's a teenager* or *he's probably taking drugs*. And, when they finally took it seriously, his incarceration in a psychiatric hospital. By the time he was released, she had lost her virginity to his best friend.

'It's not that he doesn't remember,' she replied, as patiently as she could. 'It's just that his conviction that what he believes is happening is so strong it overrides the memory.'

There was a pause. 'I know,' Suki admitted, at length. 'I know, and I know it's not his fault, but it's so frustrating! And I am so *sick* of hearing the words *Floyd never shouts at me*! Like Floyd is some sort of saint!'

'Have you tried talking to Floyd about this?'

'I've not seen much of him recently. I don't know whether he's trying to avoid more arguments with Justin, or whether he's avoiding *me*.'

Sally frowned, wondering whether Suki was exaggerating. Floyd had always been so easygoing that she couldn't imagine him actively avoiding anybody. Then again, she'd never seen him fall out with Justin, either.

'Have they really been arguing?'

'How the hell should I know?' Suki demanded, impatiently.

'Maybe you should have a word with Floyd, he might be able to shed some light on the situation.'

'What's the point? If they have fallen out there's nothing I can do about it, and if they haven't Justin's never going to take my word for it over the voices in his head!'

Sally felt anger prick. 'How can you be so flippant? Don't you think –'

'Oh – that's the door,' Suki interrupted. 'It's probably Justin. Sometimes I think the only reason Floyd hasn't tied his keys around his neck is because he might give in to the urge to strangle him with them!' There was a scuffling sound before Suki added, 'I'll see you tomorrow.'

'Suki, be gentle with him.'

'Yeah, I will,' Suki responded, carelessly, almost as she hung up. The action summed up Suki's attitude to friendship. Friends always came second to her boyfriend, and, when her relationship was going well, were lucky to get a look in. Whenever there was a problem, on the other hand – and with Justin there often was – Suki expected people to drop everything to be there for her. And Sally was close enough to get truly taken for granted.

With a sigh, she returned her attention to the selection of photographs on the screen. They served only to reaffirm her feelings. Suki hadn't even bothered to wish her luck with the interview.

'Howdy stranger!' A cheerful voice called as Alec crossed Plender Street en route home at the end of a long night in the Underworld. 'Whaddaya doin' bunkin' off?'

Alec turned to see Floyd heading in his direction, a hand raised in greeting.

'Hey,' he responded with a smile, turning back towards the pavement. 'Where've you been?'

'Oh, all over,' Floyd replied, ebulliently, waving his arms in emphasis and staggering sideways as he did so. 'I was just on my way to see you,' he jabbed a finger in Alec's direction, 'But clearly you're not there.'

'Not where?' Alec queried, as Floyd came to halt in front of him, swaying slightly.

'The club,' Floyd responded, as if he couldn't quite believe Alec needed telling.

'Mate, it's half two.'

'Is it?' Floyd looked at his wrist – a futile activity, given that he wasn't wearing a watch – then back to Alec. 'Are you sure?'

'Quite sure.'

Floyd's brow contracted. 'But I only jus' got off the tube.' He jerked his thumb in the direction of Camden Town station. The gesture threw him off balance, and Alec grabbed hold of his arm before he could fall into the road.

'Ok, mate, let's get you home, eh?'

'No, I wanna –'

'Yes,' Alec interrupted, firmly, walking Floyd towards the pedestrian crossing outside Poundland.

'When did you get so fuckin' borin'?'

'Must've been February,' Alec humoured him. Given the hour, the traffic lights proved redundant, and Alec guided his friend across the high street and into the narrow confines of Miller Street.

'What happened in Feb'ry?'

'D'you remember that little party I had in the upstairs bar at the Hawley?'

There was a pause before Floyd repeated the word *party*, more to himself than to Alec, sounding perplexed.

'My thirtieth, you div,' Alec reminded him, amicably.

'Oh,' Floyd nodded, before tripping over his own feet.

'How many have you *had* tonight?'

'Coupla pints.'

'Couple of gallons, more like.'

'I am *not* drunk,' Floyd protested, rather incoherently.

''Course not,' Alec replied, disbelievingly.

'I'm *not.*'

'Who've you been out with?'

'Elliot.'

'No wonder you're in such a fucking state.'

'We only hadda couple,' Floyd maintained.

'Elliot never stops at just a couple. Becks is going to kill him if he comes home in this kind of shape.'

'Stop lect'ring me!'

Alec sighed. 'I'm not lecturing you, Floyd. We've all been there.'

'I am not fucking drunk!' Floyd returned, belligerently.

'Ok, whatever.'

'You know fuck all!'

Alec held his tongue, checking for traffic before leading Floyd across Arlington Road and wishing he'd left work just a few minutes earlier. He could have been at home with a DVD and a bowl of instant noodles by now.

Rosa had waited up. Valentine had made her promise not to, but it wasn't as if she would have been able to sleep. It was all she could do to stop herself incessantly calling his mobile. She had gone through the motions as if it were any other night, changed into a nightie and switched out the light. And then she had sat in the dark, watching the luminous characters of the digital alarm clock blinking away the seconds. Each minute waiting for the sound of his key in the lock felt longer than the last. Each minute she felt a little bit colder. The birds had started to sing and still she was waiting. She hadn't banked on his taking so long. What if, what if, what if. *Is everything all right?*

It was a stupid question. Nothing was *all right.* She had long since passed the point of being able to explain things away, to dismiss warning signs as misunderstandings or fears as overreactions. Creeping suspicion had given way to harsh reality, and with it the torment of a decision that felt like the ultimate betrayal. It hung unspoken between them, as if each was relying on the other to act, but Rosa knew the ball was in her court. Valentine would carry on in silence, as he always did, until either circumstance forced her hand or anger got the better of him. He seemed to have no other way to express himself.

His whole world had been shattered twice before he even reached his teens, but Rosa hadn't once seen him cry, nor heard him use any of his experiences as an excuse. He'd never spoken about the day, age nine, he found his father dead of a drug overdose, or the fire that claimed the lives of his mother and sister eighteen months later. Rosa had tried many times to coax him into opening up, but to no avail. Perhaps, to him, doing so would have conflicted with the promise to be brave that his grandfather had demanded of him on the morning of his father's funeral. Or maybe he didn't know how or where to start without being overwhelmed by feelings he had no idea how to cope with.

Time and time again, Rosa had put off the inevitable. Every time she promised herself would be the last. Every time she broke that promise. Every *next* time she feared she'd left it too late. And what then?

They would both have to live with the consequences.

## Four

'Looks like Justin's still up,' Alec remarked, as he and Floyd approached the flat in Mornington Terrace.

'What time is it?' Floyd asked, grasping hold of the railings that marked the boundary between the street and the front courtyard.

'Quarter to three,' Alec replied, pausing at the foot of the steps that led up to the front door. 'Have you got your keys?'

Floyd dug into his pocket and pulled them out before instantly dropping them. Alec released him, bent to retrieve the keys, then climbed the steps and unlocked the door. Floyd stumbled up the steps behind him, and, once through the doorway, half-crawled up the stairs immediately inside. Alec followed and unlocked the door at the top of the staircase, shepherding Floyd into the flat ahead of him.

'Ok, mate, let's get you into bed,' Alec suggested, closing the front door behind himself and guiding his friend through the doorway a few feet down the corridor. Floyd fell onto the nearside of the bed and almost rolled straight off it, forcing Alec to jump forwards to catch him. Having moved him into a more secure position and removed his boots, Alec made for the living room. As he neared, he could hear what sounded like sobbing, but he arrived in the doorway before he had consciously taken this on board.

'Jesus Christ –' he breathed, as he absorbed the scene that met him. Justin was on his knees on the floor, Suki in his arms. Her head had fallen back, her eyes were glazed and her jaw hung at an impossible angle. Her face was a mess of congealed blood, and her strawberry blonde hair was dark and matted with it. On the carpet a short distance away lay the splintered and bloodied remains of an electric guitar's headstock, its body leaning against the sofa. Blood was splattered across the wall, the sofa and the carpet, and Justin's face was streaked with blood and tears. 'Fucking hell – Justin – what the hell happened?'

Justin raised bloodshot eyes from his girlfriend's body, his expression dazed. Alec moved further into the room, the reality of the situation beginning to hit home. 'Justin, what happened?'

'I don't know!'

'You don't *know*?' Alec echoed, in disbelief. 'Jesus, Justin –'

'She won't wake up!'

'She's fucking dead, Justin! Of course she won't fucking wake up!'

Justin's face crumpled, and he bowed his head. 'No – no –' he whispered, burying his face in Suki's chest, his slender frame shuddering.

'Can you keep the noise down?' Floyd's voice complained from the hallway moments before he appeared in the doorway, propping himself up against the door frame. Several seconds passed before he took in the scene in front of him, and even then he said only, 'What's going on?' sounding confused rather than concerned.

'*What*?' Alec exclaimed, incredulously. 'Floyd, are you completely fucking blind?'

Floyd blinked and slid down into a crumpled sitting position on the floor. 'I feel sick,' he muttered, at length.

Alec felt queasy himself, but somebody needed to take control, and nobody else was in a fit state to do it. 'I'm calling the police,' he decided, eventually.

Justin's head snapped up, his expression panicked. 'You can't!' He cried. 'They're going to think *I* did this!'

Alec didn't immediately respond, staring at Justin in disbelief. 'Well if *you* didn't, who *did*?'

'I don't know!' Justin answered, hopelessly. 'I don't know, I don't know!'

'Justin, what the hell else am I supposed to do?'

'I don't know!' Justin repeated, rather desperately. 'I don't know!'

Alec drew a deep breath, trying to marshal his thoughts. He generally prided himself on being good in a crisis, but he was under no illusion that on this occasion he was completely out of his depth. Caught between the knowledge there was no option but to involve the authorities and the fear endemic prejudice would deny Justin any real chance of justice, there seemed to be no decision he wasn't likely to regret. And, in the end, only one person he could think of to call.

* * * * *

By the time Rebecca registered that the sound that had awoken her was the electronic tone of Elliot's mobile, he had already answered it with, 'Fuck's sake, Alec, do you know what fucking time it is?' She wondered how he might have reacted had she answered his various calls at all hours whilst away on tour in the same manner. There was a brief pause before he passed her the phone. 'Alec wants to talk to you,' he informed her, shortly.

'Alec?' Rebecca took the mobile, rather nonplussed. 'Hello?'

'Becks, it's Alec.'

'I gathered. What's up?'

'Suki's dead.'

'Who?' Rebecca responded, still half asleep.

'Justin's girlfriend.'

This brought Rebecca wide awake, and she sat up. '*What*? What happened?'

'I don't know. I came back with Floyd a few minutes ago – found Justin on the living room floor holding her body.' He hesitated before adding, 'I wondered whether maybe you might be able to come over.'

'*Now*?'

'I'm sorry – I just – I didn't know who else to call,' Alec admitted, haltingly. 'He says he doesn't know what happened, and if I call the police they'll no doubt assume he was responsible because he has schizophrenia, so –'

'Alec, I *am* the police!'

'Well yeah, I know, but –' he trailed off. Rebecca could almost hear him shrug.

'All right,' she agreed, grudgingly, moving to climb out of bed. 'What's the address?'

Alec provided it, and Rebecca fumbled for a pen. In the absence of anything else to write on, she scribbled the details on her hand.

'Ok. Just stay where you are and I'll be over as soon as I can.'

'Thanks,' Alec sounded relieved. 'I'm sorry to wake you.'

'Don't worry about it. I'll see you soon.'

Rebecca terminated the call, setting Elliot's mobile down on the dressing table and reaching for a pair of trousers. The alarm clock on her bedside table read 02.53, and she wondered what time she would see it again. Although her job generally involved long and often irregular hours, it rarely necessitated getting up in the middle of the night, which, she thought as she pulled on a t-shirt, was probably just as well. The only part of the morning she had ever been particularly pleased to see passed before she went to bed, and she was beginning to tire of hearing *oh, but after a while you get used to getting up early, don't you?* As far as Rebecca was concerned, that was some sort of urban myth. She was thirty-two, and she *still* wasn't used to it.

Selecting a jumper from the wardrobe, she pulled it over her head and made for the door, feeling for the sleeves and trying to remember where she had left her trainers. She had half expected Elliot to ask where she was going, but he didn't, and she guessed he was too intoxicated to even notice she was up. He had been mired in severe depression for some months, and had repeatedly opted for Jack Daniels and vodka over medication or counselling. Rebecca had tried sympathy, anger, emotional blackmail and ultimatums, none of which had made a scrap of difference, and in recent months his heavy drinking seemed to have progressed to full-blown alcoholism. She had given up trying to help, and was concentrating on getting on with her own life whilst Elliot increasingly opted out of his. She had threatened to leave more than once; threats that had been met by tears and promises things would change. They hadn't, of course, and Rebecca had begun to understand how so many women became trapped in abusive relationships. Making the decision to go was one thing, but telling Elliot was quite another, and seeing someone she still cared deeply for so distraught was so difficult that it was easier to believe he might keep his promises.

Taking the car keys from the ledge in the hallway, Rebecca drew back the bolts Elliot had fixed to the front door after an intruder had entered through it one night the previous summer, wondering how he would react to it being left unsecured at such an early hour. Not, she reasoned, that there was much chance of his noticing, considering that he was unlikely to be up before lunch time. Some days, he didn't get up at all. It almost seemed to Rebecca as if someone had switched him off.

When they had met, three years earlier, he had rarely had a chance to lie in bed during waking hours, juggling a day job with DJ stints and his band, Astatine. Rebecca had been impressed by his determination to turn a dream into a career, although she hadn't ever really expected it to happen. Elliot had worked so hard to build a fan base, to raise money to pay for the first album, and to persuade a record company to take a chance on him – and now all that looked set to go to waste. In recent months, his drinking had generated more column inches than his music, and was threatening to eclipse the fact that he was an incredibly talented songwriter and musician. It seemed a terrible waste.

Not that any journalist was likely to be interested in what Elliot was doing that week if Suki really was dead. The erratic lead singer of a band called Quixotic Dystopia, Justin had also garnered more than his fair share of unwelcome press coverage in recent months, mostly owing to several prolonged stays in hospital as doctors attempted to manage his schizophrenia. The possibility that he might have murdered his girlfriend was going to make headlines in more than just the music press, and, as she unlocked the car door, Rebecca wondered what the chances were that Suki's death had been an accident. Very small, she quickly concluded. If he had been in any doubt, Alec would never have called.

For Rebecca, the look of relief on Alec's face when he opened the door to her at quarter to four was more than a little surreal. The two of them had never hit it off – partly because, for reasons nobody had ever been willing to explain, Alec didn't want Elliot to marry her, and partly because she found his repeated interference in Elliot's life and their relationship infuriating. Although, if she were honest, Alec's behaviour didn't bother her nearly as much as Elliot's response to it did. As a rule, any attempt to tell Elliot what to do proved futile, yet where Alec was concerned the proverbial *jump!* was more than likely to be met with *how high?* A recent conversation with one of Elliot's other friends had shed some light on his friendship with Alec, whom he had apparently met whilst in hospital after some sort of breakdown when he was nineteen. What Alec had been doing there, she had no idea.

At present, he looked considerably less composed than he had sounded on the phone, and his face was white. Standing back from the door to allow Rebecca to enter, he thanked her for coming.

'Where's Justin?'

'Kitchen,' Alec turned to show her the way. 'I figured we shouldn't stay in the living room, what with forensics and everything.'

'Is the body still there?'

Alec nodded.

'Can I have a look?'

Wordlessly, he pushed open the door to the room and stood back. Rebecca took in the scene before her, and, satisfied that the girl was most certainly dead, closed the door and looked back to Alec. 'So. Where's the kitchen?'

'Through there,' he nodded towards the end of the narrow corridor in which they stood.

Rebecca followed his direction. The kitchen was rather dated, but clean and tidy, and a rectangular wooden table stood in the centre of the room. Justin was sitting motionless in one of the three chairs gathered around it, his arms wrapped tightly around himself and his head bowed. His white-blonde hair was lowlighted with blood.

'Justin?' Rebecca pulled a chair out from the table and positioned it in front of him before sitting down. 'Justin, love, do you think you could tell me what happened?'

Justin didn't react.

'Justin?'

When he still made no response, she glanced around at Alec, who was hovering in the doorway, a packet of Embassy in his hand.

'I think he's in shock,' Alec offered, digging a cigarette from the box.

'So he's not catatonic.'

Alec shook his head. 'Justin's a paranoid schizophrenic.'

Rebecca frowned. 'And?'

'Catatonia isn't usually a feature,' Alec expanded, as he lit up.

'Right,' Rebecca nodded, wondering whether Alec had some level of medical or psychiatric training. She tried again to elicit a response from Justin before standing and heading back towards the hallway, indicating for Alec to follow her. Once out of view of the kitchen, she said, quietly, 'You mentioned earlier that you came back here with Floyd – where'd you been before that?'

'I bumped into him in the high street on my way home from work.' Alec leaned against the wall. 'He was mashed – said he'd been out drinking with Elliot.'

'But Elliot was home by midnight. Where had Floyd been in the interim?'

'I don't know,' Alec admitted. 'I didn't ask – I just thought they'd had a bit of a session. I assumed Elliot was in a similar state.'

Rebecca shook her head. 'I know he'd been in the pub, but he was reasonably coherent when he came home.' She didn't add that the same hadn't been true by the time they went to bed, although she had no idea what he'd been drinking after he arrived home, or how much. These days he had hiding it down to a fine art – or even, Rebecca thought, sleight of hand. She almost never saw him drinking, yet he managed to be drunk most of the time. Sometimes she wondered how he did it.

Guessing from Alec's expression that he had successfully read between the lines, she continued, 'So then what happened?'

'He was all over the place, and I was worried he might fall in front of a car or something, so I walked him back. We got inside to find Justin kneeling on the floor, cradling her body.' He sighed. 'I really didn't handle it very well. I shouldn't have shouted at him.'

'Hey, come on, if you hadn't been shaken there'd be something wrong with you,' Rebecca reassured him.

'Floyd was too far gone to notice.'

'Well then it's a good job you were here, isn't it?'

Alec managed a weak smile. 'Maybe. And thanks. For coming over.'

'I'm going to have to call someone, Alec.'

'I know,' he acknowledged. 'It's just – he was so upset before, I thought calling you first might make it easier on him. But right now he's not going to notice what happens.'

'Ok,' Rebecca nodded, reaching into her handbag for her mobile. 'You keep an eye on him while I sort something out.'

'Yuh. Thanks.'

Rebecca made for the front door, and was halfway through it when Alec's voice stopped her. 'Becca.'

She turned. Elliot was the only person to use that derivative of her name, and it sounded strange coming from someone else.

'Don't let them pin this on him just because it's convenient.'

'I won't.'

'Promise me you'll make sure it gets done properly.'

For Rebecca, this was a completely different Alec from the one she had known to date, and it occurred to her that he might also be revising his opinion of her. For all the difference it was likely to make now, given that her relationship with Elliot had all but fallen apart. The thought made her feel suddenly terribly sad. Drawing a deep breath, she pushed any further thoughts of her personal life firmly to one side and met Alec's eyes.

'I always do my job properly.'

## Five

Pulling his Honda into the space behind a familiar grey Aston Martin, Detective Chief Inspector Lawrence Forrester had two almost simultaneous thoughts. The first was to wonder how Leighton had made it to Camden from Clapham in less time than it had taken him to travel from Battersea. The other was how much he'd love to own the same car. He sighed. At present it was neither practical nor affordable, and he suspected that by the time his two children left home it might be too late. *Tragic* would doubtless be the word thirteen-year-old Jimmy would attach to the idea of fifty-something men zipping about town in two-seater sports cars – much the same sentiment Lawrence had had when he was young, unmarried and even further from being able to afford one. Ah well. Maybe by the time he *was* fifty-something he'd have changed his mind.

Switching off the ignition, he checked the details Rebecca had provided before climbing from the car and taking in his surroundings. Only one side of the street was inhabited, a blackened wall all that divided the pavement on the other from a sharp drop down to the steel spaghetti of a mainline rail route. Lawrence presumed it fed directly into Euston, less than a mile away, and wondered how loud the noise of train traffic might be inside the row of terraced Georgian houses opposite, most of which were probably furnished with only single-glazed sash windows.

Unlike many of Camden's roads, the northern end of Mornington Terrace had apparently been largely spared by the Blitz, and the imposing four-storey buildings had been well maintained since. At first-floor level a painted iron balcony ran the length of the terrace, which must have comprised some twenty properties, many of them with raised ground floors and wide staircases leading up to their front doors. As Lawrence climbed the steps of the address Rebecca had given him, he noticed every basement window in sight was fitted with security grilles. Had he lived there, he would have considered installing them at ground level, too. This might be a popular – and fiendishly expensive – location, but it was also among the capital's worst crime hotspots.

'I gather the body snatchers have preceded me,' Lawrence remarked, in a low voice, as he joined Rebecca on the landing outside the flat, where the pathologist's kit bag lay wide open in the middle of the floor, evidence bags, blue nitrile gloves and paper bodysuits spilling out the top.

'So far it's just Leighton and Anton, but there are two more SOCOs on their way,' Rebecca updated him as he helped himself to a bodysuit and set about putting it on.

'How many people were in the flat before you got here?'

'Three. Two of whom live here.'

'And where are they now?'

'Justin and Alec are in the kitchen. Floyd's in bed.'

'Lucky him.'

'Justin was completely spaced out when I arrived, but I think it's all starting to sink in now, he's pretty agitated. Leighton's trying to calm him down.'

'He's the schizophrenic?' Lawrence checked, the details Rebecca had given him over the phone earlier, while he was still half asleep, now rather hazy.

'Yes.'

'So we're going to need to find an appropriate adult before we can interview him,' he concluded. 'Could you make a note of anyone we might contact for him before you head off?'

Rebecca frowned. 'Off where?'

'Home.'

'Home?' She echoed. 'But Sir, I –'

'Becky, these guys are Elliot's friends – some of the people we end up interviewing may even be *your* friends – and there is no way you can be objective enough to be involved!'

'I know, but there must be some jobs I could do – I mean –'

'No,' Lawrence cut in, firmly.

'Please. Let me do something. Anything.'

Lawrence sighed. He wanted to refuse the request, but knew that in her position he would have felt exactly the same. 'All right,' he conceded. 'You can do any paper chasing I need, and you can liaise with Leighton and the SOCOs for me, but that's all you're going to do. Clear?'

Rebecca nodded.

'Oh, I'm sure she can be more useful than that,' Leighton remarked, as he appeared from inside the flat. An almost perennially cheerful young man in his mid-thirties, he was shorter and heavier than Lawrence, with long, thick dark hair that didn't look as if it had been brushed prior to being dragged into a ponytail. 'Someone needs to take care of the coffee and cookie runs, for starters.'

'Oh, I'm sorry, I thought that was your cardio,' Lawrence responded, drily.

Leighton waved a careless hand through the air. 'Don't worry, there's still the walk to the pub.'

Lawrence bit back a tart retort about Leighton's regular lunch-time visits to the pub. This was neither the the time nor the place, and, even if it had been, snide remarks were unlikely to achieve anything more than making *him* look unreasonable. They certainly wouldn't make any difference to the pathologist's wayward work ethic.

The problem wasn't Leighton's competence. When he engaged with something, he did an outstanding job, and was more than willing to undertake tasks that were beyond his official remit, often on his own initiative. He never uttered the phrase *that's not my job* – something Lawrence had heard all too often from one of the other pathologists – and rarely used the words *I can't*. When he did, it was more likely to be because something wasn't possible than because he wasn't prepared to do it. He was unquestionably a major asset to the pathology unit – and, by extension, the Met – the problem was, he knew it, and appeared to think it gave him carte blanche to take liberties. No. The real problem, Lawrence reflected, was that Leighton's boss *allowed* him to take liberties.

Hearing raised voices, Lawrence turned to see a tall young man with long, mousy hair striding down the hallway, closely followed by Anton, the only scenes of crime officer so far on site. Lawrence moved to block the doorway, holding up his hands.

'What's the problem?'

'You can have my clothes but I am not having someone pointing a camera at me while I take them off!'

'I'm sorry, you are?'

'Alec Hastings.'

'DCI Forrester,' Lawrence introduced himself. 'I'm sorry if it seems intrusive, but what –'

'No no no,' Alec interrupted, shaking his head. 'I've done nothing wrong and nobody has the right to take private photographs of me without my consent!'

'I'm afraid we do have that right, and –'

'You are not taking my fucking picture!' Alec exploded.

'Mr Hastings, if need be I can have you arrested for obstruction, so it would be in your interests to comply with procedure.'

'I don't give a fuck if you arrest me! You cannot force me to do anything against my will!'

'You guys are going to wake the whole street up,' Leighton intercepted, calmly. 'I've a few questions for Alec before I move anything, so perhaps you could worry about who's wearing what later?'

'Fine,' Lawrence consented, glad to be shot of the problem, if only temporarily. Alec didn't object either, and Leighton nodded towards the bedroom visible behind him before following Alec inside and closing the door.

Lawrence turned to Rebecca. 'Could you put a call in about transport?'

'But I could –'

'No,' he interrupted, guessing what she was about to say. 'Until we know what happened here you will not be getting into a car alone with anybody. As far as I'm concerned, this investigation will be conducted the same as any other. Understood?'

'Yes Sir.'

'Right.' Lawrence drew his mobile from his pocket, glancing at his watch. 'Five-fifteen. Danny's going to love his new alarm clock.'

By the time Lawrence arrived at Scotland Yard, Justin was too distressed to interview, and Lawrence decided to speak to Alec and Floyd first. After a quick coffee and some toast with Rebecca, who provided a rough summary of each man's circumstances and background, he joined Daniel in an interview room, wondering whether Floyd would be as willing to answer questions as he had been to accompany them into town.

Taking a seat beside Daniel at the table, his first thought was how striking Floyd looked. He had dead straight, jet black hair, which fell some way past his shoulders, and almost flawless porcelain skin. With prominent cheekbones and long, thick eyelashes, he would have looked stunning were it not for the dark crescents beneath his eyes and the fact his hair was desperately in need of a wash. Clad in faded blue jeans, a black, long-sleeved t-shirt and a grey jumper with so many holes in it that the sleeves had been rendered virtually obsolete, he sat slumped to one side in his chair so that his right shoulder leaned against the interview room wall, elbow on the table, head propped up with his hand. He didn't look at all well.

'I'd like you to start by telling me where you were and who you were with last night,' Lawrence began.

'I went for a drink with Elliot,' Floyd replied, wearily, every word apparently an effort.

'Whereabouts?'

'Soho.'

'What was the name of the pub?'

'The Dark Heart.'

'And what time did you leave there?'

'Closing.'

'Which is?'

Confusion clouded Floyd's face. 'What?'

'Closing time isn't all that specific,' Lawrence pointed out.

'Oh. Right. It's standard. Eleven.'

'And what did you do after that?'

'We got the tube from Tottenham Court Road. I missed my stop, so I got off at Kentish Town and walked from there.'

'Then what?'

Floyd took some time to answer, and it was difficult to know from his vacant expression whether he was trying to remember or just staring into space. 'I dunno,' he concluded, at length. 'I guess I went home.'

Lawrence frowned. 'When Alec called Rebecca, he said the two of you had only been back at the flat for a matter of minutes, and that wasn't much before three. So what were you doing in the intervening period?'

'Walking from Kentish Town.'

'And what else?'

'Nothing.'

'You must have done *something* else!' Lawrence exclaimed.

Floyd shrugged weakly, but offered no explanation.

'If the bar called time at eleven, the pub would have closed by half-past, and it can't have taken you more than about another half an hour to travel a handful of tube stops,' Lawrence observed. 'Kentish Town is the best part of – what – a mile from Camden Town? At the very minimum that leaves a couple of hours you've yet to account for.'

Floyd shrugged again.

'Did you speak to anybody? See anybody?'

Floyd shook his head slightly. 'I really have no idea.'

'Ok, let's focus on the period after you arrived home. Can you run through what happened from the moment you walked into the flat?'

'I don't remember.'

'You must remember something!'

Floyd closed his eyes, his facial muscles tensing. Bowing his head, he pressed the fingers of his right hand to his brow.

'Are you all right?'

'I have a migraine,' he replied, weakly. 'I get them all the time.'

Lawrence sighed, wondering whether Floyd was attempting to distract from his inability to account for his activities in the early hours of the morning. Assuming there wasn't a much simpler explanation.

'Were you drinking last night?'

'We had a couple of pints,' Floyd answered, reopening his eyes and dropping his hand into his lap.

'Just a couple?'

'Yes.'

Lawrence frowned. 'In that case, how is it that you don't remember?'

Floyd shrugged rather hopelessly.

'Had you been taking drugs?'

'Only my migraine meds.'

Lawrence's frown deepened. 'Let me get this straight: you weren't drunk and you hadn't taken drugs, yet you remember nothing about what happened between midnight and three o'clock this morning?'

'More or less.'

'That's rather convenient given that Suki may well have died during that time, isn't it?'

Floyd didn't respond.

'Could you tell me the truth now, please? Whatever it is?'

'I've told you,' he protested. 'I don't remember.'

'Yes, you have, but you've yet to provide me with a reason *why* you don't remember, and I don't think you're telling the truth! Now either you tell me what happened, or you tell me why you don't remember!'

'*I don't know*!' Floyd answered, rather desperately.

Lawrence sighed heavily to express his irritation. 'Let's talk about your flat mate, then,' he suggested. 'Has his behaviour been at all unusual lately?'

Floyd didn't pause to consider his reply. 'No.'

'No?' Lawrence repeated, raising his eyebrows. 'I realise he's a close friend of yours, but he is schizophrenic and –'

'He's a person, not a label!' Floyd flared, wincing with the exertion and returning his fingers to his brow. He drew a careful breath before continuing, 'Yes, his behaviour can be a bit odd, but that isn't *unusual* for Justin. I assumed what you wanted to know was whether he'd been himself recently, not whether he'd been like everybody else. He's *never* been like everybody else.'

'I understand you've known him a long time.'

'Yuh.'

'Has he ever been violent towards you?'

'No.'

'Never?'

'You do realise violence isn't a symptom of schizophrenia, don't you?'

Lawrence resisted the desire to point out that, in his experience, that wasn't always the case. 'What time did you last see Justin yesterday?' He asked, before adding, pointedly, 'That you can remember, that is.'

'Five – five-thirty – maybe six.'

'And how did he seem then?'

'He was a bit upset,' Floyd admitted. 'We had an argument.'

'About what?'

'I dunno, really. It started over something stupid and escalated into a big slanging match.'

'What did it start over?' Lawrence persisted.

'I honestly don't remember. I don't know why I got so upset about it, either, because usually I don't shout back at him when he gets worked up. I felt really bad about it afterwards.'

'What happened after that?'

'I went to the diner. I was in there until about eight.'

'Doing what?'

'Not a lot. Thinking. Writing dire song lyrics on paper serviettes. The sort of self-indulgent crap you chuck in the bin when you re-read it with a clearer head the following day.'

'And where did you go from there?'

'To meet Elliot.'

'Which brings us back to what happened after that,' Lawrence concluded. 'Are you going to tell me now?'

'I've told you, I *don't remember*.'

'And I've told *you* I don't believe you.'

Floyd swallowed, drawing a hand over his eyes. 'I can barely see straight,' he countered, weakly. 'I need to lie down. Can I do this later?'

'You're going nowhere until I've had the truth about last night,' Lawrence informed him. 'Either you tell me where you were or you tell me why you don't remember. This isn't a game, and if you refuse to co-operate you may find yourself in a great deal of trouble.' He stood to leave. 'You sit there and think that over for a while.'

Lawrence opened the door onto the next interview room along the corridor to find Alec tearing ramparts into the rim of an empty plastic cup. He stopped as Lawrence and Daniel entered, setting the cup down on the table. His long mousy hair looked as if it had been crimped, and, although Lawrence couldn't be sure, he thought he could make out traces of black eyeliner along the rims of Alec's lower eyelids.

Leighton had somehow succeeded in relieving Alec of his clothing without incident – for all his faults he was superb when it came to dealing with people – and had provided the man with a paper bodysuit to wear in exchange. Alec had since removed the sleeves, exposing toned, tattooed arms. Lawrence was impressed by the degree of depth that the tattoo artist had managed to capture in the monochrome designs, which reached around Alec's arms from his shoulders to just above his elbows. The fantasy representations were a far cry from the line drawings and block colour of conventional tattoos, with subtle shading and intricate detail that wouldn't have been out of place on an artist's canvas. When it came to body art, Lawrence hadn't been aware such workmanship was even possible, and Daniel was obviously equally impressed, observing, 'Nice work,' as he sat at the table opposite Alec.

Alec smiled, revealing untidy front teeth that had obviously seen a good deal less work. 'Cheers.'

Lawrence waited until Daniel had flicked to a clean page in his notebook before saying, 'Could you run us through what you did last night?'

'Sure. I was at work, at the Underworld. I'm a DJ – I do the music between the bands, and then the club afterwards. I was on my way home when I ran into Floyd, and –'

'What time was that?'

'About two-thirty. The club shuts at two, and then I have to tidy up the equipment and turn everything off.'

'And where's home?'

'Oakley Square.'

'What happened after you bumped into Floyd?'

'He was monged, so I thought I ought to walk him home, make sure he got there ok.'

'What do you mean by *monged*?'

'Wasted,' Alec answered, shortly, not really resolving the ambiguity surrounding his previous choice of adjective.

'By wasted do you mean drunk?'

'Yeah. Paralytic, actually, he was all over the shop.'

'He told me he only had a couple of pints last night.'

'Yeah, that's what he told me,' Alec responded, with a small shrug.

'How about you? Had you been drinking?'

'I had the odd beer over the course of the evening, but I take it slowly when I'm working. It's not a difficult job, but it's easy enough to screw up if you've had a few too many.'

Lawrence nodded. 'I'm sorry to have to ask you to relive it, but could you describe what happened after you arrived at the flat?'

'I got Floyd into bed – I figured Justin was still up because the living room light was on, so I thought I'd look in to let him know what sort of shape Floyd was in – make sure someone would be around to keep an eye on him. He was kneeling on the floor, holding her – I suppose like you might hold someone who'd fainted – and –' Alec paused. 'He was crying and saying *she won't wake up*.'

'Do you think he was responsible for her death?'

'That was my first assumption, but –' he hesitated. 'On reflection, I don't know.'

'Do you know him well?'

'Yes.'

'How long have you known him?'

'Nine or ten years, I guess.'

'If you don't mind my asking, what interest did you have in a twelve-year-old at the age of twenty?'

'Very little,' Alec replied, seemingly amused by the question. 'Back then he was just a mate's kid brother.'

'Ah,' Lawrence understood. 'So you're a friend of –' he checked the notes he had made over breakfast. 'Vinnie's.'

'That's right.'

'Have you seen much of Justin or Floyd recently?'

'No – but then I don't think many people have – they've been holed up in the studio for weeks. Justin was out last weekend, and that was the first time I'd seen him in ages. If you want much of an insight into what has or hasn't been going on lately you'd be best off speaking to the other guys in the band – maybe their manager – producer – the sound engineer at the studio –' Alec trailed off, apparently out of suggestions.

'Can you give me the names and addresses of the other band members?'

'Names yes, addresses no.'

'That'll do.'

'Ethan Taylor – he's the bassist – and Dave Hanson's the drummer.'

'We also need the name of someone who can substantiate where you were last night.'

'Sure. I could probably give you about twenty, would you like me to list them all?' Alec paused, then added, 'Best not, actually. Some of them probably don't even remember they were there themselves.'

Returning to the small interview room he had left some twenty minutes earlier, Lawrence found Floyd with his face buried in his arms, which he had folded on the table top.

'Mr Newton?'

Floyd slowly raised his head, his eyes only partially open. 'Can I please go home? My head is killing me.'

'That'll be the hangover, I presume.'

'I only had two pints!' Floyd maintained.

'Well you obviously had *something* else, because Alec told me you could hardly stand up by the time he bumped into you.'

'Please let me go home. I feel like hell.'

Lawrence said nothing, and Floyd raised a hand to his forehead, squeezing his eyes shut. '*Please*. I feel really sick. I just want to go to bed.'

'All right,' Lawrence relented, reluctantly, guessing from Floyd's pallor that he might be telling the truth about feeling unwell. 'You can't go home right now – my team hasn't finished in there yet – but if you're not going to help me any further you might as well get out of my way. We'll let you know when we're done at your flat – do you have a number we can reach you on?'

'My phone's at home.'

'Well then where will you be?'

'Probably my mate Ethan's place. Elliot'll be able to give Becks his number.'

'What's the address?'

Floyd provided a street name and number, and Lawrence asked whether he also knew what Suki's address had been. He shook his head.

'All right, then, off you go,' Lawrence concluded, coolly, handing Floyd his card. 'If anything comes to mind, please let me know.'

Floyd nodded, taking the card and struggling to his feet. He looked rather unsteady, and gripped the doorway tightly as he left the room. Lawrence turned to Daniel as the door closed. 'What do you think he's on?'

Daniel shook his head. 'I dunno. Vodka? Glue? Smack, maybe? He looks like an advert for a methadone program.'

'I thought I'd seen him somewhere before.'

'Do you want me to run a check for previous?'

'Later. First I want to see whether we can get some answers from Justin.'

Although tall, Justin was very slight, and Lawrence had been surprised to learn he was twenty-two, having thought his build more that of an adolescent than a man. He didn't respond to Lawrence and Daniel's entry to the interview room, picking at the frayed cuff of his black v-necked jumper. With his head bowed, his face was largely obscured by a curtain of bloodstained white-blonde hair, and his eyes were hidden behind dark glasses, which he had been wearing since departing his flat at six-thirty. Lawrence hoped he wasn't in for another wasted interview. Sunglasses were unnecessary enough on a wet, cloudy day, but in a windowless room seemed almost laughable. As far as he could see, there were two alternatives – either Justin was playing the part of the rock star way ahead of schedule, or he was on drugs.

Rebecca had succeeded in tracking down the young man's social worker, who had agreed to act as his appropriate adult. From what Lawrence had seen so far, Justin regarded her with the same degree of suspicion he did detectives. But Lawrence reasoned she would at least be capable of properly fulfilling the role; he wasn't at all sure the same would be true of the young man's friends. Justin apparently didn't trust lawyers, either, and all offers to provide legal representation had been met with a vigorous shake of his head.

Having finally reached a point at which the interview could commence, Daniel turned to start the audio recorder affixed to the wall at the end of the table. Before he even had a chance to press record, however, Justin jerked backwards, shaking his head and beginning to hyperventilate. His glasses made it impossible to be sure what he was looking at, but, guessing it was the recording device that had upset him, Lawrence explained, 'Recording the interview is standard procedure, Justin.'

'You can't take my thoughts away!'

'Nobody wants to take your thoughts away.'

These words seemed to have no effect, and within moments Justin's chair was pushed up against the rear wall of the room. The social worker turned her chair towards him and said something in a low voice that Lawrence didn't catch. Justin shook his head vehemently, shunting the chair away from her and into the corner.

Lawrence tried again. 'All we want to do is make a record of what's said in this room, Justin. Doing so is as much in your interests as ours, it –'

'No!' Justin exclaimed, frantically, shaking his head again and wrapping his arms around himself.

Lawrence sighed, suspecting they might get more out of the interview if he gave in and had Daniel take notes instead. 'All right, we won't record anything,' he conceded, glancing expectantly at Daniel before returning his attention to Justin. The young man was rubbing the palm of his right hand up and down his left arm, from shoulder to elbow and back again, his splayed fingers tense and trembling. He didn't respond.

'We don't want to take your thoughts, we just want to ask you a few questions,' Lawrence submitted.

If it were possible, Justin shrank even further into the corner. His rapid, shaky respirations were still audible. Lawrence wondered how best to proceed, unsure whether giving Justin a break would help calm him down or simply provide an opportunity for him to work himself up. Perhaps, he concluded, the best way to engage him might be through some form of distraction.

'Becky tells me your band is playing at the Reading Festival this summer,' he began, conversationally. Then, thinking Justin might feel less under pressure if he wasn't the focus of everyone's attention, Lawrence dropped his eyes to the folder on the table in front of him and made a show of leafing through the contents. 'Depending which day it is, I might be there as well,' he went on. 'My son talked me into taking him on the Saturday.' He paused as if reading the page in front of him before adding, 'He was holding out for a longer visit. But I draw the line at camping.' He glanced up. 'Where sleeping in a tent is concerned, anyway. A campervan with all mod cons might be a different story.'

Justin hadn't moved, but his breathing sounded slower, so Lawrence continued.

'A bit like a tour bus, I suppose. Although I'm only guessing, I've never actually been on one. What would you score them out of ten, comfort-wise?'

This elicited a small shrug, and, feeling encouraged, Lawrence added, 'I think Jim – that's my son – would rather like to be a musician someday. But I imagine it's a lot more work than he realises.'

Justin shrugged again.

'Alec mentioned that you've been putting in a lot of hours in the studio.'

Justin nodded, and Lawrence found himself wondering how the band ever managed to record anything. Assuming the phobia of recording devices wasn't just a considered ruse to make his job more difficult.

'Are you the one who writes the songs?'

'Me and Floyd,' Justin replied, his voice little more than a whisper.

'Is it difficult combining two people's input for something so creative?

'Depends.'

'On what?'

His answer was surprisingly thoughtful. 'The people.'

'I suppose that's true of many things,' Lawrence observed.

Justin nodded, then raised a hand to nudge his glasses back up the bridge of his nose.

'Perhaps you might lose the shades, since we're indoors?' Lawrence suggested.

Justin frowned. 'What?'

'The sunglasses,' he indicated his own eyes for emphasis. 'Do you think you could take them off?'

'No.'

'Why not?'

'You'll be able to see in.'

Lawrence wondered whether the comment related to Justin's conviction they were trying to take his thoughts, or whether he wanted to keep the glasses on for the very reason Lawrence wanted them removed – to make it easier to conceal the truth. He had long been curious to know what effect blindness might have on a person's ability to lie, not only in terms of what expression the eyes of a blind person might lack, but also because they wouldn't – he assumed – feel the pressure that eye contact could so successfully exert on the vast majority of the population.

'Please take them off,' he persisted, as patiently as he could.

'It's too bright. My doctor said.'

Keen to get something out of the interview, Lawrence gave up. 'Maybe you could tell me what happened at your flat last night?'

'I don't know,' Justin responded, rather dully.

'What do you mean, you don't know? Why don't you know?'

'I wasn't there.'

'Where were you?'

'Out,' Justin answered, uninformatively, pulling restlessly at the fingers of his right hand with those of his left.

'Where did you go?'

Justin's feathery eyebrows pulled into a frown. 'What?'

'Where did you go last night?' Lawrence asked, slowly and deliberately.

'Oh. The Spread Eagle.'

'Is that a pub?'

'Uh-huh.'

'And where is the Spread Eagle?'

'Parkway.' There was a momentary pause before he added, 'Although – it isn't, really.'

'What does that mean? Surely it's either there or it isn't?'

Justin hesitated. 'Sorry?'

Lawrence sighed, concluding that the matter wasn't worth pursuing: he could locate the pub easily enough himself. Instead, he asked, 'Did Suki go with you?'

'What?'

'Did Suki go with you to the pub?' Lawrence clarified.

'No.'

'Why not?'

'She shouted at me.'

'Why was that?'

'She thinks I'm stupid.'

'Did she say that?' Lawrence asked, not missing the fact Justin had referred to Suki in the present tense.

He nodded.

'And how did that make you feel?'

Justin shrugged.

'Did it make you angry?'

There was a pause before he shrugged again.

Deciding to come back to that later, Lawrence returned to the specifics of Justin's activities the night before, asking, 'What time was that?'

Justin frowned again. 'What?'

Lawrence drew a deep breath, struggling to maintain a reasonably patient tone. He had no way of knowing whether Justin really was as confused as he seemed, and was all too aware that the social worker would jump on anything she deemed to be oppressive or antagonistic. The best course of action, he decided, would be to gather what information he could, and then have a psychiatrist assess Justin whilst he and Daniel tried to substantiate the young man's version of events. Assuming, that was, he didn't admit to Suki's murder and save them the trouble.

'What time last night did you leave your flat to go to the pub?' He asked, again.

'I don't know. I don't have a watch. I did, but –' he faltered. 'Now I don't.'

'Do you have any idea what time you might have left the pub?'

'When they told me to,' Justin responded, with sudden and surprising clarity.

'When who told you to?'

'Can I have a cigarette?'

'In a minute. Who told you to leave the pub?'

'I need a cigarette.'

Lawrence looked to Daniel. 'Would you mind finding some?' He asked, more for Justin's benefit than his colleague's; Daniel would have deduced the request from a single glance. The sergeant stood and turned for the door.

'Let's go back to the pub,' Lawrence suggested, as the door closed. 'When did –'

'You weren't in the pub!' Justin interrupted. 'You're confusing me! That's how you fit people up!'

'Justin –'

'You're trying to trick me into admitting things I didn't do!'

'Justin, please,' Lawrence entreated. 'All I want to know is what you *did* do. Now can you think back to last night for me? In the pub.'

'You weren't there!'

'I know, that's why I need you to tell me about it. Ok?'

Justin looked suspicious, but nodded.

'Now why did you leave the pub?'

'They said it was time,' Justin revealed, before adding, more to himself than to Lawrence, 'Time. Breakfast. Bath. Break. Bed.'

'Ok,' Lawrence nodded, guessing that probably meant Justin had been in the pub until closing. 'So did you go home at that point?'

Justin rubbed his forehead with the heel of his right hand, shaking his head as he did so. Lawrence wasn't sure whether the action was an answer to his question, and tried a different approach.

'What did you do after you left the pub last night?'

There was a long pause before Justin said, 'Looked at houses.'

'Which houses?'

'In the windows.'

Lawrence frowned. 'Do you mean you were looking in the windows of houses?'

'No.'

'Well then which windows were you looking at?'

He never got an answer, as the door to the room opened and Daniel reappeared with a packet of Mayfairs and a cigarette lighter in his hand, disrupting Justin's erratic train of thought. Thereafter, it proved impossible to focus his attention on anything further than his desire to smoke. Despite being a fervent proponent of the workplace smoking ban, had it been a rule rather than a law Lawrence would have been sorely tempted to flout it. As it was, the only real option was to take a break.

Once outside, Lawrence flipped the lid of the cigarette packet open and held it out towards Justin. The young man took several seconds to select one, as if the process were of some importance, but eventually raised one to his lips. Reluctant to give him possession of the lighter, Lawrence fired it up for him, hoping Justin wouldn't perceive the action as having some ulterior motive. To his surprise, Justin thanked him before accepting the light, then leaned back against the wall of the building as he exhaled.

Lawrence offered the cigarettes to the social worker out of politeness rather than any expectation she would take one; when she did he immediately wondered whether she had her own and, by extension, might have saved them some time. As he handed her the lighter, Justin finally seemed to focus on the events of the previous evening, saying, rather hollowly, 'She wouldn't wake up.' He drew deeply on the cigarette, his hand shaking slightly. 'I didn't know – I –' he gulped. 'She – she –' he shook his head, sliding down the wall behind him until he was sitting on his heels. 'She's dead, isn't she?' He managed, at length, his voice rather choked.

'I'm afraid so.'

'I didn't know she was gonna get hurt!' He exclaimed, bowing his head and raising his hands to cover his face. Regardless of the cigarette that he held, he pushed his fingers roughly beneath the lenses of his glasses, which almost immediately fell to the ground. 'I wouldn't have gone!' He exclaimed, curling his fingers against his forehead and singeing his hair with the cigarette as he did so. 'I would've – I would've –'

Lawrence reached to remove the cigarette from Justin's grasp before he could do any further damage, and Justin jumped as if he'd been slapped, jerking back against the wall. Lawrence himself was more than a little startled, not least by Justin's appearance minus his glasses, for the wild eyes staring up at him were a translucent red. He looked disorientated and panicked, and Lawrence suspected his apparent confusion during the interview had been authentic. The next question to address was whether it was in any way relevant.

## Six

Obtaining Suki's home address had not proved straightforward. Neither Floyd nor Alec was able – or willing – to provide it, and although Justin apparently knew how to get there, he claimed not to recall the name of the road or the block. Alec did have a mobile number for Suki's flat mate, Sally, but Lawrence wasn't about to deliver the news of Suki's death over the phone, not least because he wanted to be there to see her reaction when he did so. In the end, Alec offered to contact a mutual friend, and, hopeful that they had the correct details, Lawrence and Daniel departed for Holloway, leaving Rebecca to contact the duty psychiatrist and to make a start on interviewing Justin and Floyd's neighbours.

The address turned out to be a council flat, which Lawrence presumed Suki had been renting privately. Given the lengths of the waiting lists in most London boroughs, an able-bodied twenty-two-year-old with no dependants would have stood next to no chance of qualifying for local authority housing. Then again, he thought as he knocked on the front door, her flat mate's circumstances might be very different.

He had been about to knock again when the door was flung open by a petite young woman in pink cotton pyjamas. Despite her state of dress, she didn't look as if she had only just fallen out of bed, her hazel eyes clear and her dark, corkscrew curls falling neatly from a perfect centre parting. Lawrence suspected she had yet to apply some make up, however, as she was minus both eyebrows, and he didn't imagine they would be missing unless she subscribed to the rather odd fashion of drawing them on. She had clearly expected to find somebody she knew on her doorstep, and stopped short, her full lips parted ready to speak, on coming face to face with Lawrence and Daniel.

'Sally Jacobs?'

'Yes.'

'I'm Detective Chief Inspector Forrester, this is Detective Sergeant Freeman. Could we come in for a moment?'

'Uh – sure –' she backed away from the door, her freckled face turning pale. 'What's happened? Is Quary ok?'

'As far as I'm aware,' Lawrence reassured her, wondering who Quary was. A lover, maybe – or brother – or sister – who could tell with the odd names people seemed to have these days. Still looking ill at ease, Sally showed them into a small kitchen with dominant red and white wallpaper detailed with tomatoes and spring onions, and gestured towards the four chairs crowded around a folding table. None of them matched.

'Sorry, we don't have a living room,' she apologised, resting a heel on the edge of one of the chairs as she sat down and linking her fingers loosely in front of her ankle to hold it in place. The pose reminded Lawrence of the way his ten-year-old daughter, Elise, sometimes sat at the breakfast table. Not that he was often home for breakfast these days. The thought made him feel more than a little guilty. He took a seat opposite Sally and waited for Daniel to join him.

'So?' Sally asked, anxiously.

'We're here about your flat mate.'

'Suki?' The skin where Sally's eyebrows ought to have been climbed by a centimetre. 'Why?'

'I'm afraid Suki's dead. I'm very sorry.'

Sally looked momentarily stunned. Then panic took over once again, and she demanded, 'Is Justin ok?'

This wasn't at all the response Lawrence had anticipated, and questions about the nature of Sally's relationship with Justin immediately came to mind.

'He's not really ok, but he's not hurt, if that's what you're asking.'

Sally's panicked expression dissipated, and she sounded calmer as she asked, 'What happened to Suki?'

'She was murdered.'

'Murdered?' Sally echoed, weakly. 'God.'

'We will need to ask you some questions, but if you don't feel up to that now we can come back later.'

'Oh – well –' Sally hesitated. 'I'm ok, but I need to go and check on Justin. Can I talk to you after that?' She moved to stand.

'I'm afraid you can't see Justin.'

'Why not?'

'We're currently holding him in custody.'

'*What?*'

'So if –'

'What are you holding Just for? He'd never hurt Suki!'

'Miss Jacobs, Suki died in his flat, and he was found holding her body. Whilst we aren't certain he was responsible, you can understand how he came to be a person of interest.'

Sally didn't respond, sinking back down onto her chair.

'Do you know him well?' Lawrence asked, keen to establish the reason for her evident concern.

'Yeah,' she nodded slightly. 'I've known him forever. We grew up together.'

'And Suki?'

'Um – I guess I've known her since she met Just, so – I don't know – maybe a couple of years.'

'Have you lived with her long?'

'About eight months.'

'Did you get on well?'

'Mostly.'

'Meaning what?'

'She was my flat mate. Anybody you live with is going to annoy you at times.'

That was true enough, Lawrence conceded – particularly, as he remembered, if they were remiss with the washing up. He had long ago come to the conclusion that once a person's student days were over their chances of living happily with anybody who wasn't their partner were limited. Then again, there seemed to be an increasing number of people who were happy doing neither.

'When did you last see Suki?'

'Sunday night. We went to a gig.'

'Did you hear from her at all after that?'

Sally nodded. 'She called. Last night.'

'From where?'

'Justin's place.'

'Why?'

'She'd had a fight with him and wanted someone to moan at.'

From her tone, Lawrence sensed Sally hadn't been a particularly sympathetic listener. 'What time was that?'

Sally took a few moments to consider her answer. 'Half ten?' She ventured, at length. 'Eleven maybe. I'm not sure exactly. Not late.'

'Did she say what the fight was about?'

Sally sighed. 'Justin tends to get rather fixated on things – particularly if they've upset him – and he ends up going round and round in circles. It drove Suki nuts.'

'So it wasn't a one-off argument.'

'No.'

'Was Justin there when she called you?'

'No, he'd gone out.' Sally paused, then, anticipating his next question, added, 'I don't know where.'

'Did you talk for long?'

'Only a few minutes. The doorbell rang, so she had to go.'

'Was she expecting anybody?' Lawrence asked, feeling sceptical. Sally clearly cared more for Justin than Suki, and he wouldn't have been surprised to learn she was trying to protect him. Her reply scotched this theory.

'No, she thought it was Justin. He's always locking himself out.'

'Always?'

'Well, quite often. He storms out and slams the door, and it's only later, when he calms down, that he realises he doesn't have his keys on him.'

Lawrence nodded. 'Had she fallen out with anybody else recently?'

'Not that I know of. But we weren't joined at the hip.'

'And is there anybody you can think of who might have wanted some harm to come to her?'

Sally thought this over, then shook her head.

'Since you grew up with Justin, I'm assuming you know Floyd, as well?'

'Yes.'

'I understand he and Justin are very close. Do you think he felt threatened by Justin's relationship with Suki?'

Sally tipped her head to one side. 'He's never said – because he wouldn't – but I think he felt relieved, more than anything.'

'Relieved? Why?'

'Justin can be hard work. He takes up a lot of time and energy, and Floyd's always given him that. I don't think he minds, but I think Suki being around provided him with more time for his own life.'

'Have you seen much of either of them recently?'

'Not really. They've been in the studio 'til all hours for weeks. Just's been round here with Suki, but mostly he came over late and they just went to bed.'

'How about her job? We've gathered she worked in a bar, but we haven't been able to get much out of Justin and nobody else seems to know which bar. Do you have any idea?'

Sally looked uncomfortable, and there was a long pause before she revealed, 'Suki wasn't doing bar work.'

Lawrence felt intrigued. 'So what was she doing?'

'Stripping,' Sally admitted.

'Is that something she kept quiet?'

'Yes. Justin's paranoid enough without –' Sally stopped herself.

'So he didn't know.'

'No.'

'How do you think he might have reacted if he'd found out?'

'He wouldn't have *hurt* her!' Sally exclaimed. 'He *wouldn't*! He *adored* her!'

'As I've said, we don't know what happened yet.'

Sally nodded slightly. 'Poor Just. He must be in bits.' She sighed. 'How's her mum?'

'We've not spoken to her yet. We were hoping you might be able to give us her address.'

'Oh – yeah, sure.' Sally rose from the table. 'It might take me a few minutes to find it, but it'll be here somewhere.'

'And we'd like to have a look at Suki's room.'

'Yeah, no problem. I was supposed to be –' she faltered. 'I had a job interview – this afternoon – but –' she shrugged. 'I don't much feel like going now, so I'll be around.'

'He's killed her, hasn't he?' Charlotte Jenson responded, hollowly, to Lawrence's initial introduction of himself and Daniel at her front door. Daniel wondered whether her conviction had any real basis, or whether it was simply a prejudiced response to the fact Justin had schizophrenia. He felt immensely relieved he wasn't the one to have to deliver the news, and held his breath as he waited for his superior to respond.

'May we come in?'

'Oh God –' Charlotte managed, pursing her lips and raising a hand to her mouth. She backed away from the door, her face crumpling, and Lawrence stepped inside and gently took her arm. Daniel followed him in and closed the front door behind himself as Lawrence guided Charlotte through the doorway to their right.

This, it turned out, led onto a tidy but dingy living room. The oatmeal-turned-grey walls desperately needed a fresh coat of paint, and the worn beige suite looked well past its use-by date. A row of framed photographs stood atop the narrow mantlepiece that overhung an old-fashioned gas fire reminiscent of the one Daniel's parents had once had in their front room. For years his sister had been convinced the flames were somehow going to escape and set the house on fire – and just as she had finally accepted it wasn't going to happen, the fire had begun leaking carbon monoxide and had to be removed anyway.

With the exception of a wedding photograph, all the pictures on the mantlepiece were of Suki, and Daniel guessed she had been an only child. Not being a parent himself, he often wondered whether having more than one child would make losing one any easier to cope with. Sometimes he concluded that it must; other times he didn't feel so sure. Not that he was ever likely to find out: kids were definitely *not* on his personal agenda. With that thought, he realised it had never occurred to him to ask whether they were on Rebecca's. Making a mental note to find out, he returned his attention to Charlotte, who was sitting forwards on the sofa, her face buried in her hands. Lawrence was perching beside her, but his eyes were on Daniel. He looked impatient, and as Daniel met his gaze, he nodded wordlessly in the direction of the hallway. Understanding, Daniel turned and headed to find the kitchen to make some tea, hoping Charlotte's preference was for something other than Earl Grey. As far as his senses could make out, the stuff tasted like disinfectant.

By the time he returned to the living room, Charlotte was a little more composed, and even managed to thank him as he set a mug of English breakfast tea down on the coffee table in front of her.

'What did he do to her?' She asked Lawrence, weakly, making a half-hearted effort to dry her reddened eyes with a pretty lace handkerchief. 'What did he do?'

'At the moment we aren't sure who was responsible,' Lawrence replied.

Charlotte swallowed hard. 'What happened?'

Lawrence hesitated, and Charlotte whispered, '*Please*.'

'We believe Suki died of a head injury, but we're still waiting for the medics to confirm that.'

'And you're telling me you don't know who was responsible?' Charlotte demanded, her voice rising. 'Her boyfriend's a psychopath! Who else could it have been?'

Taking a seat in a nearby armchair, Daniel wondered what percentage of the population knew the difference between psychopathy and psychosis. Maybe not even double figures. Then again, given that the English dictionary on his desk defined psychopath and sociopath as one and the same, perhaps it wasn't surprising mental illness and personality disorders were so misunderstood amongst laymen.

Lawrence threaded his fingers together, saying, gently, 'Mrs Jenson, we have interviewed Justin, and at the moment we are holding him in custody, but we can't just assume that because he has schizophrenia he must have been responsible.'

'But I knew this was going to happen!' Charlotte came back. 'I *knew* it! I *warned* her!' Her voice breaking, she returned her hand to her mouth, drawing a long, unsteady breath and clearly trying to choke back her tears. When she seemed to have succeeded, Lawrence continued.

'Was Justin violent towards Suki in the past?'

She nodded. 'Last year – he –' she shuddered. 'He tried to throw her off the balcony of his flat. The only reason she didn't fall fifteen storeys was because his flat mate was there!'

'Do you know why he did that?'

Charlotte shook her head rather hopelessly. 'I don't even know if *he* does! He's *dangerous*! I tried to warn her! I tried, but she seemed to be blind to the reality of it all! She said he didn't mean it – as if that made it all right! It doesn't matter what he *meant*! What matters is what he *did*!'

Lawrence nodded. After a moment he said, 'If you'd rather we can talk about this in more detail later. I realise it must be incredibly difficult.'

'No. The sooner I –' she paused. 'I want him to get – what he – deserves.'

'Can you give us any other examples of occasions when Justin behaved violently?'

Several seconds passed before Charlotte attempted to speak. 'There were – times – when – when she –' she stopped. 'She came up with excuses – for – for how she'd hurt herself – but I didn't believe her. It's not as if she was clumsy, or accident prone.'

'Do you recall any specific incidents?'

'Yes,' Charlotte confirmed. 'Yes. Last summer she broke her arm – and – at Christmas she – she had a huge bruise – here –' Charlotte indicated the left side of her forehead with trembling fingers.

'Did Suki talk much about her other friends?'

Charlotte nodded. 'We spoke every weekend,' she revealed, with tears in her voice. 'She always had so much to talk about – gigs, clubs, parties – it all sounded like such fun. I couldn't help wondering why – why she wanted to –' her voice wavered. 'He took up a lot of her time, and often it wasn't *happy* time.'

Daniel had been wondering the same thing ever since seeing the plethora of photographs on display in Suki's bedroom. She had been stunning, and, from the number of people who appeared with her in the various pictures, clearly hadn't lacked social skills. Yet she had chosen Justin. His mind wandering back to Rebecca, he sighed. Apparently it didn't matter how much of a headcase you were if you were pretty and played guitar.

'Could you name some of her close friends?' Lawrence asked, jolting Daniel back to the job in hand.

'A few, perhaps, but there were so many I found it hard to keep track.'

'Any names would be helpful.'

'Yes,' Charlotte responded, seemingly more to herself than anybody else. 'Well, there was Sally, of course – her flat mate – and Kaia, her name came up a lot. Floyd – Valentine –' she trailed off. 'I'm sorry, my mind's gone blank – I –' she gave up.

'You've been very helpful,' Lawrence reassured her. 'I'm sorry to have to ask anything further, but I do need to know about Suki's father. Is he still around?'

'No. He passed away when Suki was thirteen.'

'I'm sorry.'

'They were very close,' Charlotte added. 'He doted on her. I don't think the void he left behind ever really closed. Maybe the fact Justin made her the centre of his world went some way to filling it.' She paused, staring blankly at the fireplace, before concluding, sadly, 'Perhaps that's why she wouldn't listen to reason.'

Lawrence had dropped Daniel in Camden High Street with instructions to take a bus or tube to Soho in search of Suki's workplace. After getting caught up in the one-way system and driving around most of Camden Town twice, he managed to find his way back to Mornington Terrace, where he parked his car before setting off towards the Spread Eagle pub. It took him only a couple of minutes to reach Parkway, a commercial and residential hybrid of a road that funnelled a considerable volume of traffic east from Regent's Park. Walking down it, the first thing that struck him was the abundance of estate agents crammed into a stretch that couldn't have been more than fifty yards in length. Presumably they were what Justin had been referring to when he said he had been *looking at houses in the windows*.

The Spread Eagle was located at the junction with Albert Street, a wider, although far less busy, road flanked on both sides by carbon-copy Georgian terraces and substantial plane trees. A single line of tables and chairs hugged the building's perimeter, complete with a sign announcing that they were *for the use of Spread Eagle customers only*. Lawrence was amused to see somebody had tacked the letter *d* onto the end of the word *Eagle*.

Inside, what had presumably once been an old-fashioned pub seemed to have undergone two separate facelifts. The bar area was unremarkable – a modernised version of what had no doubt gone before it – and much like those of many other drinking holes across the capital. The main seating area, meanwhile, was furnished with a mish-mash of arm chairs and sofas, and, unusually, what looked like an antique chest of drawers, topped with a vase of flowers. The overall effect – not, Lawrence suspected, what the designer had been aiming for – was oddly reminiscent of a farmhouse kitchen.

The bar was sufficiently busy that Lawrence had to wait several minutes for the attention of any of the staff, but he was eventually approached by a young man with hefty arms and shoulders that indicated he devoted a considerable amount of time to weight training. Clad in the brewery's uniform navy t-shirt and black trousers, he gave Lawrence a perfunctory smile before saying, in an Australian accent, 'What can I git ya?'

Lawrence produced his warrant card and introduced himself before asking the man's name.

'Andy.'

'Were you working here last night?'

'Yeah.'

'Do you remember seeing a young man with long blonde hair, possibly sunglasses –'

'Oh, you mean Justin,' Andy realised, aloud.

'Do you know him?'

'You want to speak to Alicia.' Andy nodded towards a chunky red-head approaching from the opposite end of the bar with a collection of glasses in her hands before beckoning her over. 'Al, this is –' he broke off, looking to Lawrence for assistance.

'DCI Forrester.'

'He wants to ask you about Justin,' Andy added, helpfully, before turning back down the bar.

Alicia set her armful of glasses down and regarded Lawrence expectantly.

'Do you know Justin well?'

'Not particularly. But he's in here often enough.'

'How often?'

'Once or twice a fortnight, I suppose.'

'And does he always talk to you?'

'No. Some nights he barely says a word to anyone. He just sits and stares at his drink.'

'Was he here last night?'

She nodded.

'How did he seem?'

'Well – sort of drunk – but not.'

'Can you explain what you mean by that?'

'He kept saying the same things – like he didn't remember he'd already told me. But he didn't *sound* drunk.' She shrugged. 'Then again, some people don't, do they?'

'What sort of mood was he in?'

'He seemed sad,' Alicia replied. 'No, sad's the wrong word. Miserable. He'd had an argument with his girlfriend – at least, that's what he kept telling me. Is he ok?'

Lawrence ignored the question. 'Do you remember what time he arrived here?'

'Um – I think about ten.'

'And was he here long?'

''Til closing.'

'What time do you close?'

'Eleven-thirty.'

'Was there anything particularly memorable about your conversation?'

Alicia considered the matter for a moment before shaking her head. 'No. He didn't say a lot, to be honest – just the same few things over and over again. Besides, I don't have all evening to chat. I'm here to work.'

'I realise that,' Lawrence conceded, reaching into his pocket for his card. 'But if anything does come to mind could you let me know?' He set it down on the bar.

'Sure.' Alicia slid it towards herself and folded it into her pocket before gathering up the glasses she had been carrying previously and continuing on her way along the bar. Lawrence watched her go. Assuming she was correct, and that Sally was telling the truth, somebody other than Justin must have seen Suki in the hours – and perhaps even minutes – before she died. Identifying that person could prove incredibly difficult; verifying Sally's version of events less so. Drawing his mobile from his pocket, Lawrence dialled Rebecca's number. With luck, she could have an answer for him by the end of the day.

It came as no great surprise that Ethan had seen nothing of Floyd in the hours since his interview, but Lawrence was puzzled to learn Ethan had heard nothing about Suki's death, either. Although the news had yet – to his knowledge – to reach the media, he had assumed it would have travelled at least as far as Justin and Floyd's band mates. Not that Ethan looked as if he belonged to the same band. Neither Floyd nor Justin looked *ordinary*, and that was precisely how Ethan did look. He was considerably heavier, with short, thinning dark hair and what could loosely be termed a goatee, but was really little more than a week's worth of stubble. He had no visible piercings or tattoos, and was clad in black jeans and a Reading Festival t-shirt, dated several years previously. Lawrence's initial introduction of himself didn't appear to unsettle the man, but his explanation of why he was there elicited stunned silence.

'What happened?' Ethan asked, eventually.

'That's what I'm trying to establish.'

The man nodded mechanically, looking shell-shocked. 'How's Justin? Is somebody with him?'

'We're actually holding him in custody, so somebody will be keeping an eye on him.'

'Custody?' Ethan's eyebrows shot up. 'You mean – you think he –' he faltered.

'We really don't know what happened yet, but I do need to ask you a few questions. Would you mind if I came in?'

'Oh – no – no, do.' He turned from the door and started up the stairs immediately inside. Lawrence followed, emerging moments later into an open-plan living area with a kitchen built against one end wall and a chunky fireplace set into the other. With the exception of a navy velour sofa and a widescreen television, which crouched on the floor in the alcove between the fireplace and a window, the room was devoid of furniture, and, given the number of boxes stacked against the walls, Lawrence concluded Ethan was in the process of moving either in or out. He answered the question of which almost immediately, waving a hand in the direction of the fireplace and saying, apologetically, 'I have to be out by Friday.'

'I won't keep you long,' Lawrence assured him. 'First of all, can you tell me anything about why Justin tried to push Suki off the balcony of his flat last summer?'

Ethan sighed, leaning against the kitchen worktop. 'That wasn't how it sounds. He and Floyd were living in an ex-council flat, and he got it into his head the council was trying to gas them. One night he tried to *escape* over the balcony – Suki tried to stop him, and he nearly took her over the edge with him. Fortunately Floyd was there as well.'

'How about the bruise she sustained to her face in the run-up to Christmas?'

Ethan frowned. 'What's that got to do with Justin? He wasn't driving.'

'Are you saying it was the result of a traffic accident?'

'No – well, not exactly – we were on the tour bus. The driver slammed on the brakes while Suki was standing up and she went flying.'

'And do you know how she came to break her arm last summer?'

Ethan appeared to consider this for a moment before shaking his head. 'No. But I don't think it had anything to do with Justin, if that's what you're asking. He's not violent.'

'And Floyd?'

'What about him?'

'Has he ever been violent?'

Ethan almost laughed. 'Floyd rarely even hurts people's *feelings*.'

'Does he take drugs?'

'How's that relevant?'

'Well, he can't seem to remember much about how he got home last night, or what he was doing during the hours surrounding Suki's death. He claims not to have had much to drink, and, if he wasn't drunk, I'd like to know whether there might be another reason why he can't remember, other than that it's convenient when faced with questioning.'

Lawrence had expected Ethan to jump to his band mate's defence, but he didn't. Raising his eyebrows, he held out his hands. 'I dunno. He's been all over the place lately.'

'Do you think you could explain what you mean by that?'

Ethan sighed. 'Floyd's usually very reliable, but recently he's been late for rehearsals and studio sessions – that's when he's been there at all – his playing has been totally erratic –' he shook his head slightly. 'And you never know what sort of mood you're likely to catch him in. He's always been really easygoing, but these days he'll bite your head off over nothing at all.'

'Have you asked him about that?'

'He blames everything on his migraines,' Ethan shrugged, his tone such that it was difficult to know how convinced or otherwise he was by the explanation.

'Do you believe that's all there is to it?'

'Not entirely,' Ethan admitted. 'I mean, I know he gets them, and I know it's not a trivial complaint, but –' he hesitated. 'Sometimes I think he takes advantage of that, because it's difficult to challenge him without sounding like an unsympathetic twat.'

'Could he be using drugs, do you think?'

Ethan averted his eyes, clearly uncomfortable, and didn't answer the question.

'Mr Taylor, I'm investigating a homicide. Your testimony isn't going to result in my arresting him for drug-related offences.'

There was a pause before Ethan spoke. 'I think it's possible,' he allowed, digging his hands into the pockets of his jeans. 'He looks awful, he keeps forgetting things, half the time he can't walk in a straight line – and we've tried tackling him about it, but he denies taking anything and without some kind of proof there's not a lot we can do.'

Lawrence nodded. 'And how about Justin? How's he been recently?'

'All things considered he's been doing pretty well.'

'Meaning what?'

'Floyd's behaviour hasn't made life easy for him, and neither has his brother. But he's been ok.'

'So you're not aware of his having had any difficulties with Suki?'

'No. I think she's been one of the things keeping him –' Ethan stopped short. 'I was going to say sane, which is hardly an appropriate figure of speech. But you get my drift.'

'Did you know her well?'

'Not really. I don't see much of Justin outside of the band, so I never saw much of her either.'

'Is there a reason you don't socialise much with Justin?'

'I already spend days and weeks in the studio and on tour with the guys. And I do have other friends.'

'So you would count the members of your band as friends.'

'Sure. If we weren't I don't think we'd have made it past six months together. It's tough enough living on top of each other for weeks at a time even when everybody *does* get on.'

Lawrence could believe it. He knew from some of what Rebecca had said in the past that Elliot found touring incredibly difficult for that very reason, and guessed it would be all too easy to fall out over anything and everything in such circumstances. With this in mind, he asked, 'Have there been any major disagreements between the four of you recently?'

'Nothing serious,' Ethan replied, his evident discomfort betraying him.

'But there have been arguments?'

'Well – there always are. Justin takes what we do very seriously. Musically, he's a natural, and the rest of us don't always measure up.' He rubbed his chin. 'But that's normal. We're used to it.'

Lawrence sensed Ethan wasn't telling the full story, but didn't press him, asking instead what he had been doing the night before and whether he could provide an address for the band's drummer. Perhaps he would be more forthcoming.

*****

Daniel had had little difficulty locating the rather brazenly named *Skin* club where Suki had supposedly been employed, but on arrival found it closed. An A4 notice taped to the front door stated that this was due to an electrical fault, and that they hoped to be open again by the following afternoon. Persistent knocking on the front and side doors drew no response, and neither the manager of the wine bar nor the owner of the café between which the club's entrance was sandwiched was able to provide any contact details over and above those Daniel already had. Having tried a number of other businesses in the immediate area with no success, he decided to head back to the Yard to see what progress Rebecca had made.

She wasn't at her desk when he reached the office, but her laptop was on, so Daniel guessed she hadn't gone far, and sat down at his own desk, reaching for the copy of *Rock UK* that lay in her in tray. He had barely found an article he was interested in reading when the telephone on Rebecca's desk rang. He reached to answer it.

'DS Freeman.'

'Hi, this is Cerise on reception. There's a bloke down here who'd like to talk to someone about Justin Black, and –'

'I'll come down,' Daniel replied, replacing the receiver and standing to retrace the route he'd walked just a few minutes earlier.

The young man sitting in reception looked vaguely familiar, and Daniel wondered whether he'd previously seen the man's picture in one of Rebecca's music magazines. He was casually dressed in bleached denim jeans and a long-sleeved Pagans tour t-shirt, and had untidily ruffled dark hair, several rings in each ear and one through his nose. He stood as Daniel approached, offering a small smile in greeting.

'Hi.'

'Afternoon. I'm DS Freeman, how can I help?'

'I'm a mate of Justin's. Is he all right?'

'And you are?'

'My name's Tony.'

'Tony who?'

'Nash. Is he ok? What happened?'

'We don't know what happened yet.'

'Is it true Suki's dead?'

Daniel ignored the question. 'How do you know Justin?'

'He's a mate – I've known him years. Can I see him?'

'Not at the moment. But you might be able to answer a few questions for me.'

'Sure,' Tony nodded, earnestly. 'You haven't charged him or anything, have you?'

'I really can't answer that.'

'Right. Of course.'

'We'll talk upstairs,' Daniel decided, aloud, turning towards the lifts. Tony followed, saying, 'Poor Justin. He's already been through it this year.'

'How so?'

'Well, you know – all that time in hospital – and his brother going off the rails – do you think maybe it all just got to be too much?'

'Do you?' Daniel countered, spotting Rebecca heading towards them, the cardboard cup and paper bag in her hands immediately updating him on where she'd been. She smiled as she neared, then, noticing Tony, stopped short.

'What are you doing here?' She asked, sharply.

'I came to see how Justin's doing.'

'Did you,' Rebecca returned, coldly. 'Well, now you can go.'

'Becks, come on, I'm sure we can –'

'*Now.*'

'But –'

'Do I need to have you escorted from the building?'

Tony sighed, turning to leave.

Daniel looked to Rebecca for an explanation as the man walked away. 'What was that about?'

'He's a journalist, Dan.'

'Oh God.'

The lift arrived and Rebecca stepped inside. Daniel hurried after her.

'What did you tell him?' Rebecca asked, as she selected the relevant floor.

'Nothing,' Daniel replied, feeling both relieved it was true and stupid for having been taken in.

'You sure?'

He nodded. 'Yes.'

Rebecca seemed satisfied, and leaned back against the wall of the lift, saying no more.

'God. I'm such an idiot.'

'You're not an idiot. If you didn't tell him anything there's no harm done, is there?'

Daniel shrugged.

'Except perhaps to your ego,' Rebecca observed. 'Dan, you didn't know. That's not your fault.'

'You did.'

'Only because I live with somebody journalists are interested in.'

'Still.'

'Just be careful,' Rebecca advised. 'Justin's news, and so are a good many others you'll be talking to. This story is tabloid gold.'

Daniel made no reply. Rebecca was right, of course – there was no way he could have known who Tony was – he just wished it could have been somebody else there to set the record straight. *Anybody* else.

## Seven

As Lawrence reached to ring the doorbell of the address Ethan had provided for Dave, the door opened and a man emerged in a long black velvet coat, platform boots and oversized sunglasses, with fiercely bleached and back-combed hair. On coming face-to-face with Lawrence, he paused on the threshold, his gloved left hand holding the door half-open behind him.

'Can I help you?' He asked, his manner oddly genteel.

'Are you David Hanson?'

The man shook his head, turning and leaning back through the doorway. 'Dave!' He yelled, his decorum abruptly evaporating. 'Door!' Then, leaving the door ajar, he skirted around Lawrence and hurried down the steps towards the street. Some seconds passed before the door re-opened and a more normally attired young man with short, mousy hair and equally mousy stubble appeared. He didn't seem surprised to find an unfamiliar visitor on the doorstep, and Lawrence guessed either Ethan had called to give him advanced warning or, given his absence from Ethan's flat, that Floyd had elected to head for Dave's home instead.

'Good afternoon. I'm DCI Forrester. I've a few questions for you if you don't mind?'

'About Suki,' Dave assumed, partially satisfying Lawrence's initial hunch. *Somebody* had clearly updated Dave on the day's events.

'Yes.'

'Sure, come in.' Dave turned from the door, stepping over remnants of what had clearly once been a banister rail, a now naked – and dangerous – staircase climbing the wall to the right of the door. 'Sorry about the mess,' he apologised as Lawrence picked his way through the debris. 'My flat mate pulled the rail down at the weekend to get a piano up to his room. I'm still waiting for him to clear up.' He flicked a light on in the room beyond the staircase, adding, 'From experience it's probably going to be a long wait.'

Looking around the room ahead of him, Lawrence wondered how long *it* had been waiting to be cleared up. It was more of a storage area than a living room, with amplifiers, instruments and other musical paraphernalia he couldn't identify occupying at least seventy-five per cent of the floor space. A grubby yellow sofa crouched in the black sea of equipment, serving the secondary function of a table, with magazines, DVDs and an open packet of biscuits strewn across it. Dave tipped these unceremoniously onto the floor, kicking the magazines and several of the DVDs under the sofa before looking back to Lawrence. 'Have a seat.'

Lawrence did as bid and Dave perched on a trunk opposite him, his expression expectant.

'Could you tell me when you last saw Suki?'

'Oooh –' Dave wrinkled his nose in thought. 'Not in a while. Probably not inside the last month.'

'Did you know her well?'

'No. I couldn't stand her.'

'Why not?'

'For the same reason a lot of people didn't like her.'

Lawrence felt intrigued. 'Well so far I haven't come across anybody else who didn't.'

Dave smirked. 'I doubt that's true. The other people you've spoken to probably just don't have a decent alibi.'

'And you do?'

'I was at a friend's place in Acton until about four o'clock this morning. There are three other people who can confirm that.'

'We'll come back to how I can verify that later. First you can tell me what you meant about Suki.'

Despite his earlier honesty about his feelings towards the girl, Lawrence was taken aback when Dave replied, bluntly, 'Suki was a manipulative bitch.'

'Justin obviously didn't think so.'

'Justin's not a great judge of character.'

'Could you expand on what you said about Suki?'

'She used people. If she wanted something from you she could be very, very nice – but if you didn't serve any useful purpose, you generally got dumped.'

'Do you think she was using Justin?'

'Of course she was. She wanted a rock star boyfriend, and that's exactly where he's headed. He's talented, attractive and very easy to use.'

'Easy to use?' Lawrence queried. 'How so?'

'Just wants to be looked after. No, actually, he *needs* to be looked after. Suki was willing to do that, and she was beautiful. I'm sure he loved her, but I think she just loved what he represented.'

Lawrence wasn't convinced. From what he had learned that day, he doubted anybody would have attached themselves to Justin purely for reasons of status – or at least remained attached for long. Suki had been with him for nearly two years.

'Who else do you think she was using?'

Dave half smiled. 'You name someone who called her a friend, and I'll tell you why that person was her friend.'

Lawrence felt nettled by the young man's arrogance, and almost hoped he'd be proved wrong. 'How about her flat mate?' He suggested.

Dave looked blank. 'Who is her flat mate?'

'A girl named Sally.'

'Sally,' Dave echoed, his eyebrows crinkling in thought. 'Sally Jacobs?'

'That's right.'

'You heard of a band called Vicious Circle?'

Lawrence nodded. 'My son's a big fan.'

'Well Sally's brother is their bass player. So three guesses what Suki saw in her.' He paused, then added, 'But that's nothing against Sal, she's a great girl.'

'You said earlier that you thought a lot of people disliked Suki – can you think of anybody who might have wanted her dead?'

Dave appeared to give this some considerable thought. 'Not dead, no,' he concluded, at length. 'But then, besides Justin I don't know many people who were close to her. I don't waste my time hanging around with people I don't like.'

'How about Floyd? Do you think he liked her?'

'Oh Floyd likes *everybody*,' Dave responded, casually. 'He's irritatingly good-natured. For months after I met him I thought it must be an act, but I don't think it is. Or should I say was.'

'What does that mean?'

Clearly having none of Ethan's qualms about what he should or shouldn't say to the police about his band mate's activities, Dave replied, 'These days he's too out of it to care. He's fucking his life up and doing his best to take the rest of us with him.'

'How?'

'I don't know what he's using, but he's been fried on something for weeks! He's been impossible to work with, and if it wasn't for Justin, we'd have sacked him by now!'

'Meaning what? Justin won't agree to it? Or he depends on Floyd too much for it to be an option?'

'Both,' Dave responded, shortly. 'Although as far as I'm concerned, right now he needs Floyd like a hole in the head.'

'You said a moment ago that Floyd *was* irritatingly good-natured, by which I presume you mean he hasn't been lately. Has he been aggressive, at all?'

'No, just a moody git.'

'And how about Justin? How's he been recently?'

'He's been –' Dave broke off, presumably to consider his answer, before saying, rather unhelpfully, 'Justin.'

'Are you saying he's been more or less himself?'

'Yes.'

'When did you see him last?'

'Saturday afternoon. In the studio. We were recording all last week.'

'Did anything unusual happen in that time?'

'Well, Just and Floyd had several massive rows,' Dave observed. 'But that's becoming less and less unusual.' He paused, then added, 'And to be frank, if Justin didn't do it, I'd do it for him.'

Lawrence had met Greg Murray, the duty psychiatrist, before. A slender man of about five foot ten, he seemed to look exactly the same every time Lawrence saw him. Regardless of the hour he was called upon, he was always smartly dressed in a grey pinstriped suit and white shirt, with an unremarkable plain tie. His long dark fringe was swept in a gravity-defying fashion across his forehead, and his taupe eyes were slightly magnified by delicate, rectangular glasses. Even smiling, he managed to look serious. He greeted Lawrence with a familiar nod and a genial, 'Evening.'

'Hi. How's Justin?'

'He's fairly quiet at the moment.'

'When we questioned him earlier, he seemed to have a lot of trouble following what was going on. Would that have been genuine, do you think?'

'Psychosis can be very disorientating,' Greg replied. 'To give a simplistic example, try to imagine having more than one person talking to you at the same time, about different things. That alone can make focusing on one train of thought incredibly difficult. Then add the fact schizophrenia can affect a person's ability to take in, retain and utilise information, and you can see how easily even simple tasks might become confusing or overwhelming.'

'Would that also account for his occasionally coming out with bizarre things that didn't appear to make any sense?'

'Possibly, but that could also be thought disorder, which is essentially an inability to think in a coherent, logical manner.'

'And do you think in Justin's case that's genuine?'

'His behaviour certainly seemed that way to me.'

'Is that a result of what happened last night, or would he already have been in that state?'

Greg sounded apologetic as he said, 'That's hard for me to say. The symptoms of schizophrenia don't appear overnight, but he's had a very traumatic twenty-four hours, and it's quite possible that could have exacerbated things. On top of which, I don't know what medication he's been prescribed, or how good he is at taking it. Schizophrenics are notoriously bad at complying with drug treatment. His friends or family might be able to give you more insight.'

'I've spoken to several of his friends and none of them seem to think he's been behaving any differently from usual.'

'Usual doesn't necessarily mean normal,' Greg pointed out. 'But it is difficult to know what sort of impact recent events have had. Anybody in his shoes – whether or not they were responsible for it – is going to be pretty shaken up.'

Lawrence nodded. 'And at the risk of asking a stereotypical question, is it possible he attacked his girlfriend while hallucinating? Maybe thought she was someone else, or meant him some sort of harm?'

'It's possible, but –' Greg's eyebrows contracted in concern. 'I don't think pigeonholing people is particularly helpful. Even if he *was* responsible, his actions may have had precious little to do with his illness, and it's quite possible he understood the consequences of what he was doing. I would keep an open mind while you try to tease out the details of the past day or so. The only person who can really tell you what's going on in his head is him.'

Lawrence nodded. 'Do you think he's up to questioning?'

'Even if he were it wouldn't be worth it at the moment with the drugs I've given him – he's very drowsy, and it's unlikely he'd be able to concentrate or think clearly about anything.'

'How about in the morning?'

'I can't answer that until tomorrow.'

'Ballpark?'

'I'm afraid there's no way of making an accurate prediction. I really don't know.'

Lawrence sighed. 'Ok.'

'I'll pop back to see him tomorrow. If you decide to release him in the meantime, don't send him off alone. He ought to have someone keep an eye on him.'

'I'll bear that in mind. If he is up to it in the morning, would you have time to sit in on the interview?'

Greg gave the request a moment's thought, then nodded. 'I can be here from eleven until about one. I'll be in to see him first thing – I'll try to have a yes or no for you by nine.'

'Great. Thank you.'

'Have a good evening.'

'You too,' Lawrence replied, automatically, wishing he was the one heading home. *His* evening, he guessed, was still some way off.

Rebecca peered through the glass panel in the laboratory door and, seeing Leighton leaning over the bench, eased it open. As she did so, Leighton glanced in her direction before returning his eyes to the rack of tiny plastic tubes in front of him. He held a bottle of colourless liquid in one hand and a chunky pipette in the other, and was in the process of adding minuscule quantities of the fluid to each tube in turn.

'Hey Becks,' he greeted her, continuing with what he was doing. 'How's it going?'

'I've been dispatched to see where you're at.'

'Ah, you mean Forrester wants to know why the hell I've not reported back already,' Leighton interpreted, with a grin.

'Something like that,' Rebecca admitted.

'If he wants these to reach the lab tonight, he'll have to wait a bit longer.'

Rebecca nodded, perching on a nearby stool.

'How's your day been?' He enquired, giving her his attention long enough for her to answer wordlessly with a change in expression.

Leighton mock winced. 'That bad, huh?'

'Over the course of your career, have you come across anybody who died of boredom?'

'Only a couple,' Leighton answered, carelessly, returning the pipette to the bottle in his hand. 'But that was to be expected. They lived in East Anglia.'

Leighton regularly made fun of the fact Rebecca had grown up in Norfolk, and she generally returned the favour with cracks about his choosing to live south of the Thames. On this occasion, she satisfied herself with delivering a playful punch to his arm. 'Git.'

'Technically I could have you for assault,' Leighton teased, as he transferred the pipette's load to one of the tubes.

'*Technically*,' Rebecca stressed, 'It would be battery. But I wouldn't expect a tabloid reader like yourself to understand the finer points of English law.'

'Objection, your honour! I *never* read the tabloids.' He paused for effect before adding, with a grin, 'I just look at the pictures.'

Rebecca rolled her eyes in response. In reality, she knew Leighton was all too familiar with the nuances of English law where violent crime was concerned: his elder brother had served time for several such offences. At present, Tom was incarcerated in Wakefield Prison, and Leighton made the effort to visit at least once a month. It struck Rebecca as a big commitment for someone whose movements were restricted by an on-call schedule two weekends in every six, and she often wondered whether he did it by choice or out of duty. It wasn't really the sort of question one could ask.

He brought her back to the present with, 'Have the press woken up yet?'

'Yep. Word got out on social media.'

'And the news spread faster than cholera through a Victorian slum?'

'Pretty much,' Rebecca replied, smiling at his choice of analogy. 'We've already had a couple of journalists try to sneak past the radar.'

'Hmmm. Radar could be where you're going wrong,' Leighton said, with a wink. 'What you need is razor wire and an AK-47.'

'I'll see what I can find in the stationery cupboard.'

Leighton set the bottle and pipette down on the bench and began the delicate task of closing the lentil-sized lids of his tiny sample tubes. Rebecca watched him work his way along the line in silence, not wanting to distract from the process. Clipping the last one into place, he straightened up, swivelling around to face her. He looked tired, and, after their early start, Rebecca guessed he wasn't the only one.

'Did you know her?' He asked, his blue eyes concerned.

'Not really. I've seen her at gigs, and we've exchanged small talk on a few occasions, but nothing more.'

'And Elliot?'

'He knew her better than I did – the guys have all been part of the same crowd since before I knew him. And he toured with Justin last year.'

'How's he handling it?'

'Probably the same way he handles everything else these days – with whisky or vodka,' Rebecca returned, her tone harder than she had intended. Leighton didn't immediately reply, and she said, 'Sorry. That sounded harsh. I know he's probably going through hell and I should be more sympathetic, but –' she shook her head. 'I'm sick and tired of dealing with it all.'

'Have you told him that?'

'I've tried. A lot of the time he's too drunk to take what I'm saying on board, and when he does manage to get the gist –' she sighed. 'It's impossible to have a sensible conversation with him, because the moment I say anything critical or raise concerns about us, he goes to pieces. Sometimes I'm not even sure it's genuine, and I think he's simply trying to avoid the issue.'

'It's probably just more than he can cope with right now.'

'*He's* getting to the point of being more than *I* can cope with,' Rebecca returned, testily, wishing her friend would take a less impartial stance and validate her feelings about the situation. Maybe he thought badly of her for wanting to give up on someone who was, when it came down to it, seriously ill. She hesitated before saying, 'Do you think I'm being selfish?'

'No. Elliot doesn't have a monopoly on feelings.'

'It wouldn't be so bad if he didn't think the answer was at the bottom of a bottle,' Rebecca replied, feeling the need to defend herself despite Leighton's benevolent response.

He nodded slightly. 'I know.'

Rebecca wasn't sure he really did, but appreciated his willingness to listen without telling her what to do. She forced a smile. 'Thanks.' Slipping down off the stool, she added, 'I should be getting back before Forrester sends out a search party. Can I give him an ETA for your update?'

'Fifteen minutes?' Leighton estimated, hopefully. Rebecca knew that probably meant at least thirty, which was what she would feed back to her superior. On this occasion, she was possibly even more impatient than he was for the findings of the postmortem. Despite scarcely knowing him, she found herself desperately wanting Justin to be innocent.

Predictably, Leighton appeared in CID after considerably more than a quarter of an hour. Rebecca followed him into Lawrence's office, where Daniel was leaning against the wall by the window, gazing down towards the street, and Lawrence was reading what looked like an official report. He set it to one side as Rebecca and Leighton entered, looking to the pathologist.

'I can only hope you've had a more fruitful day than Danny and I.'

Leighton sat back-to-front on a chair on the near side of Lawrence's desk. 'You're probably out of luck there.'

Lawrence sighed. 'Well let's have what you've got.'

'Ok. Cause of death – as you would expect – skull fracture, brain haemorrhage, et cetera. She'd been hit so many times it's impossible to put a number on it.'

'Suggesting a very angry assailant,' Lawrence observed.

'Uh-huh.'

'How about time of death?'

'I can't really be any more specific than the time frame we already have. Sorry.'

Lawrence nodded.

'With regard to the guys who were there this morning, all of them had at least some blood on their clothing, although that's probably circumstantial where Floyd and Alec are concerned. We didn't find any other bloodstained clothes in the flat, and a couple of the SOCOs extended the search to nearby bins with no luck. As for Justin – you saw the state of the room – the blood up the walls is enough to tell you the attack severed a major artery, and although Justin was covered in blood there's no real evidence of blood spatter. Besides various smears that look like they've come from his fingers, the blood on his jumper is all in one place. If he was responsible I would have expected more splashes.'

'So what are you saying? You don't think he was responsible?'

'I don't know. Fabrics aren't particularly reliable materials where blood transfer is concerned. I certainly can't say he *was*.'

'Translation: the evidence so far won't stand up in court,' Lawrence interpreted.

Leighton nodded wordlessly.

'But Justin could have changed his clothes as easily as anybody else,' Daniel interjected.

Lawrence shook his head. 'If Justin was responsible it wasn't premeditated. I doubt he so much as moved from her side from the minute he either found her or killed her.'

'Did you see his bedroom?' Leighton enquired.

'No. Why?'

'It's wallpapered with tin foil. The ceiling too.'

'How bizarre.'

'Although I'd probably want to cover my walls, too, if they were painted magnolia.'

'So it wasn't hiding anything else.'

'Nope. We did find traces of blood in the bathroom, which could indicate someone cleaned themselves up before leaving, but even if it does turn out to be Suki's we won't know for sure because she was surfing the crimson wave.'

Noticing Lawrence's puzzled expression, Rebecca clarified, 'He means she was menstruating.'

'Right,' her superior nodded.

Leighton held his hands out, palms upwards. 'We're always being told you guys don't like long medical terms,' he said, with a mischievous smile.

Rebecca raised her eyes heavenwards.

'The only other remotely interesting thing we came across in the flat was some unlabelled pills in Floyd's bedroom. When I find out what they are I'll let you know.'

'Do you have any idea?'

''Fraid not, they've no stamp or anything else to identify them by. Although as high street chemists don't dispense tablets in ziplock bags, they're probably not over-the-counter meds.'

Rebecca felt surprised, and at the same time wondered why. She didn't suppose many – if any – of Elliot's friends were strangers to recreational drug use, and the knowledge that Elliot himself had taken cocaine whilst away on tour had caused more than a little friction between them. She didn't know Floyd as well as some of Elliot's other friends, but from what she did know she couldn't imagine his having a drug habit. He had always seemed wise beyond his years, and considerably more responsible than the majority of Elliot's crowd. Then again, applying common sense and professional experience over gut instinct, there was no such thing as a *type* where drug users were concerned. And, of course, there was a world of difference between those who bought drugs for a night out, and those who bought them to use alone at home.

Leighton pushed himself rather reluctantly up out of his chair. 'I'm not finished yet, though,' he said, as he made for the door. 'So you never know. I might have something more for you in a day or two.'

'Thank you,' Lawrence responded, looking to Rebecca as Leighton left the room. 'If you're ready, I'll give you a lift home.'

'Are you going my way?'

'Right to your door. I need to ask Elliot about Floyd's account of last night.'

Rebecca hesitated, not sure she could face being a party to the interview. Her colleagues knowing about her fiancé's drinking was one thing, but *seeing* it was quite another. Then she nodded, and headed to retrieve her jacket and handbag. If she didn't go, what went on in her imagination could, quite possibly, be even worse than the reality.

Lawrence hadn't seen Elliot in several months, and, despite all Rebecca had said in recent weeks, felt rather shocked by the young man's appearance. He evidently hadn't bothered bleaching his hair in some time, and the dark roots framing his face made him look terribly pale. His thick jumper did little to disguise the fact that he was desperately thin, his cheekbones protruded sharply, and the dark shadows beneath his brown eyes betrayed how little sleep he had had in recent days. He was slumped in the corner of the sofa, his head propped up with his right hand, elbow on the armrest, a cigarette between the fingers of his left hand. He looked anxious and exhausted, and Lawrence wondered how his doctor could even entertain the idea of allowing the record company to send him on a European tour in under a fortnight.

'Hello Elliot.'

'Hi,' he muttered, disinterestedly.

'I'd like to ask you a few questions, if you have five minutes?'

Elliot tensed, his eyes flickering in the direction of the doorway where Rebecca was standing.

'I just need you to run through what you did last night,' Lawrence explained, sitting in an armchair facing him. 'Perhaps you could start with where you were?'

Elliot was clearly still on edge, and his reply was rather stilted. 'Soho. A bar called the Dark Heart. I met Floyd for a drink.'

'What time?'

'About half nine.'

'Until when?'

'Closing. Then we got the tube home.'

'What sort of time would that have been?'

'I dunno. Half eleven? Twelve? Something like that.'

'What did you and Floyd talk about in the pub?'

'Friends, music, gigs,' he shrugged. 'Usual stuff. You know.'

'And what else?' Lawrence asked, guessing from the palpable tension that there was more Elliot hadn't told him.

'Nothing much.'

Lawrence would have challenged him, but Rebecca beat him to it, her tone sharp. 'Tell the truth for once, Elliot.' Then, as an afterthought, 'Assuming you can remember what that *means*.'

Elliot cast his eyes down, saying nothing.

Lawrence sighed. 'Elliot, come on, this may be very important.'

'I dunno,' Elliot muttered, eventually. 'I was drunk.'

'Liar,' Rebecca snapped. 'You weren't that drunk when you got home!'

'How would you know?' Elliot retorted. 'It's not like you *spoke* to me, is it?'

The atmosphere in the room told Lawrence far more about the state of Rebecca's relationship with Elliot than she had. He didn't doubt her presence would be detrimental to the interview, and, with this in mind, said, 'Perhaps it might be best if I went over this with Elliot.'

'Be my guest,' Rebecca responded, curtly. Shooting Elliot a disgusted look, she spun around and left the room, pulling the door shut behind herself with rather more force than necessary.

Lawrence returned his attention to Elliot. 'Are you going to tell me now?'

Elliot frowned. 'What – you think –' he shook his head. 'We didn't talk about Becca, we –' he trailed off, seeming to realise he had caught himself out.

'So you remember what you *didn't* talk about,' Lawrence responded, evenly. 'Now, how about you tell me what you *did* talk about?'

Elliot stubbed out his cigarette and reached for the crumpled packet of Marlboros that lay on the coffee table. He tapped one out and lit it before admitting, 'He was a bit upset.'

'Why?'

'He'd had some falling out with Justin. They've not been getting on, and he's finding that hard, because they've been close since they were kids.'

'What was it about?'

Elliot shook his head. 'I don't know.'

'Elliot –'

'I honestly don't know.' He lifted his gaze to meet Lawrence's eyes before adding, for emphasis, 'Really.'

'Has Justin ever been violent towards him?'

'If he has I've never heard about it.'

'Do you have any idea how good he is at taking his medication?'

'Pretty good, I think. Floyd makes sure he keeps on top of it.'

Whilst that might once have been true, Lawrence very much doubted it was now. Wondering why he was bothering to ask, given that the answer was hardly likely to be reliable, he continued, 'How much did you and Floyd have to drink last night?'

'A few pints.'

'And what else did Floyd have to say?'

'Not a lot.'

'You're wasting my time, Elliot. He clearly said something that worried you, and I'm going nowhere until I find out what.'

'He didn't say anything much else,' Elliot protested.

Lawrence regarded him in silence for a moment before leaning forwards and resting his forearms across his knees. 'Don't make the mistake of thinking I will afford you any special treatment on account of your relationship with Rebecca,' he warned. 'If I have to arrest you for wasting my time, I won't hesitate to do so. Is that clear?'

Elliot swallowed. Seconds passed. 'It wasn't anything particular that he said,' he admitted, eventually. 'It was just –' he faltered. 'He seemed – odd.'

'In what way?'

Elliot shook his head slightly. 'I don't know. He just wasn't himself.'

'How?' Lawrence persisted.

'Floyd's always been really laid back – he's one of those people you want to hate, because they seem to have everything, but at the same time you can't help liking them. He's fun to be around, he's thoughtful, he's empathic –' Elliot paused. 'And he's always been so content I can't help but envy him. Everybody likes Floyd.'

'And last night?'

'He seemed – I dunno – unsettled. Impatient. A bit manic.'

'Did you ask him about that?'

'No.'

'Why not?'

'I don't know. I just didn't.'

'Your friend was behaving in a manner that seemed completely out of character and you didn't ask what was up? Whether he was ok?' Lawrence responded, incredulously. 'Try again.'

There was a long pause. Elliot looked tortured, and Lawrence guessed he was on the verge of revealing whatever it was he had been trying to keep to himself since the start of the interview. Well aware of the pressure silence alone can exert, he listened to the seconds tick by and watched as Elliot's anxiety visibly increased. Eventually, just as he was wondering whether to try repeating the question, Elliot caved.

'I didn't –' he closed his eyes briefly. 'I just –' Another pause. Then, finally, 'I wasn't sure how he'd react.'

Lawrence knew his wife was angry before she even turned from the sink, and wondered how much that resulted from the length of time they had known one another, and how much it was due to his studying people's body language on a daily basis. He suspected the smell of smoke on his hair and clothing after the interview with Elliot was going to aggravate her further, as she would probably assume he'd been socialising.

After their daughter had started school, Katie had opted to return to work part time, but the demands of Lawrence's job meant she had also been doing the lion's share of the childcare and housekeeping ever since, and he was well aware she was feeling the strain. Over the past couple of years she had grown increasingly intolerant of the long hours and weekends he was frequently required to work, and he was beginning to resent constantly having to justify himself. And short of changing career – which he simply couldn't imagine doing – he had absolutely no idea how to resolve the situation.

'Sorry I was up so early,' he began. 'One of Becky's friends was in trouble.' It wasn't quite true, but he hoped it might diffuse her irritation at also having been woken in the small hours.

'Did you manage to sort it out?' Katie enquired, pulling off her rubber gloves and hanging them over the mixer tap before turning around and leaning against the worktop.

'Unfortunately not, no,' he replied, digging his hands into his pockets and thinking Katie actually looked more upset than angry. Feeling he ought to apologise again, but at the same time reluctant to do so, he added, 'How are the kids?'

'Elise is cleaning out the hamster. Jimmy's waiting for a lecture from you.'

Lawrence frowned. 'About what?'

Katie reached behind the miscellany of art-class pottery that cluttered the windowsill and drew out a ten pack of Benson and Hedges.

'Ah,' Lawrence raised his eyebrows, wondering what it said for their marriage that he had automatically assumed he had been the one to upset her. Had the issue at stake been less serious he might also have felt relieved that, for once, something wasn't *his* fault. Of course, that could easily change, and from the way Katie was looking at him he sensed she expected him to say something further. 'God. Are we at that stage already?'

'Stage?' Katie echoed. 'You make it sound on a par with wanting a smartphone!'

Lawrence sighed. 'Kate, come on, I'm not denying the seriousness of it – all I meant was that all kids do these things –'

'*I* didn't!'

'Didn't you?' Lawrence exclaimed, before cursing himself for not thinking before he spoke. He managed it perfectly well at work.

'No! Although as you obviously did there's no point my expecting you to back me up!'

'That's not fair.'

Katie turned away to face the window above the sink, resting the palms of her hands on the edge of the worktop and bowing her head.

Lawrence rested a gentle hand on her arm, half expecting her to pull away. 'I'm sorry, it's been a long day. Let's sit down and sort this out. What's been said so far?'

'Not much.' Katie turned back towards him. 'I yelled – he yelled –' she sighed, allowing him to hold her. 'I just felt so unprepared for it. They've seen what it can do – I thought that might have been enough.' She leaned her head on his shoulder. 'I don't know. Maybe that was naive.'

Both evidence and experience indicated that few people learned from the mistakes of others, but Lawrence didn't say as much. Katie's father was seriously ill with emphysema after decades of heavy smoking, and he suspected the discovery that one of her own children was dabbling with the habit was one of her greatest fears realised. He held her close for several seconds, then, with a kiss, released her.

'You sit down. I'll give him a shout.'

Nodding, Katie did as bid. Lawrence made for the hallway and, stopping at the foot of the stairs, called, 'Jim? Down here now please.'

Shortly, Jimmy came trudging down the stairs, eyes on the floor. Lawrence returned to the kitchen and joined Katie at the table. Jimmy leaned against the door frame, kicking the metal bar that separated the kitchen lino from the polished wooden floor of the hallway.

'Sit down,' Lawrence instructed.

Wordlessly, Jimmy obeyed.

'Where did you get these?' Lawrence asked, holding up the cigarettes.

Jimmy shrugged.

'That's not an answer.'

'From a mate.'

'Which one?'

Jimmy didn't reply.

'Answer me!'

'I'm not telling you,' Jimmy responded, insolently, looking up for the first time.

'Well then perhaps I should call the school and see whether they have any ideas.'

'You can't!'

'I *can*.'

Jimmy didn't respond, reverting to staring sullenly at the tabletop.

'Jim, this isn't a little thing like playing football in the flower beds, or reading after lights out! Smoking is dangerous! And if you won't tell us where those cigarettes came from, I'm quite prepared to call your headmaster.'

'Fine,' Jimmy snapped. 'Ruin my life if that's what you want.'

'Ruin your life?' Katie echoed. 'What do you think *you're* going to do if you carry on smoking? Do you want to end up like your granddad, stuck indoors with an oxygen cylinder?'

Jimmy shrugged. 'He's old.'

'He wasn't when he started, was he?' Katie returned.

'Loads of people do it,' Jimmy countered. 'Elliot does.'

'Elliot's an adult!' Lawrence exclaimed. 'Besides which, he's not my son! *You* are!'

'How d'you know that?'

Lawrence blinked. 'I *beg* your pardon?'

'It said on TV that loads of kids get brought up by a guy who isn't their dad. How d'you know you're mine?'

Lawrence clenched his fists beneath the table and forced himself to take a breath before responding. 'Ok, first of all you can apologise to your mother for what you've just said. Then you can go to your room. We'll discuss your punishment later.'

There was a long pause. Jimmy said nothing.

'I'm waiting,' Lawrence pressed, his tone dangerous.

'Sorry,' Jimmy mumbled.

'Right. Go and finish whatever homework you still have to do, and then straight to bed. Clear?'

Jimmy nodded.

'And if I catch you playing computer games there will be hell to pay!'

## Eight

When Rebecca awoke she was alone, and guessed, from recent experience, that Elliot had gone in search of a drink. Nothing else was likely to have enticed him out of bed at seven-fifteen in the morning. Reluctantly sitting up and casting the covers aside, she stood and reached for her dressing gown, hoping she might, for once, catch him awake enough and sober enough to listen to what she had to say.

The kitchen was empty, and she continued along the hallway to the living room. Elliot was sitting forwards on the sofa, dressed only in boxer shorts and a thin t-shirt, his elbows resting on his knees and his right hand cradling his forehead. He jumped as she spoke his name and hurriedly dried the tears on his cheeks with his fingers. In his left hand, Rebecca noticed, he held what looked like a small piece of card.

'What've you got there?' She asked, curiosity overcoming her desire to deliver a few home truths. She joined him on the sofa and Elliot wordlessly proffered a shabby, crinkled photograph, his hand shaking violently. Rebecca took it and flattened it out. It was a picture of two boys, one aged five or six, the other in his mid teens. The younger of the two was clutching a brightly coloured kite, and the older boy stood behind him, arms wrapped loosely around his neck. They were very alike, both slim and dark haired, with high cheekbones and matching smiles, and the sand dunes in the background suggested the picture had been taken on holiday.

'Is that you?' Rebecca asked, indicating the elder of the two.

Elliot nodded.

'Who's with you?'

'My little brother,' Elliot sniffed. 'It's his eighteenth birthday today.'

'You must miss him a lot.'

'Yuh,' Elliot admitted. 'He used to be the most important person in my life.'

'When did you last see him?'

Elliot drew a deep, rather unsteady breath. 'Ten years ago on Saturday.'

'Ten years?'

'Yuh.'

'Why so long?'

Elliot shook his head, and Rebecca guessed that was all she was going to get. Where his family was concerned, coaxing any information at all out of Elliot had always been an uphill struggle. And the more he held back, the more she wanted to know. She sometimes wondered whether that was why he did it.

'What about the rest of your family?' She probed.

'They never fucking cared,' Elliot replied, bitterly.

Rebecca rested a gentle hand on his knee. 'What happened?'

Elliot didn't respond, turning away to hide his tears and reaching for the cigarettes that lay on the coffee table. Rebecca returned her eyes to the photograph. She didn't think she'd ever seen Elliot look so happy. The thought saddened her. They'd been together nearly three years, and recently she'd begun to realise he'd never actually been happy. He'd just spent the first two years on medication that kept him from being *un*happy. All she'd ever known was a chemical smile.

'What's his name, Elliot?'

Elliot just shook his head again.

'Did you send him a birthday card?'

'No. He's better off without me.'

'What was he like?'

Elliot swallowed hard. 'He was great. We had so much fun. We used to camp out in my uncle's garden, and climb trees – I even built him a tree house. I made him a boat, too. A little sailing boat, with blue sails. We used to take it to the pond in the park. I was his hero. He was so proud of me.' He bowed his head, tears running from his eyes. 'Then I fucked it all up.'

'What happened?'

'I let him down, more than you can possibly imagine.' He drew a deep, ragged breath. 'Actually, you probably can imagine. Letting people down – seems to be – what – what I do best!' He broke down, raising a hand to shield his eyes. Rebecca didn't move. She knew she ought to hold him. These weren't alcohol-fuelled tears, they were real, and she suspected whatever was at the root of them was also responsible for both his depression and his drinking. Part of her wanted to hold him close and promise him everything would be all right, but she couldn't do it. Nothing about their relationship was all right, and she guessed that, deep down, Elliot knew it too. Doubtless it was on the long list of denials that had become his norm. So she sat and watched him cry, feeling suddenly close to tears herself. At the same time, she wondered how she could possibly have any tears left after the past few months.

She had realised weeks ago that their relationship was over, yet the pain of that realisation hadn't lessened. Perhaps because she hadn't made the final break. Perhaps because part of her still hoped he might accept help, take his medication and go back to being the man she had fallen in love with. And, she finally admitted to herself, perhaps because she was afraid she might never again feel for anyone what she had felt for him.

Meredith listened to the same Radio One headlines she had heard half an hour previously, and half an hour before that. The words had the surreal quality of a dream. Two years ago it would have felt like a waking nightmare; now Meredith wasn't sure how she felt. Numb wasn't quite the right word, but it wasn't far off.

She wondered what had happened. How it had happened. What the last thoughts to go through Suki's mind had been. Whether she had felt any regret. Any remorse. Meredith had certainly never seen her show any. Not even on that sickening wet Thursday afternoon when she had answered her boyfriend's desperate call from the hospital. She had said all the right words, but when, minutes later, she repeated his – the memory of which still left Meredith cold – there had been no sign of distress. No sense of responsibility. Just stark facts and a callous joke. At the time, Meredith had convinced herself it was her friend's way of coping; now she suspected Suki hadn't needed to cope, because she hadn't cared. And if she hadn't cared about him, or about what she had done to him, she probably hadn't cared about anyone.

Beyond how came *why*. Meredith studied the poster blu-tacked to the wall beside her bed; a rare picture of Justin without his tinted glasses. He wasn't smiling, and his red eyes and intense stare lent the image the sinister ambience of a still from a horror film. Doubtless by now that picture was wallpapering news stands and agents across London. What speculation the tabloids were legally permitted to publish at this early stage she wasn't sure, but their questions would almost certainly converge on Justin's state of mind. In all likelihood, his instability would serve to absolve Suki of any real responsibility, and Meredith wondered whether anybody would look beyond that. She suspected Suki might not be quite the victim she had thus far been painted to be.

## Nine

'You see?' An old flat mate of Daniel's had once remarked, whilst watching an episode of *Big Brother*, 'It's true. The prettiest girl *always* makes best friends with the fat ugly one.' Of course, there are always exceptions to rules, and Kaia Winters was a notable exception. Slender but not skinny, perfectly proportioned and with long, apparently naturally blonde hair, Daniel imagined she had been the girl every boy in the year had lusted after at school. Her fine fringe skimmed the lashes of pale blue eyes, and her delicate cheekbones lent her face definition without taking away its softness. Smiling, she would have been stunning.

As it was, when Lawrence and Daniel arrived to interview her on Wednesday morning, she looked to be fighting a losing battle to maintain her composure, blinking back tears that repeatedly threatened to flood her already bloodshot eyes, and biting into her lower lip to keep it from trembling. She had apparently learned of Suki's death the previous afternoon, and Daniel wondered whether she had slept since.

Leaving him to close the front door of her studio flat, she crossed the room to the bed, where she curled up against the velvet headboard, cuddling an old grey teddy to her chest. The duvet, the tracksuit she wore and the sofa standing against the wall opposite the bed were all baby pink, and, as he joined Lawrence on the sofa, Daniel noticed the curtains and rug also matched. No prizes for guessing Kaia's favourite colour, then.

'I'm sorry to put you through this so soon,' Lawrence apologised. 'I understand you and Suki were very close.'

Kaia nodded. 'She's – was – my best friend.'

'Had you been friends a long time?'

'Not really,' Kaia's voice shook. 'But it feels like it. We just – clicked. You know.'

'How long had you known one another?'

'A couple of years. Since she met Justin.'

'Do you know him well?'

'No, not really. He was more Matt's friend than mine.'

'Was?'

'Is, I guess,' Kaia corrected herself. 'But I'm not with Matt any more.'

'Matt who?'

'Quilter.'

Another beautiful girl, another screwed-up jerk with a guitar, Daniel thought, almost forgetting himself and shaking his head in disbelief. He wondered when they had split up. Whether it had had anything to do with the Vicious Circle frontman's now infamous heroin habit. A quizzical glance from his superior redirected his focus, and he hastily pulled his notebook from his pocket.

'Did Suki talk much about Justin?' Lawrence continued.

'Of course.'

'Do you know whether he ever hurt her?'

'I don't think it was intentional.'

'But he did hurt her?'

There was a long pause before she nodded.

'How?'

'She wanted to be the one in control,' Kaia sniffed. 'And Justin's hard to control when he gets –' she hesitated before settling on, 'Upset.'

'Was that always the case?' Lawrence asked. 'It strikes me as the sort of thing most people would learn fairly quickly.'

'She knew it was possible,' Kaia shrugged. 'Floyd could do it. Actually, I think that was what got to her, more than anything.'

'Was she jealous of their friendship?'

'Not exactly jealous,' Kaia ventured, after a moment. 'But she wanted to be the one he needed. I think she expected him to express his love for her the same way she did for him.'

Daniel wondered whether that spoke of inexperience or simply a lack of empathy. 'Did she say that?' He enquired.

'Sort of. We were talking once – about love – and about how a boyfriend can end up being your best friend as well. She said when she was ill, she used to want her mum, but now it was Justin she wanted. I think she viewed the fact Floyd could better control Justin in the same light, and that made her feel maybe he didn't love her as much as she did him.'

'So she was insecure,' Lawrence concluded.

'It's hard not to be when your boyfriend fronts a successful band,' Kaia answered, sadly.

'And Justin?' Lawrence asked.

'Suki never gave him reason to be insecure.'

'I don't imagine she would have needed to, given that he suffers from paranoia.'

'True,' Kaia acknowledged. 'But I don't think he ever obsessed about her leaving, or cheating on him. That would've seemed less weird than most of the things he does worry about.'

Lawrence nodded. 'You said before that he hurt her. Could you give us some examples?'

'Not really. It wasn't like he ever did her much damage – mostly he just pushed her off when –' Kaia broke off, raising a hand to her eyes. She drew several shaky breaths before she managed to choke out, 'She used to – try – to restrain him. He'd – push her away. I think – it used to shake her – more than – hurt – her.'

Lawrence paused, Daniel guessed to give the girl a chance to recover herself, before saying, 'Do you think he could have been responsible for her death?'

'I don't know,' Kaia admitted, bowing her head so that her chin rested between her teddy's rounded ears. 'I'd like to be able to say no, but –' she hesitated. 'He has schizophrenia. Who knows what he might be capable of?'

Daniel drew a large question mark in his notebook. His knowledge of schizophrenia was limited, but from the statistics he had dug out the night before it seemed Floyd had been at least partially correct when he claimed violence wasn't a symptom. Only a small percentage of homicides were committed by schizophrenics, and most murder victims know the perpetrator. That being the case, in Britain alone several hundred people a year were dying at the hands of mentally intact acquaintances, friends and relations. When it came down to it, you never knew what anyone was capable of. Daniel suspected it wasn't so much that schizophrenia *made* people violent, more that some people *were* violent, and a subset of them happened to have schizophrenia. With this conclusion in mind, he asked Kaia whether she could think of anybody else who might have been responsible.

'No,' she replied, unconsciously stroking the back of her teddy's head with her right forefinger. 'No one at all.'

* * * * *

Fin had been so preoccupied with the picture of Suki's smiling face on page three of the Metro that he'd missed his stop on the tube. He hadn't noticed until several stations thereafter, and had jumped to his feet before thinking better of it and sinking back down into his seat. He was still grasping the paper as he walked into work. Despite having no desire to keep it, something had stopped him from letting it go. Perhaps because, subconsciously, it might mean letting Suki go.

Hearing the door open, Petra glanced up from her position behind the bar, then, seeing him, her expression changed.

'Hey,' she greeted, with an uneasy half smile, as he neared. 'I wasn't expecting to see you today.' She lifted up the bar flap to join him on the near side. 'Are you ok?'

The note of concern in her tone stirred his already volatile emotions, and, not at all sure he would be able to speak without losing control, he simply shrugged. Petra moved to embrace him and he held up a hand to stop her, withdrawing by a couple of paces.

'Sorry,' she offered. After an awkward silence, she added, 'D'you want a cup of tea?'

Fin nodded, more because it would grant him a few minutes to try to gather his thoughts than because he actually wanted one.

'Ok. You sit down.'

He did as bid, then, as Petra headed for the kitchen, felt almost immediately self-conscious and pulled out his mobile phone to distract from the fact he was sitting alone in an empty bar. He scrolled slowly and unseeingly through his Facebook news feed, needlessly opened and closed several apps, and then switched to deleting a selection of duplicate photographs. He'd just completed a purge of his text messages when Petra returned, setting two mismatched mugs down on the small table beside him and perching on a stool a couple of feet away.

'Thanks.' He paused. 'And thanks for the messages. Sorry I didn't reply.'

'It's ok.'

There was a long pause. He could think of nothing further to say, and it seemed Petra was also struggling to fill the silence. In the end, she plumped for, 'I didn't think you'd be back 'til next Monday.'

'Yeah,' he acknowledged. 'But there wasn't really anything left to do at home. I was just staring at the walls.'

Petra nodded.

'And I had everything together this morning. It was only – on the tube –' he shrugged weakly. 'I saw her picture. In the paper.'

'And that made it seem real?'

'I guess.'

'I'm sorry.'

'No you're not.'

Petra looked taken aback, her heavily made-up eyes widening slightly.

'You didn't even *like* her,' Fin added, by way of mitigation.

'That doesn't mean I wished her ill,' Petra responded, sounding hurt. 'And it doesn't stop me feeling sad for you.'

Fin didn't reply.

'Do you want me to leave you in peace?' She asked, at length, more kindly than he deserved.

He hesitated: he really didn't know. The decision to come into work had been spur of the moment, and in making it he hadn't taken into account the possibility Suki's picture might be everywhere. In all honesty, it hadn't occurred to him that her death would be such big news – Justin wasn't *that* famous. Or at least, he hadn't been. He was now.

'Sorry,' he mumbled, half by way of apology for his earlier comment and half because he couldn't think of anything else to say.

'Don't worry about it,' Petra returned, the slight waver in her voice betraying the fact he probably ought to. When he didn't say anything further, she managed to combine a deep breath with a sigh. 'Ok,' she concluded, moving to stand. 'I should –' she indicated the bar with a flick of her wrist. 'Shout if you need anything.'

He nodded.

'And maybe –' she trailed off awkwardly, twisting her fingers together. After a moment, she nodded towards the paper lying on the table beside him. 'Maybe put that away.'

Lawrence's second interview with Justin was reminiscent of a long-distance telephone call, with a distinct pause between every question and response. Lawrence wondered whether that was simply down to the drugs Justin was on, or whether he was taking a moment to carefully consider each answer. He had removed the jumper he had been wearing the day before, and his exposed left arm and half his hand – from his knuckles to beneath the short sleeve of his grey t-shirt – were a mess of black ink. Lawrence couldn't make out any words, but it was clear the broken squiggles were more than just doodles, and, given that Justin's hand had been clean the previous morning, he concluded that the self-tattoo must have been penned during the past twenty-four hours. Since Justin had been searched and stripped of his possessions on arrival at Scotland Yard, Lawrence wondered how he had managed to get his hands on a pen.

The young man was still wearing his sunglasses and, although Lawrence didn't hold out much hope, he asked whether Justin would mind removing them. He complied almost immediately.

'Sorry – I'm so used to them – I forget,' he excused himself, setting them down on the table. In the moment before he squinted and lowered his eyes, Lawrence noticed that the young man's irides were tinged blue.

'Is it too bright for you in here?'

'It's ok.'

'Do you understand why you're here?'

Justin nodded mutely, and Lawrence wondered whether he really had any idea at all.

'You haven't been charged with anything, all right? We just want to ask you some questions.'

Justin nodded again.

'Ok. Let's start with Suki's job. Can you tell us where she was working?'

'A bar.'

'Any idea which bar?'

'The Dark Heart.'

The name was familiar, and it took Lawrence only a moment to realise it was same venue Floyd and Elliot had visited on the night of Suki's death. 'Do you know where that is?'

'Soho.'

'Did you ever visit Suki there?'

'Yuh.'

'Often?'

His answer was unhelpfully vague. 'A few times.'

'And was that job her sole source of income, as far as you know?'

A longer than normal pause followed before Justin replied, rather hesitantly, 'Yes.'

'Are you sure?'

'Yes,' he repeated, raising his right hand to his mouth and biting into his thumbnail.

'I'm sorry to have to put you through this again, but I'd like to recap on the events of Monday night.'

Justin didn't question why, nodding slightly.

'Could you start with what happened when you got home?'

'I put my key on the shelf.'

Lawrence waited several seconds to see whether Justin would say anything further, and, when he didn't, asked, 'Are you sure you had your key?'

Justin chewed his nail for a moment, then nodded. 'Yes.'

'You didn't ring the doorbell?'

The young man sounded perplexed rather than suspicious as he said, 'I live there.' Then, as if it had just come to mind, he added, more confidently, 'And I remember the sheep.'

Lawrence frowned. 'What?'

'On the shelf. When I put my keys down.'

Lawrence wondered whether he had had all the clarity he was going to get from Justin that day, and glanced at Greg as he asked, 'What sort of sheep?'

Justin seemed puzzled by the question. 'I don't know. I've never been to Cumbria.'

'Cumbria?'

'That's where it came from.'

'The sheep?'

Justin looked as confused as Lawrence felt as he said, 'The postcard.'

Lawrence sighed. 'So there was a postcard of a sheep on the shelf?'

'And a Chinese menu.'

'Right.' Lawrence drew a long breath and tried not to sound impatient as he said, 'Could you tell me what happened after you left the shelf?'

'I went to the living room.'

'Do you know what Suki was doing at that time?'

'She was on the rug.'

'And what happened next?'

Several seconds passed before Justin shook his head slightly. 'I don't know,' he answered, rather flatly.

'What do you mean, you don't know?'

'I don't know,' he repeated, still with a remarkable lack of emotion. 'I don't remember.'

Lawrence felt immensely frustrated. Justin might have a mental illness, but that didn't necessarily make him any less able to lie or withhold information than the next person, and ordinarily Lawrence would have continued to push for answers. In Greg's presence, he felt unable to do so. He wondered whether he was being overly sensitive, or whether in the past there had been occasions when he had been more aggressive than he would publicly like to admit. Making a mental note to ask Greg what the likelihood was of Justin's having no recollection of the events surrounding Suki's death, he continued, 'You said yesterday that you didn't know she was going to get hurt. What did you mean by that?'

'I didn't know,' Justin echoed, uninformatively. 'I'd have stayed. I didn't know.'

'Was Suki dead when you arrived home?'

There was a long pause before Justin nodded.

'Do you have any idea who might have killed her?'

'No.'

'Have you ever hit her?'

'No.'

'Ever wanted to?'

'I didn't,' Justin shook his head, looking anxious for the first time that day. 'I didn't hurt her, I didn't, I –'

'All right,' Lawrence acknowledged, quickly, holding up a hand for emphasis. He gave Justin a chance to calm down before asking if he knew whether Suki had fallen out with anybody recently.

Justin coughed. 'She shouted at me,' he said, his voice hoarse.

'Other than you.'

He shrugged, then coughed again, raising a hand to his throat.

'Would you like a drink?'

Justin nodded before saying, in all seriousness, 'Vodka.'

'I meant of water.'

'Oh,' Justin responded, evenly. 'Ok.'

Lawrence glanced expectantly at Daniel, who rose and turned for the door. As it shut behind him, Lawrence drew a deep breath before posing his next question. He was rapidly losing the battle to convince himself this interview wasn't a waste of time.

Daniel joined Rebecca in the office shortly after one. She was sitting at her desk with her laptop open in front of her, hands clasped around a mug of coffee. Daniel often joked that she must have polystyrene fingers, because there was no way he could hold a mug that way until the drink was too far down the road towards cold to be worth having.

'Hey.'

She looked up with a smile. 'Hi Dan. How's it going?'

'Hard work. Your boyfriend has some fucked-up friends.'

'Well, you know what they say. Like calls to like.'

Daniel sat at his desk. 'Are things at home still a bit –' he hesitated, not sure how to conclude the question.

Rebecca's irritation was evident as she said, 'Dan, you read the papers, I'm sure you can add two and two.'

'Sorry, I didn't – I mean – I –'

He was interrupted by Lawrence's arrival. 'That was like pulling teeth,' he observed, sitting at the unoccupied desk opposite Rebecca's.

'Learn much?' Rebecca asked.

'No. But I am starting to feel less convinced he was responsible. I don't think he has the presence of mind to successfully maintain a false account of his activities, and nothing he's said today conflicts with what he told us yesterday. Although he claims not to remember much of what happened after he arrived home, which hardly helps.'

'Does schizophrenia affect memory?'

'Greg attributes it to the trauma. He says it's quite possible Justin's blocked the whole thing out.'

'Do you think that could mean he actually believes an erroneous sequence of events?'

'I don't know. I suppose it might.' Lawrence sighed. 'Have you heard back from the phone company yet?'

Rebecca nodded. 'Somebody did call Sally's number from the flat. The call lasted for about three minutes and was terminated at –' she rifled through a heap of papers and drew out a fluorescent pink Post-it. 'Ten thirty-seven.'

Lawrence reached for a pen to add this information to the wall-mounted timeline that he and Daniel had estimated for the hours surrounding Suki's death. 'So, assuming Sally's telling the truth about the doorbell – which I think she is – somebody saw Suki whilst Floyd and Justin can both be accounted for elsewhere. We need to identify that person, even if it's only to eliminate them.'

'That's going to be easy,' Daniel remarked, sarcastically. 'Half the people involved so far probably don't remember whether or not they were even in Camden! Years from now – if they live that long – they're all going to be reading their own band biogs trying to work out what happened to their twenties!'

Lawrence's eyebrows rose in response to this outburst. Rebecca cast her eyes down, and, too late, Daniel realised the significance of what he had just said. There was an awkward silence, and he felt he ought to apologise, but wasn't sure what to say. Shortly, Lawrence spoke.

'We also need to have another word with Alec, because he neglected to mention that nobody would be able to account for his activities between nine-forty-five and eleven. According to the club's manager, he disappeared off to the office while the headline band were playing. And we're missing Leighton's photos of him, as well. Can you chase those up, please, Becky?'

Rebecca nodded, looking as grateful as Daniel felt for the change in subject.

'Did you manage to get through to Skin?' Lawrence continued.

'Yes. They should be open at three.'

Lawrence glanced at his watch. 'That gives us plenty of time to check out the pub Suki told everyone she was working in first,' he said, briskly. 'Next stop, Soho. Becky, can you grab Jamie or –' he hesitated.

'Noel?' Daniel prompted.

'Yes, Noel – or whoever's free – and do a second round of door to door?'

'Sure,' Rebecca consented, unenthusiastically. Daniel could understand why. Making door-to-door enquires was almost always a tedious and unrewarding job, and, keen to make amends for his earlier comment, he impulsively offered to help. Both his colleagues looked nonplussed. Door to door wasn't a job anybody tended to *volunteer* for. The surprise wearing off, Rebecca brightened, and Daniel felt relieved. The feeling was short lived.

Turning to their superior, she asked, hopefully, 'Can I come with you, then?'

Lawrence sighed. 'We've been through this.'

'Oh come on, I barely knew Suki. And I certainly didn't know her work colleagues.'

It wasn't an unreasonable argument, and only a moment passed before Lawrence conceded, 'All right. Given we'll presumably be talking mostly to women I suppose it might be beneficial to have one on my side.'

Rebecca smiled, reaching for her handbag.

'What about Justin?' Daniel asked.

Lawrence frowned. 'What about him?'

'Do you want me to apply for further detention?'

'No, not at this stage. We'll hang onto him until this evening, and unless anything further comes up in the meantime I think we'll have to let him go. I'll give a couple of his friends a call later on this afternoon, see whether somebody can collect him.'

'Ok.'

'Right,' Lawrence reached for his car keys. 'We'll see you later. Good luck.'

'You too,' Daniel replied, rather half-heartedly, as his colleagues headed towards the lifts, silently cursing himself. Somehow he'd succeeded in upsetting Rebecca and landing himself with the dull job all within the space of about a minute. What an idiot. In the grand scale of things, it made the incident with the journalist seem almost insignificant.

The Dark Heart lived up to its gothic-sounding name, with vintage red wallpaper, black curtains cloaking the booths, and intricately carved chairs and tables. Much of the room's limited light was provided by flickering LED candles set in elaborate candelabra, and the bar's counter was fronted by embossed metal plates featuring wolves and crows. Although it was well into the average lunch hour, there were few customers, and the girl behind the bar was perching on a stool, leafing wearily through a magazine. She responded to Lawrence and Rebecca's approach without even glancing up, sliding down off the stool and tossing her magazine onto a shelf behind the bar before stepping forwards to serve them.

Model thin, she had an angular face and very fair skin, which she had inadvisably chosen to combine with black hair dye and thick black eyeliner. Her long-sleeved wrap top and flowing velour skirt were also black, the only colour visible anywhere on her person that of her nails and lips, both of which were painted dark purple. She regarded Lawrence with some surprise: clearly customers in suits and ties were few and far between in this establishment. He introduced himself and Rebecca before asking whether the pub's manager or owner was available.

'My manager's not in this week,' the girl informed him, apologetically.

'Do you not have an acting manager in the meantime?'

'Usually the owner oversees things, but this week wasn't planned – his mother – my manager's, I mean – passed away last Thursday.'

'Maybe you can help us. Can we take your name?'

'Petra,' she smiled nervously, then, in response to Lawrence's expectant look, added, 'Rowntree.'

'Have you worked here long?'

'A year or so.'

'Do you know a girl called Suki?'

Petra nodded. 'Are you – is this about her death?'

'I'm afraid so. When did you hear about it?'

'Yesterday. It was all over the web.'

'And how did you know Suki?'

'Through Fin. That's my manager. They were old friends.' She lifted her eyebrows expressively. 'What a week, eh?'

'Did Suki ever work any shifts here?'

'Not any real ones. She wasn't employed by the pub – she worked at Skin, up the road – but she didn't want her friends knowing she was stripping, so she told a lot of people she worked here. If anybody came in asking for her we'd tell them she was on a break, or stock-checking, or whatever – and then we'd call her mobile and she'd run down the alley at the back and slip in the side door.'

'That's some length to go to,' Lawrence remarked, hoping to encourage further comment.

Petra simply shrugged and agreed with him. 'Yeah.'

'Did she ever get caught out?'

'I don't know. She didn't exactly have friends coming in and out on a daily basis, but her boyfriend must've thought it was a bit strange she was never behind the bar when he came in.'

'Was he in here a lot?'

'Yeah, we saw quite a bit of him.'

'How often did he visit, would you say? Weekly? Monthly?'

'Somewhere between the two, I guess,' Petra offered, after a moment's consideration.

'Did he ever say anything to imply that he knew what she was doing?'

'He never really said anything at all. Just asked where she was.'

'And do you know whether the owner knew anything about the arrangement?'

'I've no idea, but I don't suppose she did – it's not as if she's around much. Will you have to tell her?'

'Why? Would that cause trouble for you?'

'No, but it might for Fin, and he's got enough on his plate right now.'

Lawrence nodded. 'Well, at this stage I don't think there's any need for us to speak to her. But I would like Fin's address, if you have it?'

Petra hesitated and, guessing what was on her mind, he added, 'We'll try to make it as painless as we can.'

Petra cast her eyes along the bar, then turned towards the counter behind herself, and, guessing she was looking for a pen and paper, Lawrence pulled his notebook from his pocket and flicked to a clean page before laying it on the bar and offering her a pen. As she took it, the flared sleeve of her top folded back on itself, revealing a bandage wound around the base of her hand and her wrist.

'What did you do there?' Lawrence asked, conversationally.

'Huh?' She glanced up, then followed the line of his gaze back to her wrist. 'Oh,' she realised, aloud. 'Sprained it lugging beer crates. Occupational hazard.'

Lawrence sensed she wasn't telling the truth, but he didn't challenge her, waiting in silence for her to write down the address and feeling intrigued that she apparently didn't need to look it up.

'Did you know Suki well?' He asked, as she returned the pen.

'Not really. She often came in when she had a break from work, but mostly she hung out with Fin.'

'Do you know whether he saw much of her in his own time?'

'I don't think so. She always seemed to be busy when he suggested doing something. To be honest, I don't think he'd have seen much of her at all if she hadn't needed the job alibi.'

'You're saying she took advantage of him,' Lawrence summarised.

'Totally.'

'Do you think he would have liked to be more than friends?'

'You must've seen her picture. What do you reckon?'

There was an undercurrent of resentment in her tone, and Lawrence sensed Petra had envied Suki's relationship with Fin. As he retrieved his notebook, he wondered why he hadn't previously questioned who – beyond their immediate circle of friends – might have envied her relationship with Justin. And Rebecca, he suspected, might hold the answer.

'Do you and Elliot have much trouble with groupies?' He asked, as they departed the pub.

Rebecca seemed surprised by the question. 'In what way?'

'I'm just wondering how likely infatuation is to turn into dangerous obsession.'

'You mean is it possible some crazy fan killed Suki because she wants to take her place?'

'Well, I know theoretically it's possible, I'm just trying to establish how possible.'

Rebecca nodded. Several seconds passed before she answered. 'I don't know, but I imagine Justin has his fair share of unhinged fans. When you're very obviously troubled it attracts a lot of screwed up and unhappy individuals who think they identify with you.'

'How persistent are they?'

'Mostly they're just a part of the live music scene. Some of them send letters and presents. A few turn up at the front door.'

'And what's their attitude towards you?'

'Generally they blank me,' Rebecca shrugged. 'Even if I'm holding Elliot's hand they'll carry on a conversation with him as if I'm not there. And some of them try to do more than that.'

'But I assume they speak to you if you open the front door to them?'

'Oh, the ones who turn up at the flat think I'm a possessive bitch,' Rebecca replied, matter-of-factly. 'They assume I'm the one who doesn't want them to talk to him.'

'Have you ever felt threatened by any of them?'

'No. Just irritated.' She hooked her thumbs into her trouser pockets. 'And, on occasion, embarrassed. It's incredible how little self-respect some girls have.'

'I can imagine.'

They walked in silence for several seconds before Rebecca concluded, 'I've never really had a problem, but that doesn't mean it wouldn't be worth following up. Especially because Suki was so much a part of the scene – she probably knew all the hardcore fans.' She paused. 'If only to look down on.'

## Ten

'She was friendly, but she didn't really talk about herself. She always wanted to know about us.'

It was a familiar-sounding statement. Lawrence and Rebecca had already interviewed four of Suki's colleagues, and, although she had been working at the club for almost a year, none of them seemed to know anything about her.

'Do you have any idea why she kept her life a secret?'

Janne, a pretty Swedish girl with stereotypical blonde hair, blue eyes and long limbs, appeared puzzled by this interpretation. 'It didn't seem like she was keeping secrets, she just –' she paused briefly. 'She just seemed like she was interested in everybody else. You know?'

Lawrence nodded. It seemed to him that Suki had succeeded in coming across as one of several different people depending on whom she was dealing with. So far that afternoon, not one person they'd spoken to had even known she had a boyfriend, much less recognised his name, and Lawrence wondered whether Suki had kept that to herself out of concern for Justin's wellbeing or for fear of what he might do should he find out how she was earning a living. Whilst he didn't believe her relationship with Justin had been built on ulterior motives, he suspected Dave had been right when he called Suki manipulative.

'Do you know whether she fell out with anybody recently? Either here or elsewhere?'

'Fell where?' Janne asked, confusion written across her face.

'Argued with,' Rebecca clarified.

'Oh,' Janne understood. 'No.'

Her expression gave a different answer, and Lawrence said, 'You don't look very sure about that.'

'It's not important,' the girl protested, clearly uncomfortable.

'You don't know that.'

Janne didn't respond, twisting her hands together.

'We will try to keep your name out of it if we can,' Lawrence reassured her.

'You can't,' Janne replied. 'I was the only other one there.'

'Where?'

Several seconds passed before the girl yielded. 'She had a fight. With Allegra. Oliver's girlfriend.' She paused momentarily before adding, helpfully, 'He's the manager.'

Lawrence nodded. He and Rebecca had spoken to Oliver on arrival at the club, and if he knew anything about the altercation between the two women he had kept it to himself. 'What was the fight about?'

'Allegra thought Suki wanted Oliver.'

'Do you suppose she did?'

'No!' Janne answered, emphatically. 'He's very –' she lowered her voice. 'Sleazy. I don't think any of the girls here would – with him.'

'So what led Allegra to think otherwise?'

'If you're nice to men, they do what you want,' Janne responded, simply. As if it were that easy. Of course, for girls as attractive as Janne, Lawrence guessed it often was. As a young man he had frequently felt irritated by the way his sister, Carla, had played his friends for favours, although, looking back, he had to admit there were women in his past who had beaten him at the same game. Katie had not been one of them, and she and Carla had clashed more than once over whether Carla's behaviour demeaned women – Katie's argument – or whether the fact she generally succeeded in getting her way was demeaning to men. Knowing which side his bread was buttered, Lawrence had always sided with Katie. Privately, however, he had never reached a definite conclusion.

'How nice are we talking?' He enquired.

Janne's pale eyebrows wrinkled. 'I'm sorry?'

'Do you mean she flirted with him, or did she go further?'

'Oh no,' she shook her head, evidently disgusted by the idea. 'Just flirting.'

'Why do you suppose Allegra believed there was more to it?'

'I think she doesn't – like herself – so she expects him to go – to someone else,' Janne explained, haltingly, clearly struggling to find the words with which to express herself.

'You're saying she's insecure,' Lawrence summarised, more for his own benefit than Janne's, thinking it was hardly surprising, given Oliver's occupation.

'Yes.'

'And where did this argument happen?'

'Here. In the afternoon. Before work.'

'When?'

'A few weeks ago.'

'Can you remember much of what was said?'

'I wasn't there the whole time. I came in in the middle. Allegra said Suki was a whore, and Suki hit her – Allegra hit back, and –' Janne waved her hands to and fro and pulled a face to indicate the fight hadn't ended there before adding, 'But it wasn't for long. Oliver came in and stopped them.'

'What did he have to say about it?'

'He told me and Suki to get changed for work and took Allegra to the office.'

'Do you know whether anything has happened between Suki and Allegra since?'

Janne shook her head, and, when Lawrence didn't immediately pose another question, asked, 'Can I go?'

Unable to think of anything else worthwhile to ask, Lawrence agreed, handing her his card on the off-chance she might remember something more and asking if she could find Oliver for him. He wasn't interested in hearing why Oliver hadn't mentioned the fight; from experience he could already guess what excuses the man might have to offer. All Lawrence wanted was Allegra's address.

Frustratingly, Allegra had turned out to be on an overnight trip to Geneva, so, once finished at Skin, Lawrence sent Rebecca home and headed up to Camden to pay Alec a visit.

The north side of Oakley Square was lined by a grand Georgian terrace, which, like its slightly less-imposing neighbour in Mornington Terrace, had suffered little in the Blitz. The buildings were pleasingly uniform, with identikit columns framing each front door and neat rows of windows running the full length of the block. The rest of the square apparently hadn't been so lucky – assuming it had been a square in the first place. As things stood, it was more of a squashed polygon, its three other sides occupied by a mishmash of council housing that looked to have been built in at least two different eras.

Arriving at the address Alec had supplied, Lawrence found the young man standing at the foot of the front steps with an elbow resting between the railings, smoking a cigarette and talking on his mobile. On seeing Lawrence, he rapidly brought the conversation to a close and slid the phone into the pocket of his black jeans, but didn't extinguish the cigarette or move towards the door.

'All right?' He opened, pleasantly.

Lawrence was never sure how to respond to this greeting, and on this occasion opted for a nod and a cordial, 'Evening.'

'What's up?'

'Might we go inside?'

'I'd rather not, I've just locked up,' Alec objected. 'I'm due at work in fifteen minutes.'

'Whereabouts?'

'KoKo.'

Given that he appeared to be equipped with nothing more than a mobile phone and a packet of cigarettes, Lawrence felt sceptical. 'Do you not need any music?'

Alec wordlessly thrust his free hand into one of his jacket pockets and pulled out three USB sticks of differing colours and shapes. Then, perhaps anticipating Lawrence's next question, he said, 'My laptop's over at the club.'

'Well, before you go, I've a few more questions.'

Alec glanced uneasily at his watch before conceding, reluctantly, 'What is it you want to know?'

'I finally caught up with your manager at the Underworld earlier today. He wasn't able to verify your whereabouts for a chunk of Monday evening because apparently you were in the office.'

'He manages the club, not me,' Alec replied, sounding rather put out. 'I work freelance.'

'Well, regardless of the details of your employment, it seems nobody can account for where you were between about nine forty-five and eleven on Monday night, which is something you neglected to mention yesterday.'

'It wasn't intentional. I didn't really think about it. I'm at the club from six until two, so unless I particularly want to see the headline act I usually take a break during the set to grab something to eat and have a few of these.' He held up his cigarette before putting it to his lips.

'So you actually left the venue.'

'Technically speaking, I suppose. I stood a couple of feet outside the door.'

'Did you not have to go further afield to buy dinner?'

'Nah, I take that with me.'

'In that case I can't imagine eating dinner occupied the best part of an hour.'

'It didn't. I spent most of the set putting three hundred words together for *Rock UK*. I write a column called DJ Culture.'

'And did you see anybody during that time?'

Alec thought this over for a moment. 'I saw the guys on the door when I went outside, but otherwise no.'

'What time did you go outside?'

'I've no idea. I suppose they might have a security camera on the door, which would answer that for you, but if not –' he shrugged.

Unless it captured him at frequent intervals, Lawrence doubted the footage – if it existed – would be much help. He'd already established that the Underworld had several exits, one of them leading into the pub above, and suspected it wouldn't be impossible to leave the venue undetected. Making a mental note to ask someone to look into it anyway, he changed tack.

'How would you describe Suki? In terms of her personality.'

As Alec considered his answer, he pulled a packet of cigarettes from his pocket, drew one out and set about lighting it from the stub of the previous one. 'Sociable,' he began, dropping the spent one to the ground, and stamping it out. 'Confident.' He flicked the butt over the narrow ledge at the base of the railings and into the lightwell beyond with the side of his shoe. Clearly seeing Lawrence's expression, he said, 'I'll pick it up later. That's my front door,' he nodded towards the basement flat. Then, apparently continuing on the original theme, 'Assertive. A bit reckless.'

'Reckless? How?'

'Last weekend I caught her cutting through an alleyway alone in Soho at about midnight. She knew better.'

'So she didn't always have a lot of regard for her own safety,' Lawrence concluded.

'Or Justin's mental health. She begged me not to tell him because she knew how much it would worry him.'

'And did you?'

'What, tell him? No. It's not as if it would've stopped her doing it again, so there didn't seem much point in upsetting him.'

'That implies a rather selfish – or thoughtless – outlook on her part.'

'Maybe. But she was only – what? Twenty-one? Twenty-two? I guess she still had some growing up to do.' Alec checked his watch. 'I really need to get going. Was there anything else?'

'Not right now.'

'Great,' Alec flashed a smile before turning and heading towards the main road at the end of the terrace, some thirty yards away. Lawrence watched him go, wondering whether he really had been on his way out. USB sticks were neither heavy nor bulky, and for all he knew Alec kept them permanently in his jacket. He waited until the man had turned the corner, then descended the staircase leading to the basement flat in the hope of getting a glimpse of what lay behind the retractable security grille on the front window. He was out of luck. Despite the fact that, at six-fifteen in late May, it was still broad daylight, all that was visible was the lining of the curtains.

Owing to the intense media interest in the investigation, Chief Superintendent Angus MacLennan had requested an update at the end of the day, and Lawrence was heading in the direction of the man's office when he spotted Leighton engaged in conversation with a young detective constable. Seeing Lawrence approaching, he raised a hand in greeting. 'Any progress?'

'Not really,' Lawerence admitted. Then, given he'd not received an email from the pathologist, nor found anything on his desk on his return to the Yard, he added, 'Did Becky call you about those photographs?'

'Bollocks,' Leighton cursed. 'Yes. Sorry, I completely forgot.'

'Oh for goodness' sake, you're as bad as Jimmy with his homework!' Lawrence exclaimed, exasperated. Possibly worse, in fact; in Jimmy's case Lawrence wasn't at all convinced it wasn't just a convenient excuse to avoid doing the work. 'Do you think you might try writing things down?'

'Then I'd just spend all day looking for the bit of paper I wrote everything on.'

Lawrence sighed. 'Why were the photos not with the others in the first place?'

'Different camera.'

Lawrence frowned. 'Again, why?'

'I carry a compact digital camera in case we have a problem with the main one. I had it on me at the crucial moment. Getting the pictures seemed like more of a priority than the choice of equipment.'

Given Alec's reluctance to be photographed, it was a valid point, and Lawrence nodded. 'Fair enough.'

'I'll get them to you for tomorrow morning.'

'I'd appreciate it,' Lawrence replied, starting away before stopping and looking back around. 'Do you have any idea why he was so resistant to having his picture taken?'

Leighton shrugged. 'A lot of people don't like being photographed. I can't say I'm wild about it myself.'

'Really?'

'I never know what to do with myself and always end up looking like a prat,' he replied, with surprising candour.

'In a social setting I can understand people feeling self-conscious in front of a camera, but it's not as if we're going to put police photographs up on Facebook or what have you, is it?'

'You're right, human neuroses are completely logical,' Leighton returned, facetiously. 'That's why there are people out there with phobias of things like buttons and oranges.'

Lawrence had to smile. 'Point taken,' he acknowledged, before repeating, 'Buttons,' with a lift of his eyebrows. 'People are bloody strange. Being afraid of spiders or snakes at least makes some sort of sense, but buttons –' he shook his head.

'There's nothing out there that you've an irrational fear of, then?'

'I don't think so,' Lawrence replied, before considering the matter and joking, 'Besides perhaps my mother-in-law.'

Leighton laughed. 'I'm not sure there's anything irrational about that.'

'Probably not,' Lawrence agreed, turning to go. 'How about you?'

Leighton didn't miss a beat, replying, with a completely straight face, 'The prerequisite for *having* a mother-in-law.'

Vinnie was sitting alone in the dressing room, and glanced up hopefully as Elliot peered around the door, then his face fell and he muttered, 'Hi.'

'Don't look so pleased to see me,' Elliot remarked, sarcastically.

'Sorry. I thought you were Matt.'

'Silly me,' Elliot snapped. 'What are friends worth in comparison with smack?'

'Don't be such a fucking hypocrite,' Vinnie returned, tersely, glancing anxiously at his watch.

'You've a lot to learn if you're relying on another junkie for your gear.'

'Yeah, well, I don't have a whole lot of choice right now.'

'How come?'

'A.J. went and got fucking busted, didn't he?'

'Like he's the only dealer in London.'

'Most of them seem to be avoiding me, which I'm guessing has something to do with the fact A.J. reckons my fuckwit of a brother is the one who shopped him to the filth.'

Elliot's eyebrows jumped. 'Is that true?'

'How the hell would I know?' Vinnie retorted. 'Anything's possible with Justin, really, isn't it? He needs a fucking good slap.'

Elliot shook his head slightly. 'Do you have any idea what he's been going through this week? Or have you been too out of it to see past the end of your nose?'

'I really don't need a lecture, Elliot.'

'Yes you fucking do! Justin has been to hell and back over the past couple of days, and you've not even *noticed*!'

'Frankly, I'm amazed you *have*,' Vinnie bit back. 'Elliot, the problem with you and Justin is that you seem to think life is harder for you than it is for everybody else! It isn't! Life is fucking difficult! Stop making excuses for yourself and fucking grow up!'

Elliot was momentarily lost for words. 'I cannot believe you just said that!' He managed, eventually. 'You used to adore him! And now he's just one more distraction between you and your next fix! Isn't he?'

Vinnie didn't reply, and Elliot yelled, 'Isn't he!'

Vinnie shrugged.

'You should have been there, and you weren't! And when you finally start thinking about that rather than stuffing smack up your veins, you're going to fucking hate yourself!'

'Do you honestly think you have the right to –' Vinnie broke off as the door opened, and the look on his face told Elliot that Matthew had arrived before he even had a chance to turn around.

'Elliot, mate,' Matthew smiled. 'All right?' He closed the door behind himself and leaned against it before pulling a small packet of heroin from his pocket and tossing it in Vinnie's direction.

Elliot didn't answer, watching Vinnie pocket the drugs and move to stand. Matthew wandered across the room and helped himself to the crate of beer that stood on the table.

'Becks with you?'

'Um – no –' Elliot reached behind himself and fumbled with the door knob.

Matthew nodded, flipping the lid off the bottle in his hand. 'Well, Vin and I are off to see a man about a dog, so we'll catch you later.' He lifted the bottle to his lips, then paused, adding, 'That's assuming you don't want to join us, of course?' He raised his eyebrows expectantly.

Elliot knew what the real question was, and hesitated, hand still on the now open door, struggling with the conflict of what he *wanted* to do and what he *ought* to do. As he opened his mouth to answer, a fierce grip on his arm jerked him backwards, and before he had even registered what was happening, Alec was standing between him and Matthew.

'You fucking arsehole!' He began, giving Matthew a violent shove. 'Sooner or later you're going to kill yourself with that crap, but if you so much as *think* about dragging Elliot down with you, I'll kill you myself!'

'He's over eighteen, Alec, it's his choice.'

'That's not a *choice*! That's no more a choice for Elliot than it is for you, and you damn well know that!' Alec turned to go, pulling Elliot with him. Slamming the door behind them, he looked around. 'You all right?'

Elliot didn't answer, feeling shaken.

'Elliot?'

'I need a drink.' He started in the direction of the bar.

Alec followed. 'What the fuck were you thinking in there?' He demanded. 'Were you planning on sharing their needles as well as their drugs?'

'I'm not a total fucking idiot!'

'What, you got your own?'

'Get off my back.'

Alec seized hold of his arm and spun Elliot around to face him. 'Are you still clean?'

'What sort of question is that?'

'I'm sorry, mate, but you can't blame me for asking!'

Elliot didn't reply, turning away.

Alec pulled him back. 'Elliot, answer me!'

'Of course I fucking am!' He returned, angrily. 'What, d'you think I want to completely fuck my life up twice?'

Alec held his gaze. 'You seem to be doing a damn good job of *that* anyway!'

'Fuck you,' Elliot responded, coldly, turning to go.

'Elliot, please,' Alec sounded seriously concerned this time. 'Please tell me you're clean.'

Elliot swung back around to face him. 'I'm Persil *fucking* white, ok?'

Alec nodded. 'Ok.'

'And now, I'm going to go and have a drink. Is that all right with you?' He turned and walked away without waiting for a reply, feeling dizzy and sick, his chest so tight that he could scarcely breathe. Alec was right. Not that he wasn't already well aware his life was unravelling all over again. He had been trying not to think about it for weeks. It wasn't as if he'd *planned* this. The plan – if that was what you could call it – had just been to make things more normal. Or at least comfortably numb. A few shots to blur the hard edges. Enough to stop the panic attacks. Enough to sleep at night. And it had almost worked, for a while. Except that there really was no such thing as *enough*. The idea was just a signpost on a well-disguised road to hell. At least with heroin he'd have known where he was headed.

Lawrence had hoped to hand Justin over to someone who at least *seemed* relatively responsible, but in the event the only person he had been able to get hold of was Floyd. When the young man arrived, shortly after eight, he was on considerably better form than he had been the previous morning, and also appeared to be sober. Lawrence took the opportunity to ask whether he would mind answering a few more questions, and, when Floyd consented, showed him up to the office, hoping he might be more forthcoming in a less formal environment. Floyd declined his offer of tea or coffee, and, as he sat behind his desk, Lawrence began, conversationally, 'I understand Justin's bedroom is wallpapered with tin foil. Do you know why?'

'To stop people from stealing his thoughts,' Floyd responded, casually, as if it were a perfectly normal explanation.

'Has that concerned him for long?'

'Several years. Last year he did the entire flat.'

'And does he normally wear his sunglasses indoors?'

'Yes,' Floyd confirmed. 'Although usually not the dark ones, he has blue lenses at home.'

'Are his eyes that sensitive?'

'No, but the colour of his eyes bothers him, and he has to wear glasses anyway, so I asked the doctor to suggest he wear tinted lenses all the time, because it makes life easier for both of us.'

'Would contact lenses not be more effective?'

'The whole point is to avoid drawing his attention to his eyes. Contact lenses would do the opposite.'

Lawrence frowned. 'But surely he knows what colour his eyes are?'

'Well of course he does, and when he's thinking clearly it's not a problem. But when he's not, he only has to catch sight of his reflection in the wrong light to be convinced he's been possessed by a devil.'

'I imagine that could make him quite frantic.'

'It can do.'

'Has he ever hurt you whilst in that state? Maybe even unintentionally?'

'No,' Floyd shook his head. 'The only person he ever hurts is himself.'

'For example?'

'Sometimes he bangs his head against things, trying to stop the voices. And often he's so desperate to get away from a situation that he takes dangerous risks.'

'Like trying climb over a balcony,' Lawrence remarked.

'Yeah.'

'He wasn't the only one at risk on that occasion, from what I gather.'

'No, but that wasn't by design.'

'That doesn't necessarily make it irrelevant,' Lawrence observed. 'Anything else?'

Floyd thought for a moment before saying, 'One time he sliced a layer of skin off his arm because he thought he'd been branded and could be tracked, and –'

'By whom?'

'I've no idea. You don't entertain the delusion any more than you deny it, you just agree that what he's feeling must be very frightening, reassure him that he's safe and try to calm him down. Once he's calm you have some chance of explaining that it isn't real – trying to do that when he's distressed just makes him worse, and, as far as he's concerned, makes you part of the problem.'

'Did Suki ever become part of the problem?'

There was a long pause before Floyd nodded. 'A few times. I don't think she ever understood how real his delusions seem to him, and I think she found his inability to listen to reason very frustrating.'

'Did he ever hurt her?'

An even longer pause passed. Eventually, Floyd admitted, 'I don't know. Not that I saw. But I can't be with him twenty-four seven.'

Lawrence nodded. 'I gather that in recent weeks you and he have fallen out a number of times.'

'Yes.'

'Can you tell me why?'

'Not really. It's easy to fall out with Just over nothing at all – he often misinterprets things, or reads something into what you've said that isn't there, and –' he sighed. 'Recently I haven't always handled those situations as well as I might.'

'Why not?'

Floyd shook his head slightly. 'I don't know. I feel really bad about it, because I know it's not his fault, but there are days when I just don't seem to have much patience.'

He sounded genuine, and Lawrence didn't press him, saying instead, 'You said it's easy to fall out with Justin. Has he fallen out with anybody else lately?'

'Probably, but I can't give you any examples, because it tends to happen more when I'm not there, and his version of events often isn't particularly reliable – just because he thinks somebody's been having a go at him doesn't necessarily mean they *have*.'

'I imagine being so paranoid must make it very difficult for him to trust people and form relationships.'

'He copes really well, actually. I know to you he's probably seemed impossible, but for someone with chronic schizophrenia to have friends, and a girlfriend, and a career – of sorts – is really something.'

'From what I've gathered over the last couple of days, you have a lot to do with that.'

'I just look out for him.'

'That must be hard work, day in, day out.'

'Well I suppose that depends whether you class your friends as work,' Floyd replied, sounding nettled. 'Justin isn't just a schizophrenic, you know. He has a personality of his own, and as a rule I enjoy his company. Of course he has bad days, but he isn't a basket case, and when he's on his meds he generally has sufficient insight into his illness to be able to understand when I explain what is and isn't going on. He just needs it explained to him in the right way.'

'The fact that you're happy to look after him isn't the point,' Lawrence countered. 'It's still a big responsibility, and at times it must be quite a strain.'

'I'm used to it.'

Lawrence had his doubts, but didn't voice them, saying instead, 'One of our scenes of crime officers came across some unnamed tablets in your bedroom. Could you tell me what they are?'

'Oh I see,' Floyd responded, tartly, sitting forwards in his chair. 'You think I can't cope with Just, and I'm taking drugs as a result! Well I'm not!'

'So what are the pills?'

'I've no idea!' Floyd exclaimed, sounding exasperated. 'Our flat's full of different drugs!'

'What sort of drugs?'

'Justin's prescriptions, mainly!'

'And?'

Floyd frowned. 'And what?'

'You said mainly.'

'Well I didn't think Lemsip and Nurofen would be of much interest,' he retorted, sarcastically.

'The pills we found wouldn't have had anything to do with your rather convenient memory loss on Monday night, then?'

'No.'

'So what was responsible for your losing several hours of your time?'

'I don't know!' Floyd returned, angrily.

Lawrence raised his eyebrows. 'You *still* don't know?'

There was a moment's silence before Floyd seemed to deflate, sinking back into the chair. 'I don't know,' he repeated, rather hopelessly this time. 'The only thing I can think of is that maybe I shouldn't have taken anything for my head after I'd been drinking.'

'What did you take?'

'Imigran.'

'Is that available over the counter?'

'Um – I don't know – I don't think so.'

'So it was prescribed by your doctor.'

'Yeah.'

'Were you warned not to mix it with alcohol?'

'Not that I remember, but I could've forgotten – or the chemist might have forgotten to mention it,' Floyd shrugged.

'Have you been taking it for long?'

'A few weeks.'

'And in that time have there been any other occasions when you've noticed any strange side effects?'

'No, but it doesn't actually seem to be working, so most of the time I feel like I'm being kicked in the head.'

'Does the doctor have any idea what could be causing your migraines?'

'My mum gets them, so it's probably genetic.' He frowned. 'How is this your business, anyway? I only came to collect Justin.' He sounded suddenly impatient, and, after the past few minutes, Lawrence understood exactly what Ethan and Dave had meant about his erratic temper.

Lawrence pushed his chair back from the desk. 'Justin's downstairs. Would you like me to call you a cab?'

Floyd shook his head. 'He won't get into cabs. The radios freak him out.'

'But buses and trains have radios as well,' Lawrence observed. 'So how will you get home?'

'Walk, I expect,' Floyd answered, seemingly unconcerned by this eventuality.

Thinking it might be interesting to see Floyd and Justin together for more than a couple of minutes, Lawrence offered to give them a lift. Floyd looked surprised.

'Are you sure?'

'I'm heading home, and it's not far out of my way.'

'Thanks,' Floyd smiled, getting to his feet. 'We might take you up on that.'

'Might?' Lawrence queried.

Floyd blinked, then responded, as if it should have been obvious, 'Well it's not up to *me*, is it?'

Lawrence made no reply, gathering up the papers on his desk and reaching for his briefcase. He suspected that, in those few words, Floyd had summed up his relationship with Justin. Suki had believed Floyd was the one in control. Lawrence wondered whether he was under the same illusion.

## Eleven

Elliot hadn't come home by the time Rebecca went to bed on Wednesday night, and her sleep had been rudely interrupted by his drunken arrival home shortly after two. She had had little to say to him, further than that he could think again if he was planning on joining her in bed, before slamming the bedroom door. To her relief, the rest of her night passed undisturbed, and on Thursday morning she emerged from the bedroom to find Elliot sprawled on the sofa, an empty half bottle of vodka and an ashtray on the floor beside him. She shook him, hard.

'Elliot, wake up.'

He grunted, but didn't open his eyes, and Rebecca tried again. 'Wake up! Now!'

He batted her hand away, muttering, 'Leave me alone.'

'Come on, you need to pack!'

'Eh?' He opened his eyes for the first time, his expression one of confusion. 'What do I need to pack for?'

'You're moving out.'

There was a moment's silence while Elliot absorbed her words. He opened his mouth as if to speak, then closed it again. Swallowing hard, he tried again. 'But – I –' he shook his head slightly, struggling to sit up. 'You're *leaving* me?'

'Ten out of ten, Elliot,' Rebecca snapped, sarcastically. 'Except you're the one who's leaving.'

Elliot didn't respond, casting his eyes down, his breaths coming in shallow gasps. He raised a fist to his mouth, his hand shaking. Rebecca turned to go, and was almost at the door before he spoke.

'Becca, please, can't we talk?'

Rebecca turned on him. 'Talk about what? The *pathetic* state you were in last night? The fact I clearly mean less to you than a bottle of booze?'

'But I love you –'

'That's what you call love, is it?'

'Becca, I'm sorry, I – I –' he stopped. '*Please*. It won't happen again. I promise!'

'Damn right it won't happen again! We are finished!' Rebecca threw back, making for the bedroom.

Elliot followed, and caught up with her as she was rummaging in the wardrobe for the jacket that matched her skirt.

'Becca, please.'

'No!' She spun around to face him. 'Elliot, I've given you a hundred chances, and every time you've thrown it back in my face! I've tried to be sympathetic and I've tried to help you, but you don't want to be helped, you just want to get drunk! I've had enough!'

Elliot looked panicked. 'How am I supposed to cope without you?'

Rebecca completely lost her temper. 'This is not *coping*, Elliot! You haven't been *coping* for months! I've just had enough of watching you *not* coping and being dragged down by it!'

'I can't live without you,' he responded, weakly.

'Oh grow up!' Rebecca spat, contemptuously, wrenching her jacket from the wardrobe and pushing past him to leave the room.

'I *can't*,' Elliot repeated, as she made for the front door.

'Fine!' Rebecca turned one last time. 'Go kill yourself if that's what you want! Just get the hell out of my life!'

Elliot stared at her, speechless with shock. Even in her anger, Rebecca knew she'd gone too far, that she should apologise for what she'd just said, but instead she turned back to the door, yanked it open and slammed it shut behind herself. This time, Elliot didn't follow her, and she marched down the street with no real idea of where she was heading. Ordinarily, at eight a.m., she would still have been running around the flat, tossing belongings into her handbag and trying to drink a too-hot cup of coffee, in danger of being late for work. Now she wasn't sure she could face faking normality for her colleagues.

She considered calling in sick, then wondered what she would do with the day if she did. She couldn't very well return home, and her friends would all be busy with their own jobs. She could visit her twin sister, Angela, who had given up work in favour of motherhood a few years earlier, but Angela had never liked Elliot, and Rebecca was in no mood to hear the words *I told you so*. In fact, recently there hadn't been many occasions when she *had* been in the mood to talk to Angela. Another relationship she hadn't been able to hold together. The thought saddened her, and as she approached the tube station, she found herself blinking back tears. Pausing at the top of the steps, she came to a decision. She dug her mobile from her handbag, started to dial, then stopped. She wasn't sure she would be able to say the words. Not without crying, and she wasn't ready to do that yet. And technology offered an easy way out: text message.

If – and it was still a big if – neither Justin nor Floyd had been responsible for Suki's death, several potentially significant questions remained to be answered. Had the attack been premeditated, the first question was how Suki's killer had known where to find her. She hadn't made or received any calls via her mobile in the hours before she died, nor written any text messages or comments on social media that alluded to her location, and, with the exception of her brief conversation with Sally, Justin and Floyd's landline had seen no activity that night. The second question was why the perpetrator might have chosen to murder Suki in her boyfriend's home. If her death hadn't been premeditated, meanwhile, that raised even more questions, because presumably anybody dropping into the flat unexpectedly wouldn't have been there looking for Suki. Either way, Lawrence reasoned, even if Justin hadn't killed her, he probably fitted into the picture one way or another.

Given that she had known both Suki and Justin well, Lawrence decided to start his next line of enquiry with Sally. He and Daniel arrived at her flat at eight-thirty, hoping to catch her before she left for work – assuming she had work to go to. If she didn't, Lawrence had no qualms about getting her out of bed.

In fact, she was up and dressed, and, on this occasion, complete with two identical Kohl eyebrows. Lawrence could only guess at how much practise it must have taken to get them so perfectly symmetrical. She invited them in, saying as she turned down the hallway towards the kitchen, 'I'm just having breakfast, do you want some coffee?'

Both Lawrence and Daniel took her up on the offer, and made themselves comfortable at the kitchen table while Sally attended to the coffee and finished a slice of toast spread with Marmite. Setting two mugs down on the table, she asked, 'Toast?'

Lawrence declined, and Sally reached for a chair.

'We'd like to ask you a few questions about Justin,' Lawrence began, as she sat down.

Sally frowned. 'But – I thought –' she faltered. 'Floyd said you let him go. I was going to go over to see him.'

'At the moment we don't know what happened on Monday night. I'm just trying to build up a more complete picture of the circumstances surrounding Suki's death.'

Sally nodded, but said nothing, and Lawrence continued, 'Do you know whether Justin has fallen out with anybody recently?'

'Justin falls out with people quite often,' Sally admitted, reluctantly. 'He gets upset about things that aren't really happening – he always thinks people are talking about him, or listening to his thoughts –' she raised her artificial eyebrows expressively. 'It's not his fault, but that doesn't mean everybody else can deal with it, either.'

'I understand that. What I'm really interested in are any rows he's had over something more concrete.'

Sally chewed her lip as she thought this over. 'Well, he hasn't been getting on well with Vinnie for months, not since –' she left Lawrence to assume the remainder of the sentence, then, after a brief pause, finished with, 'But that's hardly an unusual reaction, is it?'

'You're referring to Vinnie's drug habit,' Lawrence assumed.

'Yes.'

'Were they close before?'

'Very. Justin worshipped Vinnie, and Vin was fiercely protective of him. Now he's as likely as anyone else to give him a kicking.'

'Are you saying their arguments have been more than verbal at times?'

There was an uncomfortable silence before Sally nodded. Then she added, hurriedly, 'I only know about one time. I don't know if it happened more than that.'

'And what happened on that occasion?'

'Justin ended up in A and E with concussion. Suki said he was covered in bruises.'

'How do you know Vinnie was responsible for that?'

'My brother told me they'd had a fight.'

'Was he there at the time?'

'No. His flat mate told him.'

Lawrence sighed, guessing he was in for a game of tracing a Chinese whisper back to source. 'When was this?'

'A couple of months ago. I don't remember exactly.'

'Do you have any idea which hospital Justin was treated at?'

'Probably the Royal Free.'

Lawrence nodded, hoping patient confidentiality wouldn't preclude the hospital's sharing the relevant date. Perhaps Rebecca could look into that whilst he and Daniel tracked down somebody who might be able to tell them more about the altercation. With this in mind, he asked Sally for her brother's address and whether he – or his flat mate – was likely to be home.

'Yeah, I think so,' she responded. 'I mean, I don't know about Val, but Quary's got a couple of days off before his band flies out to the States, so he'll probably be recreating the Glenfinnan Viaduct, or something.' Then, apparently seeing Lawrence's puzzled expression, she added, 'He likes his model railways.' She smiled impishly. 'He and his ilk might look like rock stars, but most of them are really just geeks with guitars.'

Leighton had evidently received Rebecca's text message, and was sitting at a table in the corner of *Spike's Place* – a small independent café a few minutes' walk from Scotland Yard – when she arrived. She felt touched. Ordinarily he didn't get to work until at least half an hour after she did, and she knew he'd been working late the night before. He glanced up from his mobile screen as she approached, and, as he tucked it into his pocket, gestured towards the table, which held two mugs of coffee, a bag of miniature pains au chocolat and a packet of cookies.

'I ordered caffeine, fat and sugar. Where d'you want to start?'

Rebecca forced a smile. 'I think biscuits before eleven might conflict with convention.'

'I'll have to take your word for that,' Leighton responded, pulling open the nylon tie securing the croissants. 'I'm afraid etiquette classes were sadly lacking in my university timetable.'

'You'd never know,' Rebecca replied, grateful for the joke, joining him at the tiny marble-effect table.

'You're too kind,' Leighton quipped, offering her the pastries.

'Thanks,' Rebecca took one. 'And thanks for coming.'

'Spike's still in shock. He thought the clocks had changed and no one had told him when I rolled up at twenty to nine.' He helped himself to a pain au chocolat. 'So. Should I ask how you're doing, or is that going to make you cry? Not that you shouldn't cry – if you want to – but if not I can bore you with last night's match or something.'

Tears immediately filled Rebecca's eyes and Leighton wordlessly wrapped his arms around her. Rebecca couldn't remember the last time Elliot had held her like that. For months, she'd been the one trying to comfort him, and the realisation made her cry all the more. Their relationship hadn't always been so one-sided. A couple of years earlier, when her younger brother had been rushed to hospital with meningitis, Elliot had paid for a taxi from London to Norwich at one a.m. to be there with her. And that had been before Astatine had a record deal, when he was working six days – and several nights – a week. It was impossible to imagine his going to such lengths now.

'I'm sorry,' she whispered, at length, pulling away from Leighton and raising a hand to dry her tears.

'There's no need to apologise.'

Rebecca reached into her handbag for a tissue, glancing at her watch. 'God. I feel exhausted already, and it's not even nine.'

'If you want to take the day off I'm sure nobody would mind.'

'No. I need the distraction. Besides, Elliot's probably still at home.'

'How did you leave things?'

'I told him he was moving out.' She sniffed. 'And then – we –' she gulped. 'I was so horrible to him. What if he –' she faltered.

'You can't live your life for him, Becks.'

'I know, but –' she sighed. 'I just wish I could call him. Make sure he's ok.'

'You can if you want to.'

'But then he'll think it's not over, and I don't know if I can do it again. End it, I mean.'

Leighton nodded slightly. 'You still love him,' he concluded, aloud.

'I don't know,' Rebecca managed, trying to swallow her tears. 'I love the way he was. Before.' she blew her nose. 'I've never felt like that about anybody. Ever. I finally understood that whole *you know when you find the one* thing. I didn't really believe it before. And I've spent the last year watching him destroying it. And himself.' She paused. 'I feel so angry with him. And I feel – horrible – for feeling like that – and – like – like I've abandoned him – I mean, he's not just a bit down, he's seriously depressed and – and I couldn't help him!'

'Hey,' Leighton rested a hand on her forearm. 'Becks, he clearly has some big problems, and if he's not ready to face those yet there's nothing you can do. It's not your fault. It's probably not his fault either, but you can't put your life on hold forever.'

'I feel like I've abandoned him,' Rebecca repeated.

'He abandoned you every time he got drunk and opted out. Anyone drinking like that has got to be having a fucking rough time, but that doesn't change the fact it's hell to live with.'

Rebecca looked up, struck by the conviction with which he spoke.

'My dad's an alcoholic,' Leighton revealed, after an awkward silence.

The admission took Rebecca by surprise. It was, she realised, all too easy to take cheerful, happy-go-lucky characters at face value – not because you believed there was nothing more beneath their carefree exterior, but because they rarely gave you reason to think about it. She struggled to come up with a reply.

'That must've been tough as a kid.'

'Yes and no.' Leighton reached for his coffee. 'I mean, to me it was normal. Like everything you know is when you're young. And he's generally all right when he's sober.'

'And drunk?'

'Like a different person. But then you know all about that.'

Rebecca wasn't so sure she did. In Elliot's case, alcohol just seemed to accentuate whatever mood he was already in. These days that almost invariably meant descent into introspection, melancholy and tears. She didn't say as much, asking instead, 'Has he ever tried to stop?'

'Oh yeah. Quite often he'll go for days without a drink. Especially these days, because his body can't take it any more. But once he gets started it's like he doesn't know how to stop.'

'I used to think that once Elliot realised he has a problem, he might be able to start sorting himself out. But it's made him worse.'

'Come on, Bec, Elliot's problems don't start and finish with alcohol. He has a serious mental illness and from the way he's been drinking I'd guess he's trying to block something out.'

'I know,' Rebecca acknowledged. 'But I don't know what that *is*. He's always kept so much from me. And if he can't trust me enough to tell me, what does that say about our relationship?'

'Maybe that's just how he copes.'

'He isn't coping, though, is he?'

Leighton didn't reply.

'I've always had so little sympathy for women who stay with abusive partners. I never realised how much you can want to believe someone when they promise to change.'

Several seconds passed before Leighton asked, hesitantly, 'Has he ever hurt you?'

'No,' she shook her head. 'No, that's not what I meant. I can just see how hard it is to walk away from a bad situation when you really care for someone.'

Leighton nodded.

'Did your dad hurt you?'

There was a pause before he nodded again.

Rebecca didn't know how to respond. The question had entered her head and she had blurted it out without giving any thought to how she might deal with the answer. 'I'm sorry,' she offered, eventually.

'You didn't do it.'

'I know, but –'

'That was another lifetime.' He drained what remained of his coffee and reached for the menu wedged between the salt and pepper shakers at the centre of the table. 'Now, more caffeine, or something else?' He mused, running his eyes down the drinks list. 'Choices choices.' He glanced up. 'We're not planning on heading into work yet, are we?'

'I don't know – it's nearly nine.'

Leighton waved a careless hand through the air. 'Ah, still early. In the circumstances I reckon we can justify skiving 'til at least half past. And maybe a long lunch.' He leaned back in his chair, waving the menu in Spike's direction. 'After all, all I have waiting for me are corpses. And it's not like they're going anywhere in a hurry.'

Tracking down Valentine Wright took considerably longer than Lawrence had anticipated. He and Daniel had tried his home address in Hampstead first, finding his flat mate crouching in the drive of the red brick Victorian villa, cleaning one of the innards of a vintage navy Jaguar that stood, bonnet open, behind him. Lawrence recognised Quary immediately from the Vicious Circle posters Blu-tacked to Jimmy's bedroom walls. His muscular arms were tattooed with engine oil, his athletic frame emphasised by a red tank top and tight leather trousers, and his long, dark hair was draped over his shoulders. As Lawrence and Daniel neared, he raised his eyes to meet them, his expression wary, and Lawrence guessed this was far from the first time he'd been disturbed at home by uninvited visitors.

Unlike the other bands whose members they had come into contact with that week, Vicious Circle had recently succeeded in making it out of the underground music scene and into the mainstream, and were well on their way to becoming a national phenomenon. Over the past six months they had racked up two number one singles – an achievement frontman Matthew Quilter had decried publicly as "fucking meaningless" – and a double platinum album, and had featured on just about every chart and chat show going. Matthew's blatant disregard for the law and authority – and, in fact, more or less everybody else as well – had been well documented, and Lawrence could only hope Quary had a different outlook.

In the event, he was more than helpful. Having confirmed that his knowledge of the fracas between Justin and Vinnie was limited to the little Valentine had told him, he added, rather apologetically, that Valentine was away on tour, and offered to call him to find out where his band was due to play that night. Just under two hours later, Lawrence and Daniel drew up behind the tour bus parked directly outside Southampton's Guildhall, mistakenly expecting to be well on their way back to London by lunch time.

The early hours of the afternoon came and went while they watched Cheap Appeal's road crew unload the band's equipment and start setting up the stage, and by two o'clock Lawrence had managed to speak to every member of the band *but* Valentine, and their irate tour manager, a thirty-something Glaswegian named Ben. If his band mates were to be believed, nobody knew where Valentine had gone, but given their lack of concern about his absence, and the increasing frustration of their manager, Lawrence suspected this wasn't the first time Cheap Appeal's lead singer had gone AWOL on tour.

By the time he did show up, at twenty to three, Lawrence was not in the best of tempers. Neither, it soon became clear, was Valentine. A slight figure of about five foot nine, he managed to look dishevelled despite being clean shaven, clad in jeans and t-shirt that were neither ripped nor crumpled, and having his long mousy hair fastened away from his face. He was arguing on his mobile as he wandered in through the back door of the venue, his pierced eyebrows drawn into a vicious scowl, almost every other word an expletive. Terminating the call with the words, 'Yeah, well, when you want to stop being a cunt, get back to me!' He glanced at Lawrence and Daniel, demanding sarcastically, 'Can I help you?'

'Yes, as it happens,' Lawrence answered. 'We're –'

He got no further. Valentine had apparently not expected a response, and shook his head, saying, 'Oh fuck off!' before turning to walk into the club.

Lawrence was in no mood to negotiate, and seized Valentine's left arm, pulling him sharply back around to face him and ignoring his yelp of protest. 'Police,' he informed Valentine, shortly, as he released him.

'Jesus!' Valentine exclaimed, raising his right hand to his arm. 'There's no need to dislocate my fucking shoulder!'

'There's really no need to tell complete strangers to fuck off either, is there?'

'Well I thought –' Valentine stopped, shaking his head again. 'Never mind. What d'you want?'

'I'd like to ask you a few questions about Justin and Vinnie Black.'

Valentine raised his eyebrows, but said nothing, and after a moment Lawrence continued. 'I understand you witnessed a fight between them a couple of months ago.'

'You *understand* wrong,' Valentine snapped.

'All right,' Lawrence replied, as reasonably as he could manage, 'I'll rephrase that. You told your flat mate they'd had a fight.'

'Uh-huh,' Valentine confirmed, still rubbing his arm. 'If I can't play tonight can I sue you?'

'If you can find any witnesses.' Lawrence turned to Daniel. 'Danny, you see anything?'

Daniel barely suppressed a snigger. 'No, Sir.'

'Shame.' Lawrence returned his attention to Valentine. 'Now, how about you? If you didn't witness the fight, how did you hear about it?'

'They were in the toilet at the pub. I walked in to find Justin in a heap on the floor – I asked what was going on and Vinnie stormed out.'

'Justin was on the floor?'

Valentine nodded, pulling a pristine packet of Marlboros from the pocket of his jeans. 'I asked if he'd had a row with Vinnie and he said yes.'

'Did he say anything else?'

'No, but he was obviously upset, so I took him home.'

'I assume if you were in the pub with him that you saw him before whatever happened with Vinnie?'

'Briefly,' Valentine raised the cigarette packet to his mouth and extracted one with his lips before finishing, through it, 'I wasn't actually there *with* him. I bumped into him at the bar.'

'And how did he seem then?'

'Ok. A bit anxious, but that's not unusual for Just.'

'So he wasn't upset before the row with Vinnie?'

Valentine searched his pockets for a lighter, lit up, and only then answered the question. 'No, not really.'

Lawrence was more interested in the row between Justin and Vinnie than in enforcing the smoking ban, and decided to defer that pleasure by a couple of minutes. 'Do you think it would be fair to assume that that was what had upset him?'

'I don't know,' Valentine admitted. 'Justin's a mate, but I don't know him all that well. Floyd or Quary might be able to tell the difference between Justin upset for a reason and Justin in a state over the voices in his head, but I can't.'

'Was he hurt?'

'He was a bit unsteady on his feet but he said he was ok. After we got home I realised he'd cut his head, and then he started puking, so I dragged him to the hospital. I think he'd been given a good kicking, but I didn't like to ask. Part of me didn't even want to know.'

'Why not?'

The look Valentine gave Lawrence inferred that he shouldn't have needed to ask. 'You don't beat up someone smaller and younger than you! Especially not your kid brother! And I'd like to think none of my mates would do that!'

'You mean that by not asking you can pretend it might not have happened?'

Valentine sighed. 'Yes. And yes, hearing it out loud I am aware of how pathetic that sounds.'

'And do you –'

'Where the *fuck* have you been?' A voice behind Lawrence interrupted. He turned to see Ben bearing down upon them, clearly furious.

'Went to get some fags,' Valentine answered, sounding bored.

'And that took *four hours*?' Ben responded, in disbelief. 'Who the fuck d'you think you are? Axl fucking Rose?' He snatched the cigarette from between Valentine's fingers and threw it to the floor. 'You can't smoke in here. And I told you yesterday there would be no more disappearing acts on my time!'

'And I told you to fuck off,' Valentine retorted, tersely, turning for the door through to the club. 'What part of that was unclear?' He didn't wait for a response, marching through the door and flinging it shut behind himself. It swung straight through one hundred and eighty degrees, and slammed into Ben's knee. He swore loudly, giving the door a retaliatory kick before seeming to remember he had an audience.

'Any chance you could arrest him for wasting *my* time?' He asked, ruefully, bending down to massage his knee.

'Do this a lot, does he?'

'This week he does. It wasn't funny on Monday night, but at least he finished playing before he disappeared. Yesterday he cut it so fine I almost had to pull the gig.'

'Where was he?'

'Good question.' Ben straightened up. 'None of my business, apparently, despite the fact it impacts on mine.'

'Do you not have some sort of contract?'

'We do, but Val's response to the word *lawsuit* generally involves words of four letters. Not that I think the record company would ever risk it.'

'Why not?'

'It's a small label, and the chairman probably can't afford to lose.'

'And Valentine can?'

'Yes.'

From what he had learned about Cheap Appeal over the past few hours, Lawrence guessed the money hadn't been made through the band, and, curious, asked, 'How?'

'Inheritance.'

'Ah,' Lawrence nodded, adding two and two to make one spoiled little rich kid.

'Anyway, I'm going to pin him down to sound check before he has a chance to wander off again. Are you done?'

'Yes,' Lawrence confirmed, feeling uneasy. Something – besides Valentine's attitude – was bothering him, although he couldn't have said what. With this in mind, he added, as Ben turned to go, 'For now.'

## Twelve

Petra stood staring at the blinking cursor on her smartphone screen, her mind blank. She couldn't think of anything appropriate to say that she hadn't said already, and it was too soon to revert to meaningless chatter. Silently, she castigated herself for agonising over it at all: Fin didn't deserve her concern. He probably wouldn't even care that she was thinking of him. Too busy moping over the two-faced bitch he'd never been able to see for what she was.

'Hello there.'

Petra looked up sharply to find a customer waiting at the bar. He seemed vaguely familiar, although she couldn't have said whether she had ever actually set eyes on him before – in a venue where the majority of men sported long hair and wore leather jackets, one had a tendency to blur into another. She wondered how long he had been standing there.

'Sorry,' she apologised, feeling her face flush and setting the phone down. 'What would you like?'

'I was actually hoping to speak to someone about this,' he presented a flyer for a Saturday night event that was now several weeks past.

'That was last month,' Petra replied, awkwardly.

This was met with an amused smile. 'I know. I was wondering whether it was a one-off or whether you're looking to do more of this kind of thing.'

'I'm not sure, to be honest. But you should be able to find out what's coming up from our Facebook page, that's always fairly up-to-date.'

In fact, she reflected, *fairly* was an unnecessary inclusion: Fin was meticulous about maintaining the feed.

'I'm more interested in organising something myself,' the man in front of her revealed, presenting flyers for a couple of club nights and planting a forefinger on the name *Alec* in the list of DJs for the right-hand one. 'That's me.'

'You DJ at Mausoleum?' She exclaimed in surprise, wondering why he didn't look more familiar. Then again, she hadn't made it to the monthly goth night since – when? November?

'I do.'

'And you want to play here?' She asked, sceptically.

'I like small venues,' he shrugged. 'Platforms are for knobheads with oversized egos. I prefer being at ground level where I can talk to people.'

Petra couldn't help smiling in response to this blunt appraisal.

'So, what are the chances?' He asked.

'You need to speak to Fin, really. He's not in this week, but I can pass on your details if you like?'

'Fin,' Alec's eyebrows crinkled in thought. 'Which one's he?'

'White shirt,' Petra offered, succinctly, recycling a description she'd used several times before. Fin's odd wardrobe choice stood out in a venue that was invariably filled with multiple shades of black.

'Oh yeah, I know,' Alec nodded. 'Is that supposed to be ironic?'

'I don't think so.'

'Maybe he's colourblind,' Alec joked.

His smile was infectious, and Petra found herself returning it as she said, 'Maybe.'

He added a business card to the flyers already on the bar, saying, 'I'll leave these here. Maybe you could put a good word in for me.' He winked. 'Otherwise, I'll just have to come back and make a nuisance of myself in person.'

Vinnie Black bore no obvious resemblance to his younger brother. He was several inches taller and considerably broader, with olive skin and thick dark hair. He didn't look much like the stereotypical gaunt, unkempt heroin addict either, which Daniel put down to the short duration of his habit. His eyes were the colour of wet cement, and his pupils, although perhaps slightly constricted, were not the pin-pricks indicative of an opiate high. He was clad in blue jeans and an indigo V-necked jumper, and three parallel scratches that looked like fingernail marks were visible in the crook of the V. Lawrence's first question on sitting down in Vinnie's cramped, untidy living room was to ask where they had come from. Vinnie glanced down, as if he hadn't previously been aware of their existence, then broke into a lazy smile.

'My girlfriend's an animal.'

Lawrence scarcely even blinked in response to this remark, saying, 'And can you tell me where you were on Monday night from ten p.m. onwards?'

Vinnie lay back in his chair. 'In bed with aforementioned girlfriend.'

'In bed with your girlfriend?' Lawrence echoed, with heavy scepticism.

Vinnie raised his eyes to the ceiling for a few moments. 'Well, possibly not *in* bed,' he conceded. 'We shagged in the kitchen and on the sofa before we did it in the bedroom. I couldn't give you an exact time frame.' He smiled again, and Daniel concluded from his expression that, while not sky high, Vinnie certainly wasn't sober.

'How about your brother's girlfriend?' Lawrence continued. 'Did you know her well?'

'Not *that* well,' Vinnie sniggered.

Lawrence regarded him in silence for a moment before saying, 'A young woman is dead, Mr Black. I don't think that's very funny, do you?'

'You wouldn't,' Vinnie retorted, his smile vanishing. '*You* didn't know her.'

'So you and Suki didn't get along.'

'I already have one mother to tell me what I ought and ought not to be doing. I didn't need another.'

'Could you expand on that?'

Vinnie rubbed his jaw. 'Every time I saw the girl there was something I either wasn't doing or wasn't doing right. Like Justin's the epicentre of the universe, or something. I do have my own life.' He paused. 'I wouldn't have minded so much if she'd had the first fucking clue how to deal with him.'

'You don't think she did?'

'She wanted to control him, and she wanted to fix him. You can't do either of those with Justin.'

'Suki seems to have been under the impression that Floyd could control him.'

Vinnie shook his head. 'Floyd's very good with Just, and he knows how to handle him, but knowing how to handle him and controlling him are two different things. You can't control someone who doesn't have control of himself.'

Daniel revised his first-impression opinion of Vinnie. The bloke might be a twat, but he wasn't an idiot.

Lawrence moved smoothly on to his next line of enquiry. 'I understand you and Justin had a fight in the Spread Eagle pub a couple of months ago.'

Vinnie shrugged, lowering his eyes to the glass-topped coffee table that crouched between them. In places the glass was noticeably scratched, and Daniel could guess how that might have happened. It was the perfect surface for racking up lines of cocaine.

'What was the fight about?'

Vinnie shrugged again.

'That's not an answer.'

'Justin causes fights every time he opens his mouth,' Vinnie responded, unhelpfully.

'What was it about?' Lawrence persisted.

'Nothing much.'

'He deserved to wind up in hospital with concussion over nothing much, did he?'

'*What*?' Vinnie exclaimed, clearly shocked by this revelation.

'A few hours after your fight, a friend was so concerned about Justin that he took him to A and E! According to hospital records, he was concussed and had some serious bruises! Is that how you usually respond to arguments with him?'

'I didn't do that! He's my brother, for Christ's sake!'

'Well then who did?'

His moment of animation apparently over, Vinnie returned to shrugging and saying nothing.

'Valentine Wright saw Justin go into the toilets perfectly all right. A few minutes later he found the two of you in there, and he says Justin was in a heap on the floor. Now, if you didn't hurt him, you must know who did.'

Vinnie didn't respond.

'Ignoring the question won't make it go away,' Lawrence remarked, not bothering to disguise his irritation.

'Why don't you ask Justin?'

'I'm asking you.'

Once again Vinnie said nothing.

Lawrence sighed pointedly. 'Look, I'm really not interested in how you live your life, but if you don't start to cooperate I might have to develop an interest.'

'What's that supposed to mean?'

'You know what it means. Now answer the question.'

Only a couple of seconds passed before he capitulated. 'Guy called A.J.'

'Full name?'

'Aaron Jenkins.'

'Is he a friend of yours?'

'I guess.'

'So why did he attack Justin?'

'I dunno.'

'Don't be pathetic.'

'I don't fucking know, all right?' Vinnie exclaimed, angrily. 'I have no idea what goes on in Justin's head! *He* probably has no idea half the time! He believed the council were bugging his last flat so they could listen to his thoughts! And sometimes he sits up all night worrying that the sun might not rise in the morning! He doesn't live in the same world as the rest of us! And none of us can be there every bloody second to keep him out of trouble! I know he's my brother, I love him to pieces, and if anybody really hurt him I'd probably kill them, but that doesn't stop him being a fucking liability!'

*I'd probably kill.* Page one, stupid things not to say during a police interview. Daniel re-revised his opinion. The guy *was* an idiot.

Five twenty-seven. It was incredible how quickly a dull afternoon at work could pass if you didn't want it to end, Rebecca thought as she selected yet another human interest story she wouldn't normally have bothered to read on the *BBC News* website. Sooner or later she was going to run out of ways of procrastinating, and would actually have to go home. And at home she would either have to deal with Elliot – if he'd decided to try his luck with sticking around – or she would have to deal with his absence. Neither option appealed. Nor was either familiar. She had never cohabited with a boyfriend before, so her home and her relationships had previously always been two separate entities. In days gone by she would have headed back to a sympathetic flat mate, a couple of bottles of wine and a selection or combination of chocolate, ice cream, pizza and Pringles. This time, getting drunk was the last thing she wanted to do. She sighed. Actually, going home was the *last* thing she wanted to do. But getting drunk came a close second.

'Hey.'

She glanced up. Leighton was standing a few feet away, jacket on, his long, silky dark hair spilling over his shoulders. 'You done?'

Rebecca nodded.

'Cubana?'

'No, I don't want to drink – it'll only remind me of –' she faltered.

'Sorry, stupid idea. Milkshake?'

'Spike closes up at four.'

Leighton wrinkled his nose, looking thoughtful. 'Maccy D's?'

Rebecca managed a smile. 'Classy.'

'My middle name.'

'I might need one of their apple pies as well.'

Leighton pulled out his wallet and peered inside. 'I think I can just about cover that. But if you want a Big Mac I'll be in trouble.'

Rebecca stood and reached for her handbag. 'Thanks. I was –' she stopped as she was interrupted by a muffled bee-beep bee-beep. Leighton muttered an expletive and drew his mobile from his pocket. Reading the message, he swore again before placing a call and glancing at Rebecca. 'Sorry, give me two minutes.'

She nodded.

'Hello? Yes ... Oh come on, Roddy, you know I'm –' he paused as Roddy apparently cut in, adding after a moment, 'Oh for Christ's sake, what sort of a system is that? I'm not even supposed to be –' Another pause. 'Ok, ok, but Jon is so dead when I catch up with him ... yeah, tell him that ... ok. Laters.' Leighton terminated the call and thrust his phone back into his pocket with a sigh. 'I'm sorry, Becks, I'm going to have to go.'

'It's ok,' Rebecca responded, forcing a smile.

'Some girl's been topped in Somers Town and apparently I'm the only person daft enough to have their phone switched on. If I turn up to find an eight-year-old with a chemistry set could have handled it there'll be another sodding murder!'

'It's all right,' Rebecca reassured him. 'Really. I'll be ok.'

'Do you want to come?'

'Are you serious?'

'Ah, silly idea,' he remarked, with a shake of his head. 'I just thought –' he shrugged. 'Anyway, I'll see you tomorrow. Take care, yeah?'

Rebecca nodded. Leighton turned to go, and she watched him walk down the corridor that ran along the side of the open-plan office. Then she grabbed her jacket and bag, and hurried after him. Home, or crime scene. No contest.

'Aaron Jenkins?' Lawrence asked the scruffy, unshaven young man who opened the door to him and Daniel dressed in distressed blue jeans and a once black, now faded to grey t-shirt with what looked like tomato stains down the front. He shifted position uneasily and raked a hand through his lank brown hair as he answered.

'Yes.'

'DCI Forrester,' Lawrence displayed his warrant card. Tipping his head in Daniel's direction he added, 'DS Freeman. Could we come in for a minute, please?'

'Oh for fuck's sake, what *now*?' Aaron demanded, sounding exasperated.

Lawrence frowned. 'What?'

Aaron hesitated. 'What's this about?'

'We'd like to ask you some questions about the death of Suki Jenson.'

'I didn't have nothing to do with it!'

'I didn't say you did. I'd simply like to ask you a few questions.'

'Oh. Ok,' Aaron consented, grudgingly, turning and starting down the hallway. Lawrence followed, leaving Daniel to close the door.

From without, the basement flat had appeared dirty and unkempt – much like Aaron himself – but behind the run-down facade it looked like a lived-in show home. Aaron led Lawrence and Daniel through to the back of the building, where a large, open-plan living area overlooked a well-maintained garden complete with a terrace and smart wrought iron garden furniture. A compact kitchen nestled to the left of the patio doors, and the room was dominated by three plump leather sofas, which were gathered around a carved wooden coffee table, and an expansive plasma screen that occupied the right-hand wall.

Sitting on one of the sofas, Lawrence wondered what Aaron did for a living.

'I'd like to start with an incident that occurred in the Spread Eagle pub a couple of months ago,' he began, as Aaron dropped onto the opposing sofa.

Aaron's eyes narrowed marginally. 'I don't remember an incident.'

'I'll refresh your memory, then. I understand you gave Justin Black quite a beating in the mens' toilets at about eleven o'clock on March the seventeenth.'

'Who told you that?'

Lawrence ignored the question. 'Is it true?'

'No.'

Lawrence raised his eyebrows. 'No?'

'I expect that happened inside his head,' Aaron replied, nastily, leaning sideways against the arm rest and tipping his head in the opposite direction to compensate.

'If it happened inside his head I'd be interested to know how he came to spend the early hours of the following morning in A and E with concussion.'

Aaron clearly hadn't anticipated that there might be any evidence of the fracas, and hesitated before saying, disingenuously, 'What?'

'And it wasn't Justin who told me.'

'You mean *Vinnie* –' Aaron began furiously.

'So you *do* remember the occasion,' Lawrence concluded for him. 'Great. Now, how about you tell me why you felt it necessary to do that degree of damage to someone smaller and younger than you?'

His derisive tone had the desired effect of riling Aaron. 'It was self defence! He knocked me flat and then laid into me – I didn't have much choice but to defend myself!'

'Why did he attack you in the first place?'

'How the hell would I know?' Aaron demanded, his cheeks flushed. 'He's a fucking headcase!'

Lawrence felt irritated. Over the past couple of days, several people had used Justin's schizophrenia as a means of circumventing questions they didn't want to answer, and he was rapidly running out of patience.

'So you're saying it was completely unprovoked.'

'Yes.'

'Have you and Justin ever been friends?'

Aaron managed to make a simple snigger sound sarcastic. 'No chance. Unfortunately I have to see him from time to time because Vinnie's a mate, but as a general rule I give him a wide berth.'

'Any particular reason why you and he don't get on?' Lawrence asked, expecting to receive an abrupt and uninformative reply. He was wrong.

'Justin's your stereotypical tortured genius,' Aaron responded, rather contemptuously. 'Which is great – for selling records. But it's not so great for the people who have to deal with him day to day. He's talented and enigmatic, but he's completely fucked up with it. He's going to be a star, but not before he's caused himself and most of those who love him a great deal of pain, and, when he gets there, if it doesn't kill him it'll come damn close.'

Lawrence absorbed this before saying, 'Does he often attack people at random?'

Aaron shifted slightly in his seat. 'I don't know. Like I said, I don't see much of him.'

'So not to your knowledge?'

A long pause passed before Aaron finally replied, 'No.'

'Where were you after ten on Monday night?'

'Here.'

'Doing what?'

'Watching DVDs. Drinking beer.'

'Can anybody substantiate that?'

'Um – I was here when Jake – my flat mate – came home from work, but I'm not sure what time that was.'

'Is Jake here now?'

Aaron nodded.

'I'd like a word, if it's convenient.'

He nodded again, moving to stand. 'Are you done with me?'

'I don't know,' Lawrence returned, still not satisfied that the altercation with Justin had been without basis. 'That rather depends on what Jake has to say, doesn't it?'

To Lawrence's surprise, he and Daniel were joined a couple of minutes later by a petite young woman in skin-tight blue jeans, a long-sleeved white top and a faux-fur gillet. She had olive skin of such perfect tone that Lawrence guessed she couldn't be over twenty-five, brown eyes and close-cropped dark hair – shorter, in fact, than that of most of the men Lawrence had spoken to in the past couple of days. She was attractive, although he wouldn't have said *pretty*, and exuded a surprising degree of sexual confidence for her age. She closed the door behind herself before sitting on the sofa that Aaron had recently vacated, drawing her legs up and folding them to one side with the easy grace of a cat. Leaning an elbow on the armrest to her other side, she looked directly into Lawrence's eyes.

'What did you want to know?'

'First of all I'd like to take your full name, I'm guessing it's not Jake?'

She gave a mischievous smile. 'No. It's Jacqueline. I have five elder brothers.'

'Jacqueline –' Lawrence raised his eyebrows expectantly.

'Brady.'

'Do you remember what time you arrived home on Monday night?'

'I think just after midnight,' Jacqueline offered, after a moment's thought. 'But I didn't check my watch. It might've been later. Is this about Suki?'

'Yes. Did you know her?'

'Not really. I've seen her around, but we've never spoken.'

'How about Justin?'

'Well, we're not mates, if that's what you're asking, but yes, I know him.'

'Why are you not friends?'

'We're not actively *not* friends, we've just never –' Jacqueline shrugged rather than complete her sentence. 'Conversation with Justin can be hard work, and I have enough high-maintenance friends already, if you know what I mean.'

'We've heard several reports of a fight Aaron had with Justin a couple of months ago. Do you know anything about that?'

Jacqueline shook her head.

'Aaron claims Justin instigated it. Do you think that's likely?'

'Yes, very.'

'What makes you say that?'

Jacqueline frowned and sounded incredulous as she asked, '*What*?'

'Most of the people we've spoken to so far have said they don't believe Justin to be violent. I'd like to know why you have a different opinion.'

'I hardly think you need to be violent to want to smack the guy who's *selling* smack to your brother,' Jacqueline responded, bluntly.

Lawrence managed to contain his surprise at this revelation, but only just. 'Aaron's been selling heroin to Vinnie?'

Jacqueline's expression indicated that she had expected Lawrence to know this already, although she appeared puzzled rather than horrified that she had been the one to spill the beans. Even more surprisingly, she continued, after a pause, 'Vinnie and half the other smackheads in North London. There's hardly a shortage of them around here.'

'That's a serious allegation.'

'I'm hardly breaking new ground, he's already been charged with possession with intent.'

Immediately understanding her openness about Aaron's misdemeanours, Lawrence asked when that had happened.

'Saturday.'

'When was he released on bail?'

'Monday afternoon.'

'Do you know who provided the surety?'

'His mate Val.'

'Valentine Wright?' Lawrence guessed.

'Yes.'

'And was Aaron home on Monday evening?'

'I wouldn't know, I was out 'til gone midnight.'

'Was he here when you got in?'

Jacqueline nodded.

'Can you give us some idea of his frame of mind at the time?'

'No,' Jacqueline responded, levelly.

Lawrence frowned. 'What do you mean, no?'

'We didn't speak,' she clarified. 'After the drug squad had been through everything I own, including my underwear, I wasn't in the mood for his self-pitying *why me* drivel. Given he'd ruined my weekend as well as his own, I'm pretty sure that should have been *my* line.'

## Thirteen

Leighton's first thought on seeing the mangled body splayed on the cheap parquet flooring of the Euston bedsit was that it was just as well they weren't going to be reliant on dental records to identify the girl. There were several substantial injuries to her head and upper face, but her teeth and jaw had been reduced to little more than a pulp. And he didn't need to look far for the weapon responsible: a spherical glass ornament the size of a small cantaloupe lay inches from the girl's head, smeared with blood and fragments of tooth and bone.

'Who found her?' He asked the young police constable hovering in the doorway as he crouched beside the body.

'Boyfriend.'

'Where is he now?'

'Next door. My Guv's taking a statement.'

Leighton nodded. Then, noticing Rebecca appear behind the man, he added, 'She's with me.'

The constable obligingly stepped aside, allowing Rebecca through. Taking in the scene that met her, she raised her eyebrows. 'Pretty.'

'Uh-huh,' Leighton acknowledged, lifting the dead girl's arm to find it stiff with rigor mortis. He was about to observe that she certainly hadn't died within the past few hours when Rebecca exclaimed, 'Oh give me a *break*!'

Leighton glanced up. 'What?'

Rebecca tipped her head towards something behind him. Turning, it took him a moment to realise what she was looking at. The wall was plastered with posters, and to the right of the door frame was an approximately two-by-three-foot picture of Elliot. After pausing for a moment to absorb the details of the accompanying posters, Leighton cast his eyes around the room. The other walls were similarly attired, the space above the bed given over to a photographic collage. The subjects of many of images looked familiar, and he turned back to Rebecca.

'Good thing they didn't rely on that eight-year-old and his chemistry set. I think we might be interested in this.'

Tearing her eyes away from the Astatine poster and scanning the rest of the room, Rebecca nodded.

'And at a guess, someone liked Matt Quilter,' Leighton indicated the photographs. 'She's not his girlfriend, is she? That'd make for an interesting twist.'

'Um – no – I don't think so. What's her name?'

'Meredith Armstrong.'

Rebecca shook her head. 'I don't recognise it. I know his ex – girl called Kaia – from when Matt and Elliot shared a flat, but if he's been seeing anyone since they split I haven't heard about it.'

'Elliot used to live with Matt Quilter? I didn't know that.'

'A couple of years ago. They were pretty close until Matt found a new mate called heroin.'

Leighton couldn't help thinking Elliot had done much the same with a *mate* called Jack Daniel, but he didn't say so. Resting his forearms across his knees, he said, 'Well, whoever her boyfriend is, he was the one who found her. Do you want a word?'

'Is he still around?'

'Next door, apparently.' Leighton shifted his attention to the uniformed officer stationed at the door. 'Can you make sure the boyfriend doesn't disappear off once your guv's done?'

The young man nodded mutely before ducking out of sight.

'Christ. He's like a mouse. Am I that scary?'

Rebecca smiled, and for the first time that day it didn't look forced. 'You're about as scary as a teddy bear.'

'Oh thank you. Do I at least get to be one with a growling mechanism inside?'

'I see you more as one of the ones with a pot of honey or marmalade in their paws.'

Leighton struggled not to laugh. 'It'll have to be honey. Marmalade's a crime against oranges.'

'I'll investigate that later,' Rebecca joked, moving towards the wall of photographs. 'Just as soon as I've found a link between our two girls.'

'What, aside from the fact they knew a whole bunch of the same people?'

'Yeah, doesn't help narrow it down much, does it?' She replied. 'Hopefully the boyfriend will be able to give us some clues.' She inspected the pictures at close range. 'Otherwise, from the looks of things, there are going to be an awful lot of interviews to get through.'

*****

Katie was halfway down the front steps of the house by the time Lawrence had climbed out of the car, and he immediately gathered from her expression that something was wrong.

'What's happened?'

'Where've you *been*?' She demanded. 'I've been calling you for hours!'

Lawrence felt thrown. His mobile hadn't rung once, but even if it *had* gone unanswered he wasn't sure why Katie would have been so concerned. It was only quarter to nine. 'Calm down, I'm here now.'

'Well Jim isn't!' Katie exclaimed, answering the question of why she looked so panicked. 'He hasn't come home, and he's not answering his phone! I've called everyone I can think of! I even tried going to the park, but –'

'Ok, ok, let's start at the beginning,' Lawrence stopped her. Feeling bad that he didn't know, he asked, 'What time does he usually get home?'

'Four – half-past sometimes – always by six. When I call his phone it just rings and rings. I called you, as well, but all I ever got was your voicemail. You weren't at the office, and nobody knew where you were! I tried calling Becky, but –'

'Have you contacted the school?'

'Of course I have! I've even called the hospitals!'

'How about the police?'

'I called *you*! I left messages for you everywhere!'

'All right, I'm sorry, I don't know why my phone is off, it shouldn't be.' He retrieved it from his pocket on the off-chance Jimmy had sent him a message. 'Was he at school today?' He asked, as he tried the power button.

'Yes,' Katie confirmed, tears in her voice.

'Flat,' Lawrence concluded, when the phone didn't respond. 'Right, I need to plug it in in case Jim's been in touch – let's do that first, and then I'll try calling him.'

'I've already tried a hundred times! What if something's happened to him? What if –'

'I'm sure nothing's happened to him,' Lawrence soothed, trying to sound confident. 'He's probably just sulking about being denied his allowance.'

'Maybe,' Katie allowed, sounding far from reassured.

Lawrence guided her into the house, then climbed the stairs to the second floor two at a time and connected his mobile to the charger at his bedside. It beeped and came back to life, taking seven long seconds to boot up. He immediately called his voicemail and the disembodied voice informed him he had four new messages.

'How many messages did you leave?' He asked, as Katie joined him.

'Um – three, I think.'

The first three were indeed from her, and he held his breath while he waited for the fourth. There was a pause before Rebecca's voice spoke. He cut her short after just a few words and immediately dialled Jimmy's mobile. It rang nine times before going through to voicemail and, with a frustrated sigh, Lawrence hung up, looking to his wife. 'Are all his school friends accounted for?'

She nodded.

'And you're sure he doesn't have some sort of sports match?'

'Of course I'm sure!' Katie exclaimed, sounding slightly hysterical. 'And even if he *did* he'd be home by now!'

'Kate, I'm not trying to find fault with you, I'm just making sure we haven't missed anything before we involve the police.'

'I've been through every possibility time and again!' Katie responded, beginning to cry. 'I'm just so scared – I –' she gave up, raising a hand to her eyes.

'Sit down,' Lawrence suggested, pushing her gently down onto the bed before joining her and slipping an arm around her. 'I'm sure there's a simple explanation and we'll be telling him off for worrying us in no time. I'm going to put a call in to the local police station, and when I've done that we'll see whether we can think of anything else. All right?'

Katie nodded. 'Ok,' she managed.

Lawrence returned his attention to the phone and launched his web browser to search for the number, praying that he was right. Any alternative didn't bear thinking about.

For Rebecca, Neil Shaw served as yet another reminder of Elliot. Not because they looked in any way alike, but because seeing Neil brought to mind a comment Elliot had once made. *It takes more than safety pins and a mohican to be punk*. Similarly, a convincing goth clearly required something more than black eyeliner, pinstriped combat trousers and a Celtic silver cross. The difference was that Elliot's point had been about attitude, whereas in Neil's case the issue was aesthetic. Much as Rebecca hated to admit it, to her mind gothic fashion just didn't suit chubby men. Big girls could carry the look off no problem, especially those accentuating their curves with the help of a corset, but men without cheekbones hadn't a hope in hell of getting away with eyeliner – they just looked ridiculous.

Although it didn't suit him, Neil had made a good job of applying his make up, and the fact it was still intact indicated that he hadn't been overly distressed at finding his girlfriend's body. Given the state of the corpse, Rebecca might have expected him to appear more shaken even if he *hadn't* known Meredith. Perhaps he hadn't yet taken it in. He was sitting in an armchair, and was fiddling with one of many cheap metal bangles that encircled his wrists as Rebecca entered the room. He glanced up in response to her arrival, drawing his long, frizzy black hair away from his face and giving an anxious smile. 'Hi.'

'Hi,' Rebecca returned the smile. 'I'm Detective Sergeant Palmer. I'm so sorry about Meredith.'

Neil nodded by way of acknowledgement before returning his attention to the bracelet. Rebecca perched opposite him.

'Do you feel up to answering a few questions?'

'Sure,' Neil replied, his tone rather flat.

'Had you and Meredith been together long?'

'About eight months.'

'Was it a close relationship?'

He shrugged.

Rebecca frowned. 'You must have some idea.'

No reply.

'Did you love her?'

Neil shrugged again. 'Who knows. Love's really just what people call the rut you get into when you're sentimental about sex that used to be good, isn't it?' He remarked, paraphrasing a Cheap Appeal lyric. Given the band's relative obscurity, Rebecca wondered whether his intention was to pass off Valentine's rather warped perspective as his own.

'Is that really how you feel?'

Neil answered a different question. 'She didn't love me. I *know* she didn't love me.'

'What makes you so sure?'

'I was a camouflage she wore to disguise her desperation,' he replied, bitterly. 'An understudy whose feelings didn't feature in her equation.'

Another familiar lyric. This time Rebecca chose not to ignore it. 'Quarks fan?'

Neil looked up sharply, clearly surprised she knew the origin of the line. Recovering himself quickly, he said, 'They're ok.' Then, after a brief pause, 'Mez liked them.' And, after another moment, 'At least, she *said* she did, but then Mez liked any band whose audience might include Matt Quilter.'

'Is that what makes you so sure she didn't love you?'

Neil didn't reply.

'Did Meredith's interest in Matt come between you?'

'It was more of an obsession than an interest. And yes, obviously it came between us.'

'Did she know him well?'

'Sort of, I suppose. She knew a lot about him. But as far as he was concerned she was just a particularly persistent and annoying groupie.'

He spoke with some contempt, and Rebecca replied, 'You say she didn't love you, but I get the impression you didn't even *like* her.'

'No,' Neil observed, his tone thoughtful. 'I don't think I did. I think screwing each other after a few drinks on a night out just became a habit. And it took a while for me to realise it wasn't a healthy one.'

'When did you realise that?'

'Sunday night.'

'What happened on Sunday night?'

'We went to a gig.'

'Which one?'

'Cheap Appeal. At the Barfly.'

'And what happened?'

'Nothing. Well, nothing in particular. I just – remembered something. Something that got me thinking.'

'Did you accompany Meredith home afterwards?'

'No. We had a row.'

'About?'

'Take a guess,' Neil retorted, sourly.

'Did you see or hear from Meredith again after that?' Rebecca went on, surprised, in the circumstances, by his overt resentment towards the dead woman.

'She texted me on Monday evening like nothing had happened.'

'Was that unexpected?'

'No, that was how she usually dealt with my feelings,' Neil remarked. 'Ignored them.'

'Had you arranged to meet tonight?'

'No. But she was supposed to be at a gig last night, and she wasn't. I wanted to do it properly. Not just send her a text.'

'Do what properly?'

'Finish it,' he revealed. 'I wanted to get it over with. Get on with life. So when I couldn't get hold of her I just came over.' There was a momentary pause before he added, quickly, 'Finish our relationship, I mean. I didn't kill her, I –' he sighed. 'That came out wrong.'

Bearing in mind that Leighton's initial estimate for time of death had been some time during the previous evening, Rebecca asked which band Neil had been to see.

'Quarkonia. At KoKo. It's a venue in Camden.'

'What time did you get there?'

'Um – about eight.'

'And were you there until the end?'

'Yuh.'

'Can anybody substantiate that?'

'A couple of Mez's friends were there,' he offered. 'Iona and Laura.'

'Do you have contact details for either of them?'

'No. But Iona's at UCL. She's studying geography. I guess you could probably trace her through them. She'll have Laura's address.'

Rebecca nodded. 'Did Meredith know Suki Jenson?'

'I don't think so.'

'How about Justin Black or Floyd Newton? Did she know either of them?'

'Not personally. She saw them play plenty of times.'

'And what did you do after Wednesday's gig?'

'I tried calling Mez, but she didn't answer, so I went home.'

Rebecca asked where he lived and how he had travelled there. She wondered whether Neil really had intended to end his relationship with Meredith, or whether he was simply attempting to distance himself from the investigation, and whether he was as unmoved as he appeared by her death. Whatever the reality, she intended to have someone check his route home on Wednesday night very carefully.

Alec's lungs felt raw as he sprinted around the corner into Mornington Terrace. He couldn't remember the last time he'd had to run for more than a bus, and he suspected this might not be the only time he'd be required to do as much tonight. Sally's call had come just as he was about to leave for the Garage, and he had less than twenty minutes before he would be running late for work. He and Storm – real name Ricky – who ran the club on a Thursday hadn't been on good terms since Alec had spent the night with Storm's sister six weeks earlier. Given that the girl was twenty-eight, Alec was of the opinion Storm was taking the protective elder brother role rather too seriously. Of course, Storm couldn't fire him for sleeping with his sister. He could fire him for failing to turn up to work without a decent excuse. And, having at least temporarily lost Polaroid's revenue, Alec couldn't afford to lose another job.

Sally hadn't been able to tell him much. But then, by all accounts, Justin hadn't told her much either. 'He just kept crying and saying *Floyd's dead, I don't know what to do,*' she'd imparted, breathlessly. 'If I lived closer I'd go round myself.' Alec felt glad she didn't. Granted, it was often impossible to know whether there was anything genuinely wrong when Justin was upset, but after everything else that had happened that week Alec wouldn't have taken any chances.

On arrival at the house, it took him several minutes to persuade Justin to open the building's main door to let him in. Once inside, he raced up the stairs. Justin was hovering in the doorway to the flat, tears on his pale cheeks. He was shaking.

'I didn't – I don't – I –'

'Where is he?'

Justin tried to answer, but couldn't manage a coherent sentence, and Alec hurried down the hallway, checking each room in turn. He found Floyd slumped against the wall just inside the kitchen doorway, his face half obscured by blood running from a deep gash along his hairline. Alec felt sick. Suki's death had been horrific, but when it came down to it she had been merely an acquaintance. Floyd was much more than that. Drawing a deep breath, he crouched down and reached for his friend's wrist. Finding a pulse left him feeling almost faint with relief, and he fumbled in his pocket for his mobile.

'No!' Justin cried, frantically, making a grab for the phone. 'You can't! I didn't! I *didn't*!'

'I'm not calling the police, Just,' Alec explained, guessing what his friend was thinking. 'I'm calling an ambulance. He's still alive.'

Justin blinked. 'What?'

'We need to get him to hospital.'

Justin half collapsed into a chair at the table, his respirations audible. He watched in silence as Alec made the brief telephone call and then moved Floyd into the recovery position, and, having made sure Floyd was still breathing, Alec turned to him. The red reflected through his irides made his eyes look impossibly bloodshot.

'What happened?'

'I don't know!' Justin insisted. 'I came to get a drink and –' he gulped. 'He was on the floor – I didn't know – I –' he shook his head.

'Do you have any idea how long he'd been there?'

Justin continued to shake his head. 'Before – earlier – he seemed really out of it – but when I asked if he was ok he told me to fuck off – I didn't – I –'

'Ok, come on, calm down,' Alec said, firmly.

Justin sniffed. 'He wanted me to leave him alone,' he revealed, rather hopelessly. 'So I did.' He blinked, sending tears scurrying down his cheeks.

Alec nodded, turning to check Floyd's breathing and pulse again.

'Why is this happening to me?' Justin whispered, desperately. 'Why is everyone I love getting taken away?'

'Floyd will be all right,' Alec reassured him, wondering whether, if he were, he would be able to shed any light on what had happened.

'He hasn't been all right for weeks!'

'Well I'm sure they'll be able to get to the bottom of that when we get to the hospital.'

'We?' Justin exclaimed, sounding panicked.

Alec bit back an expletive. He couldn't take Justin with him, because he was terrified of hospitals and was in no state to listen to reason. But he couldn't leave him alone. Mentally, he ran through a list of people who knew Justin well enough to cope with him in this state. Six months ago he might have called Vinnie, but even asking would be a waste of time now. And he wasn't about to leave Sally alone with Justin – she wouldn't be strong enough to fight back if things did get physical. He reached for his mobile and scrolled through his contacts. Selecting *call*, he willed Quary to answer. If he didn't, Alec wasn't sure what else he could do.

## Fourteen

Lawrence left Lavender Hill police station and walked the short distance to his car, one emotion running into another. He disabled the car's central locking system and climbed in, then sat in silence, the key still gripped in his hand. The past ninety minutes had been among the most difficult of his life; he was accustomed to dealing with anxious relatives, not *being* one, and the fact he hadn't been able to take charge of the situation had been almost unbearable. And now it was over, and he was in a position to take control, he had no idea how to proceed.

'Sorry,' Jimmy muttered, at length.

Lawrence turned. 'What for?'

Jimmy looked up with a frown. 'Eh?'

'As far as I can make out, you have several things to apologise for. I just wondered where you'd like to start.'

Jimmy didn't answer.

'Do you have any *idea* what you've put your mother through this evening? She's been beside herself!'

'I'm sorry.'

'What on earth possessed you to withhold your name?'

Jimmy shrugged.

'Perhaps you'd prefer to explain why I'm facing a bill to cover the removal of graffiti from private property?'

Jimmy made no reply.

'Well?'

'I'm sorry.'

'I asked for an explanation, not another apology.'

Jimmy simply shrugged again.

'What does that mean?'

There was a pause before Jimmy mumbled, 'I dunno.'

'Jim, you scrawled *God is gay* on the walls of a church! Some level of thought must have gone into it!'

'It's bollocks,' Jimmy responded.

'What is?'

'Religion.'

'And you think that gives you the right to commit criminal damage?' Lawrence exclaimed.

Another shrug. 'Wasn't my idea.'

'So then whose was it?'

'Seb's.'

'Who's Seb?'

'A mate.'

'From where? School?'

Jimmy shook his head.

'Well where did you meet him?' Lawrence persisted.

'Just around.'

'Around *where*?'

Several seconds passed before Jimmy answered. 'Online.'

'If it was his idea, how is it that you were the one who ended up at the police station?'

'He dared me.'

'Oh, well, that's all right then,' Lawrence responded, sarcastically. 'For a moment I thought you might have broken the law, worried your mother sick and completely embarrassed me for nothing!'

'I'm *sorry*.'

'Sorry you got caught I don't doubt.' Lawrence slid the car key into the ignition. 'Whether you're sorry for your actions is another matter.' He started the engine. 'And seeing as you clearly can't be trusted to get yourself to and from school without smoking, defacing churches or goodness knows what else, I'll have to drive you myself from now on.'

'You don't have to do that, I promise I won't –'

'It's not up for discussion,' Lawrence returned, shortly.

'But you *can't*! You'll make me look like a total loser!'

'Given that I can't remember the last time I felt as mortified as I did in that police station, that seems a fair exchange.' Lawrence glanced over his shoulder before pulling out into the road. 'Besides which, I think you've already made yourself look like a loser. In case you're under any illusion, deliberately defacing other people's property isn't clever or admirable. It's malicious and it's hurtful. How would you like it if someone scribbled all over your posters?'

Jimmy didn't reply.

'Needless to say you won't be seeing your PlayStation or your allowance for some time.'

'Why, you going to take them with you to work?'

'What?'

Jimmy turned his head towards the window, saying nothing.

Lawrence indicated left, then pulled the car to the side of the road. 'We're not moving until you explain that last comment.'

'Well I never see you either. Except when Mum needs you to bollock me.'

Lawrence sighed. 'Is that what all this is about?'

Jimmy wrinkled his nose scornfully. 'As if!'

Lawrence didn't know what to say. He felt guilty and angry all at once. Yes, he worked long hours and often weekends, but Katie's – and now Jimmy's – complaint he was *never* around was something of an exaggeration. He wondered whether Jimmy really felt neglected, or whether he had adopted his mother's frequently aired grievance to deflect attention from his own misdemeanours. In recent months he had shown little enthusiasm for spending time with Katie and Lawrence, preferring to fill his hours at home playing computer games or surfing the net. And, until Easter had brought the season to a close, a good many of his evenings and Saturdays had been spent playing football for his school team.

'Look, Jim, I'm sorry if –'

'Oh like I care!' Jimmy interrupted.

'I don't think you really mean that.'

'Whatever.'

'Fine,' Lawrence snapped, flicking the indicator back on. 'Have it your way. But don't for one second think this is the end of the matter.' He steered the car back out into the road. 'You just let me know when you're ready to drop the attitude. The longer that takes, the longer I will be driving you to school.'

As Rebecca slipped her jacket on in the hallway on Friday morning, she noticed the light on the answer machine blinking. Wondering whether she had missed it the night before, or whether it had rung a short time ago whilst she was in the shower, she hit play. The machine's electronic voice informed her that the message had been left at twelve thirty-nine a.m. A brief crackle followed before Alec's voice spoke. 'Becca?' He paused. 'Becca, if you're there can you pick up?'

There was an urgency in his tone, and in the moments that followed, Rebecca felt cold, convinced something must have happened to Elliot. She held her breath, waiting for the machine to continue.

'Ok, look, I'm at the hospital –'

Rebecca's heart jumped.

'Sally called earlier – Justin had called her. Floyd's unconscious – I don't know what happened, but he's got a massive cut on his forehead, and –' he trailed off. 'I dunno – I just thought I should let someone know, so –' he hesitated. 'That's it, really. Maybe I'll speak to you in a bit.'

Feeling relieved, and at the same time apprehensive about speaking to Elliot's closest friend only twenty-four hours after she had ended their relationship, Rebecca quickly dialled Alec's number. He answered after just one ring.

'Hello?'

'Alec?'

'Becca. Hi.'

He sounded almost pleased to hear from her, and Rebecca felt surprised. She had expected at least veiled hostility.

'I'm sorry, I only just got your message. I was at a crime scene half the night.'

'Oh, right.'

'How's Floyd?'

'Not good.'

'Has he managed to tell you anything about what happened?'

'Yeah. He passed out and hit his head on the kitchen table.'

'Do you think that's true?' Rebecca asked, sceptically. 'You don't think he's just trying to protect Justin?'

'No.'

'What makes you so sure?'

'They had to do a CT scan to check there wasn't too much damage, and –' Alec took a deep breath. 'He has a brain tumour.'

'God.'

'Yeah.'

'Do they have any idea of the prognosis?'

'I'm not sure. They're going to operate today, and they should know more after that. If it's malignant then –' Alec's voice sounded strained, and he paused before saying, 'Well then he's basically screwed.'

'How's Justin?'

'I think he's ok. Upset, obviously, but I left him with Quary and he seemed to have a handle on things when we spoke earlier.'

'Ok. Thanks. For letting me know.'

'No problem. And I know he won't be up yet, but could you ask Elliot to give me a call when he is?'

The pieces fell into place. *Alec didn't know*. Rebecca hesitated before revealing, 'He's not here.'

'Isn't he?' Alec exclaimed. 'Well then where is he? I haven't heard from him since Wednesday.'

'I don't know where he is, Alec. We split up.'

'What? When?'

'Yesterday morning.'

'And it didn't occur to you to let me know?' He demanded.

It wasn't at all the reaction she had expected. 'Why would it? Our relationship is none of your business!'

'I think you'll find Elliot generally *makes* it my business!'

'Well, if that was what he wanted he could have told you himself, couldn't he?'

'You're like the local fucking authorities!' Alec returned, furiously. 'The more vulnerable and lost people are the less they want to help! What the fuck is wrong with you?'

'Alec, I can't cope with Elliot any more! Maybe you can, but –'

'I'm not asking you to fucking cope with him! All you had to fucking do was call me before you chucked him out! So I could be there to prevent him from slitting his fucking wrists!'

'Alec –'

'You'd better pray nothing's happened to him, because if it has it'll be your fucking fault!' Alec finished, ringing off before Rebecca could respond. She closed her eyes, inhaling deeply and feeling shaken. She would have expected Alec to have been Elliot's first port of call, and that he hadn't been worried her more than she wanted to admit, even to herself. Because if he wasn't with Alec, he was probably alone.

Daniel entered Lawrence's office on Friday morning to find him picking through a stack of crime scene photographs with Leighton. The pathologist looked as if he'd been up half the night, which, Daniel quickly learned, he had been. At Lawrence's request, he filled Daniel in on the events of the previous evening and the information he had collected so far from the scene, as well as his initial estimate for time of death, which he put at some time on Wednesday evening.

Daniel turned to Lawrence. 'What time did you let Justin go in the end?'

'I dropped him and Floyd back home in Camden at about nine. Maybe a bit before.'

'Great. Interviewing those two again will make for a fun start to the day.'

'We won't be talking to Floyd,' Lawrence replied. 'Becky called just now to say he's in hospital about to have surgery to remove a brain tumour.'

'God. Poor kid.'

'Yes,' Lawrence concurred. 'Certainly explains a few things.'

'Could it have any bearing on the investigation?'

'In what sense?'

'Well, brain tumours can affect your personality, can't they? Wasn't there a case where a normal guy became a paedophile as a result of one?'

Lawrence's eyebrows climbed and he looked to Leighton. 'Is it possible a brain tumour could turn someone into a killer?'

'Possible, I suppose, but very unlikely. And given you've no more than circumstantial evidence against him I wouldn't stake much on the idea.'

'Understood. But when you have a moment could you look into it, please?'

Leighton sighed. 'I think it'd be a waste of time.'

'Well, I didn't ask if it would be a waste of time, I asked if you could look into it,' Lawrence returned, sharply. 'So I'd be obliged if you could at least expend the minimal effort you usually devote to anything non-urgent on it. All right?'

'All right,' Leighton echoed, sounding taken aback.

'And whilst we're on the subject of wasting time, I am *still* waiting for those photographs! I am sick and tired of running around after you!'

'Ah,' Leighton replied, uneasily. 'Yes. I meant to tell you. I accidentally killed the memory card.'

'You did *what*?'

'I put it down on the mass spectrometer, and the electromagnets corrupted it. I'm really sorry. If it's any consolation, there wasn't anything to see.'

'It's not,' Lawrence snapped. 'Is there no way of recovering the data?'

'I've tried. It's well and truly buggered. All I can do is apologise.'

'Which is hardly good enough!'

'I'm aware of that.'

Lawrence regarded the pathologist in silence for a second before shaking his head in exasperation. He looked furious. In an effort to dispel the increasingly tense atmosphere, Daniel asked, 'Where do you want me to start?'

It took Lawrence a moment to collect his thoughts and provide an answer.

'Becky's offered to speak to Meredith's parents, and I'm going to try to get some sense out of Justin. I'd like you to run background checks on everybody we spoke to yesterday, and the people in these pictures.' He handed Daniel a list of names and a wad of photographs in individual evidence bags. 'Meredith had them Blu-tacked to her wall. That's her.' He indicated a flat-chested brunette wearing unnecessarily bright red lipstick posing with three other girls. 'Becky's managed to provide names for about half of them – once we've tracked down a few of Meredith's friends we'll see whether they can help with the rest.'

'And what about whoever found the body? Do we need to speak to them?'

'Not at this stage. Becky spoke to him at the scene last night.'

'What was she doing there?'

'We were on our way out for a drink when they called me, and I don't think she really fancied going home,' Leighton explained.

'What, Elliot misbehaving again?' Daniel guessed, aloud.

Leighton's brow furrowed slightly. 'They split up.'

'What?' Daniel exclaimed. 'When?'

'Yesterday morning.'

Daniel nodded slightly, trying to maintain an expression of shock. Privately, he felt elated. Finally Rebecca had seen sense. He was glad she hadn't been the one to tell him; this way he had time to think about what to say to her, time to minimise the chance of winding up with his foot in his mouth. Right now, he didn't have a clue how to respond to the news. Thankfully, Lawrence's mobile interrupted the brief silence, and he checked the display before standing to leave the room.

Leighton leaned back in his chair, glancing at Daniel as Lawrence closed the office door behind himself. 'Don't even think about it.'

Daniel turned in surprise. 'What?'

'You know what. I've seen the way you look at her. Give her some time, yeah?'

'What, time for you to get in there first?'

'No, you twat, time to get over losing the love of her life.'

'What – you mean –' Daniel stopped. 'I assumed she finished it.'

'She did, and that's not what I meant.' Leighton reached for his leather jacket, which was flung over the back of a nearby chair. 'Never mind. You do what you want.' He stood and turned for the door. 'I've a postmortem to do, so I'll be in the mortuary if anyone wants me. Good luck.'

Daniel frowned. 'What with?'

Leighton nodded towards the pictures spread across Lawrence's desk. 'Getting your man.' He met Daniel's eyes momentarily before raising one eyebrow and finishing, pointedly, 'Or woman.'

Having raised no answer at Justin and Floyd's flat, Lawrence had contacted Rebecca, reasoning that she had more chance than anyone of locating Justin. She called back within a matter of minutes to inform him that, with his flight to the US only hours away, Quary had taken Justin home to his mother. On learning that she lived just a few miles away in Harlesden, Lawrence wondered why on earth it hadn't occurred to anybody else to do so before now. And why she hadn't previously bothered to check up on Justin herself.

The address Rebecca provided turned out to be on a council estate crowded with characterless post-war brick blocks so similar that it felt almost like a maze. Wondering whether his car lights and windows would be intact when he returned, and at the same time whether such thinking was unduly prejudiced, Lawrence approached the building Justin's mother apparently called home. A security door – doubtless intended to deter drug addicts – safeguarded the stairwell leading to the upper tier of maisonettes, but on arrival Lawrence found the lock had been forced and broken, and the only thing now holding the door shut was a powerful spring. Moments later, he arrived at the frosted glass front door of number twenty-two, and, given the absence of a knocker or doorbell, rapped sharply on the glass.

The woman who opened the door looked none too pleased at the interruption. She stood almost six foot tall, and that was without heels, Lawrence observed, noticing the grubby pink velvet slippers on her feet. She was thin – almost scrawny – and her greying brown hair was pulled taught into a pony tail, making her angular features look severe. Her lips were surrounded by the deep grooves of a long-term smoker, and when she spoke her sandpaper voice confirmed she had yet to kick the habit. 'Yes?'

'Mrs Black?'

'Miss,' she corrected. 'And no, you can't see him.'

'I'm DCI –'

'I know *who* you are,' came the blunt retort. 'If you were another journalist I wouldn't still be standing here.'

Lawrence sighed. 'Miss Black, I'm not here to negotiate. I need to ask Justin a few questions. It won't take long.'

'The kid's in no state to answer questions!'

'Well, if you like I can call a doctor to establish whether that's really the case,' Lawrence offered. 'But in the meantime, I'm afraid I'm going nowhere.'

Lucy Black glared at him for several seconds before stepping back from the front door to allow him in. 'I'm not leaving him with you,' she snapped, as Lawrence entered. 'He's in a bad enough way as it is.'

The living room was directly opposite the front door, the air heavy with cigarette smoke, and Justin was huddled on the sofa with what looked like a giant piece of kitchen foil wrapped over his head and around his torso. Close up, Lawrence recognised it as an emergency blanket, as sold by camping and outward-bound stores. He could only assume Justin's reason for clutching it tightly around himself related to his conviction that silver foil could prevent people from stealing his thoughts. The young man's head was bowed, and he was chewing viciously at the skin that bordered the fingernails of his right hand. His fingertips looked raw. Lucy sat beside him, taking his arm and gently pulling his hand away from his mouth.

'Don't do that, love.'

Lawrence perched opposite them. 'Hello Justin.'

Justin raised his head sharply. He wasn't wearing his glasses, and with his eyes exposed the look of panic on his face was acute. 'You can't lock me up! You can't! I didn't hurt Floyd! I didn't! I just –'

'Hush,' Lucy soothed, rubbing his back as he began to hyperventilate. 'I'm not going to let anyone lock you up, love.'

'I know you didn't hurt Floyd, Justin, that's not why I'm here,' Lawrence explained, thinking the young man clearly needed stronger medication than whatever he was on at the moment. Assuming he was on anything at all. 'I realise how worried you must be about him, and I'm sorry to have to add to that. But it would be a great help if you could try to answer a few questions for me.'

Justin tugged at his lower lip with his teeth for a moment before nodding, whether by way of acknowledgement or in agreement, Lawrence wasn't sure.

'Could you tell me what happened after I dropped you and Floyd home on Wednesday evening?'

'Floyd cooked.'

'And what happened after you'd eaten?' Lawrence asked, when Justin said nothing further.

'I didn't,' Justin responded, flatly.

'You didn't what?'

Justin blinked. 'Eat.'

'Ok, well what did you do after Floyd had eaten?'

'Had a beer.'

'Anything else?'

Justin appeared to think this over for some time. 'Talked,' he whispered, eventually.

'And after that?'

'Nothing.'

Lawrence frowned. 'What do you mean, nothing?'

The question – or perhaps Lawrence's expression – clearly unsettled Justin, and agitation set in again. 'I didn't do anything!' He exclaimed. 'I was asleep! You can't lock me up! You *can't*!'

'When you said you were doing nothing, did you mean you were sleeping?'

Justin nodded vigorously. 'I didn't do anything! I didn't, I –'

'I'm not saying you did anything,' Lawrence interrupted, firmly.

'You're *thinking* I did!' Justin returned, his fingers tightening on the blanket as his breathing quickened.

'Justin,' Lucy intervened, her tone sharp. To Lawrence's surprise, this seemed to be enough to quiet him, and his respirations slowed. In the interests of giving him a few moments' respite, Lawrence drew his mobile from his pocket and pretended to focus on it. After scrolling through several emails at random, he tucked the device back into his pocket and continued.

'Do you know a girl called Meredith Armstrong?'

Justin appeared puzzled by the question. 'What?'

'Meredith Armstrong. Does the name mean anything to you?'

He shook his head slightly, clearly more confused than alarmed by the question.

'Does she look familiar?' Lawrence asked, displaying Meredith's photograph.

Justin continued to shake his head. Then panic kicked back in. 'Why? What's she said?'

'She hasn't said anything, Justin. She's dead.'

'Oh,' Justin responded, rather blankly, seeming oddly unmoved by this piece of information.

Lucy had more to say. 'Do you have any evidence he might have been involved? Or is he just an easy target?'

'I'm not accusing Justin of anything, Miss Black. The circumstances of Meredith's death indicate that it may be connected to what happened to Suki, and as a result we need to speak to everybody who might be able to help us establish a link between the two women. Justin is far from the only person we'll be talking to.'

'Oh, right, you just thought you'd start with him, I suppose,' Lucy snapped, coldly. 'Well now you've finished! Not only has he lost his fiancée this week, his oldest friend is now in intensive care! I think that's enough for him to have to cope with, don't you?'

'Fiancée?' Lawrence echoed. 'Were he and Suki engaged?'

'Yes.'

'This is the first I've heard of it. When did they get engaged?'

'A few weeks ago. He took her to Paris.'

'Did she have a ring?'

'Yes. Just had one made specially.'

Lawrence looked to Justin for confirmation. He didn't appear to be listening, focusing instead on twisting one corner of the foil blanket around and around his forefinger. Lawrence wondered whether Leighton had omitted the ring from the list of Suki's personal effects in his postmortem report, or whether it had been missing before his arrival at the crime scene. And, if it had been, where it might be now.

'Blimey, you still awake?'

Leighton glanced up from his monitor just in time to see Jon drop into the chair at the next desk.

'Barely,' he returned, with a half-hearted smile.

'What you doing?'

'Staring blankly at the screen, since you ask.'

'Serious stuff, then,' Jon came back. 'If it's not too engrossing, I'll be in the market for a pint and a game of pool in five minutes.'

'Sold.'

'Outstanding,' Jon responded, enthusiastically, before launching a search through one of his filing trays. As he neared the bottom, he added, 'I don't suppose you've seen a padded envelope stuffed with slides lying around, have you?'

'No. Sorry.'

Jon tutted to himself and Leighton returned his attention to the research paper on the screen. It wasn't telling him anything he didn't know, and he hit backspace to return to the list of search results. As the browser refreshed the web page, a small box popped up in the bottom right-hand corner of the screen to inform him he had a new email from his boss. It was titled 'Memory card??' He sighed, clicking through to see what Max had to say about the incident and cursing himself for getting involved in the first place.

He had guessed the reason for Alec's reluctance to remove his clothes in front of the camera more or less immediately: evidence pertaining to a crime was hardly the only thing a person might want to hide. Having exchanged a few pertinent pieces of information and promised to conduct a physical examination and take pictures only if there were marks or injuries of possible relevance to the investigation, he had succeeded in parting Alec from his t-shirt. Fine white lines ran at angles across his back, overlapping in places, from his shoulders to below the line of his belt. When Alec removed his leather trousers, Leighton had been able to make out more marks across the tops of his thighs, and guessed there were others concealed by his underwear. The roadmap of scars spoke of a sustained campaign of abuse. Leighton wondered who had been responsible for that.

If he stretched in certain directions, he could still feel the pull of scar tissue in his own back from the worst of the violence he had endured at the hands of his father. Hours after his elder brother had been handed a two-year prison sentence for causing serious injury by dangerous driving, Glenn Campbell had taken his fury out on his younger son, slamming Leighton against a wall and holding the iron he'd been using on his school uniform to his back. Twenty years on, Leighton couldn't remember whether he'd cried or whether he'd been too stunned; his mother's tears he recalled all too well. She hadn't dared take him to A and E, and had given him a handful of painkillers before sitting him in the bath and spending the best part of an hour dribbling water down his back and trying to separate his t-shirt from his skin. By the end of that time he had been shaking with cold as well as shock, and Lorna had telephoned her sister in a panic.

His aunt Suzy had duly arrived, and the first thing Leighton remembered hearing her say was that she was calling social services. Lorna had begged her not to; she'd just lost one son, she couldn't lose the other. Suzy had capitulated only when Lorna agreed that she and Leighton would move out. That had lasted all of nine days. After that, they had moved back home and Leighton had returned to school with a note excusing him from physical education on account of his asthma. Given that at the time, living with two parents both smoking up to forty a day, he could scarcely run fifty yards without wheezing, nobody had even questioned it. He sometimes wondered what might have happened if they had.

'You're going to love this,' Daniel remarked, looking up from his computer monitor as Lawrence approached his desk.

Lawrence regarded him expectantly.

'Guess who has a history of assault, ABH and wounding?'

'Who?'

'One Valentine Wright.'

'Do you have any other details?'

'Yep. He's been pulled in several times for what appear to have been straightforward fights – none of which resulted in charges actually being brought – but he is currently facing charges for what initially seemed to have been an unprovoked attack.'

'But turned out to be?'

'Not entirely unprovoked,' Daniel expanded. 'The guy's a journalist, and Valentine's in the process of suing him and the newspaper he was working for at the time.'

'For what?'

'Breach of privacy.'

'What did they publish?'

'Details of his financials. Or, rather, a guestimate thereof.'

Lawrence sat in the unoccupied chair at Rebecca's desk. 'And why was that worthy of publication?'

'You heard of Gordon Wright?'

The name was familiar, but Lawrence had to think for some seconds before he could place it. 'Yes. He was pianist. Or was it a composer?'

'Both. And Valentine's father.'

'Ah,' Lawrence nodded. 'I see. A story for a slow afternoon in the newsroom: let's see how he's spending Daddy's money.'

'Or not spending it, as appears to be the case,' Daniel passed him a computer printout of the article in question. 'From what I can gather from the fairly limited press coverage of the assault – and that's assault in tabloid rather than legal terms – none of his friends knew anything about his inheritance or his family, and he didn't much appreciate it being broadcast.'

Lawrence scanned the first couple of paragraphs. 'I can understand why,' he remarked. 'But that doesn't excuse his actions. Ok, we don't know where he was on Monday night or half of Wednesday evening, and he clearly has a violent streak – I want to talk to him again. Do we have any idea where he is at the moment?'

Daniel reached for the copy of *Rock UK* on Rebecca's desk and flicked through the back pages until he found the relevant list of tour dates. 'Oxford.'

Lawrence glanced at his watch. 'I'm not wasting my whole afternoon messing about getting there and back to find he's disappeared again. Find someone who fancies a sprint up the motorway, give Valentine five minutes to cooperate, and if he doesn't, arrest him and bring him back here. All right?'

Daniel nodded.

'I will not be made to dance around some spoiled rich kid who thinks he's above the law.'

## Fifteen

Rebecca arrived back from the Suffolk home of Meredith's parents to find a Post-it note from Leighton stuck to the lid of her laptop. Spotting a similar one on Lawrence's desk, she wondered where he was. The notes were succinct – *PM done, call me, L* – and, at the bottom of Rebecca's, the additional words *hope you're ok x*. A quick call was sufficient to establish that Leighton was in a pub just around the corner. He offered to return to the office, but Rebecca had yet to have lunch, so instead opted to join him. Having put in an order for a chicken salad sandwich and curly fries, she joined Leighton and Jon in a corner behind the pool table.

'It's quiet in here for a Friday,' she observed, conversationally, as she sat down.

'That's why we're here,' Jon replied. 'Someone's got to keep the place in business.'

'How very philanthropic.'

'You have no idea,' Leighton smiled lazily, lying back in his armchair. 'Not only are we keeping the bar staff in wages, I even let Dr Adeyemi here win at pool. How's that for generosity?'

'In your dreams, Campbell,' Jon returned, amiably, moving to stand. 'I'm going for a whizz. Can I get you another on my way back?' He nodded to Leighton's almost empty pint glass.

'Sadly no, I have the car.'

'Schoolboy error,' Jon remarked, looking to Rebecca. 'Becks?'

'No, fine thanks.'

'Right,' Jon nodded, heading towards the toilets.

Leighton waited until he was out of earshot before asking, 'How are you doing?'

'All right.'

'You look about as tired as I feel.'

'I didn't sleep well.'

'Have you got much more to do today?'

'I don't know, I'm not sure where things are at,' Rebecca admitted. 'Nobody was about when I got back to the office, and yours was the only phone that didn't go straight to voicemail.'

'Well Forrester rang to put a rocket up my arse earlier and said something about a meeting at Jimmy's school, so at a guess that's where he is.'

'How about Danny?'

'No clue, I'm afraid. Although if he's any sense he'll be lying low. Forrester just about took my head off this morning.'

'How come?'

'Your guess is as good as mine. I didn't like to risk asking *why* he was in such a foul mood.'

At that moment, Rebecca's mobile began to ring. 'Maybe someone's feeling his ears burning,' she remarked, as she fished it out of her bag. Then, finding Elliot's name on the screen, she sighed. 'Or not.'

Elliot had already called twice that day and, after her earlier conversation with Alec, the first time Rebecca had felt relieved to hear from him. But as he had been drunk on both occasions, relief had quickly given way to impatience. She wanted to ignore him, but knowing that doing so might result in his calling the office, she answered.

'Yes?'

'Becca, I need to talk to you,' he slurred, sounding even more intoxicated than he had done previously.

'We're not talking about anything while you're in this state, Elliot.'

'It's important.'

'Give me a call when you're sober, and we can talk then.'

'No no no, you don't understand, I –'

'Elliot, listen to me. Go and sleep it off, and call me when you wake up. Ok?'

'But –'

'*No*,' Rebecca pre-empted, firmly. 'I'm at work. I need to go now, so I'm going to hang up. I will speak to you later.' She terminated the call, shaking her head. 'Sorry,' she said, looking back to Leighton. 'You wanted to talk about the PM.'

'Are you all right?'

'Yes. Just irritated. Go ahead.'

'Ok. You remember I –'

Rebecca's mobile interrupted again. She glanced at the display. 'Oh for pity's sake,' she muttered, cancelling the call before reducing the volume to zero. 'Right. Sorry. Do I remember what?'

'I initially put time of death at some point on Wednesday evening. I still think she died in that window, but I think it's possible she was attacked earlier.'

'How much earlier?'

'It could just have been an hour or two, but I think it was probably longer – enough time for fairly extensive bruising to develop. She died of a brain haemorrhage, but that must've happened sometime after the attack. It's unlikely she was conscious in the interim, but she wasn't dead either.'

'So what sort of time frame do we need to look at?' Rebecca asked, as her lunch arrived.

'Probably mid-afternoon onwards. I'm sorry I can't be more specific.'

'Well that puts rather a different slant on things,' Rebecca observed.

'How so?'

'Justin was in custody until after eight.'

Leighton nodded. 'I can't be specific enough about time of death to rule him out, but from what I've seen and heard, he doesn't strike me as a likely contender for premeditated murder. Two deaths a couple of days apart all seems a bit too organised.'

'Anything that might help us work out who we should be focusing on?'

'Not yet. I've left a bunch of samples with one of the technicians, I was starting to see double. But I won't get much back on those 'til next week. I don't think –'

He was interrupted by a voice calling his name, and Rebecca glanced around as he did to see Jon standing at the bar, looking expectantly in their direction.

Leighton righted himself from his near horizontal position and mouthed 'what?' at his friend, but Jon beckoned him over.

'Sorry, hold on a minute,' Leighton sighed, taking hold of the chair's arms and pushing himself to standing. Rebecca nodded, reaching for a triangle of sandwich as he headed for the bar and feeling her mobile vibrate. This time it was a text from the voicemail service. She supposed she might as well get it over with, and dialled the three-digit number, taking a bite of sandwich as she listened to the standard greeting from the phone company, and wondering how long a message Elliot had left. If this was going to go on for long, she would have to change her work number.

When the recording began, it was in much the same way as his previous call: 'Becca, I have to talk to you ... I have to tell you something ... it's important.' Rebecca sighed heavily, taking another bite of her sandwich. There was a pause before Elliot continued, and, when he did, his words stopped her mid-chew. 'It's about Justin.'

Lawrence hadn't been surprised to learn that Valentine had been less than cooperative. Being arrested had apparently come as a shock to Valentine, however, and his first words to Lawrence on his entrance to the interview room were that he planned to sue for wrongful arrest. Taking a seat opposite him, Lawrence asked whether two court cases weren't enough for him, and received a predictably abrupt response.

'Ok.' Lawrence set a photograph of Meredith on the table. 'Do you recognise this girl?'

Valentine gave it his attention for a fraction of a second. 'No.'

'Are you sure?'

'Quite.'

'You see, that's strange, because here you are with her.' He laid a photograph from Meredith's collage beside the first one.

Valentine shrugged. 'So?'

'You have your arm around her, Mr Wright.'

'I play in a band,' Valentine replied, shortly. 'Groupies wanting photos taken with you comes with the territory.'

'How about sleeping with them? Does that come with the territory?'

Valentine's expression was suspicious as he said, 'That one's optional.'

'Have you ever opted for it?'

'No.'

Lawrence's eyebrows rose. 'Never?'

'I don't get turned on by girls throwing themselves at me. It's irritating and it's pathetic.'

'So you've not been involved, in any way at all, with this girl?' Lawrence indicated the photographs.

'No.'

'Where were you on Wednesday afternoon?'

'Norwich.'

'Doing what?'

'Knitting mittens for the homeless, what else?' Valentine snapped. 'You've interrupted me in the middle of a bloody tour! What the hell d'you *think* I was doing?'

'I don't know, but according to your manager you disappeared for much of the afternoon and evening, so it certainly wasn't what you were *supposed* to be doing.'

Valentine didn't respond, he just glared back defiantly.

'What were you doing on Wednesday afternoon?'

Several seconds passed before Valentine answered. 'Watching the football.'

'Where?'

'A pub.'

'Which pub?'

'I dunno,' Valentine retorted, carelessly. 'One near the venue.'

'Who was playing?'

'QPR.'

'And?'

'Newcastle.'

'Who won?'

'Newcastle. Two nil.'

'Where did you say you were?' Daniel interrupted, before Lawrence could ask his next question.

'Norwich.'

'What, and the pub had the QPR game on when Norwich City were playing the same night?'

Lawrence could barely conceal a smile, but Valentine wasn't easily beaten and came back, without a moment's hesitation, 'Landlord was a Geordie.'

'He must have had a pretty empty pub,' Daniel observed.

Valentine didn't reply, but his expression said *like I care.*

'How about Monday night, after eleven?' Lawrence continued. 'Because I'm well aware you weren't on the tour bus.'

'I went out in Kingston after the gig.'

'Where did you go?'

'A club.'

'What sort of club?'

'A rock club.'

'And what time were you there until?'

Valentine shrugged. 'I dunno. About two.'

'Then what did you do?'

'Went home with a girl.'

'What was her name?'

'Jenny.'

'And where did she live?'

'I've no idea, it's not exactly familiar turf for me down there.'

'But you managed to find your way back to London in time to get back on the tour bus the next morning.'

'Yeah, there are these things called taxis, generally the driver knows the way.'

Lawrence regarded Valentine in silence for some moments before saying, 'Ok, story time's over. Where were you?'

'I've told you. Kingston.'

'No you weren't. Don't waste my time.'

'If you know more about my life than I do, you really don't need me here to answer your questions, do you?' Valentine returned, insolently. 'You can just answer them yourself.'

'This isn't a game, Mr Wright, and I'd advise you not to treat it as one.'

'I make it a rule not to take advice from the law.'

'*Where were you*?' Lawrence pressed. 'And *don't* make me ask you again.'

'How about you ask me something I haven't already answered?'

'Ok,' Lawrence turned to Daniel. 'Mr Wright obviously wishes to spend the night, so if you could show him to –'

'What?' Valentine exclaimed. 'You can't do that!'

'I think you'll find I can,' Lawrence smiled, rising from the table. 'See you in the morning.'

'No, you can't,' Valentine sat forwards in his chair, sounding suddenly panicked. 'Please, you don't understand, I can't be here – I have *responsibilities* – you *can't* –' he trailed off, visibly distressed. '*Please*.'

Lawrence reclaimed his seat. 'All right. You tell me where you were on Monday night – and Wednesday afternoon – and I might reconsider.'

Valentine sank back into his chair, looking defeated. Some seconds later, he muttered, 'Willesden.'

'Doing what?'

A long pause preceded his answer, and Lawrence wondered whether he was frantically trying to think of one. Eventually, eyes fixed on the table, he said, 'I was trying to find my granddad.'

'In the middle of the night?'

'Yes.'

'Would you like to tell me why?'

'Not really.'

'Wrong answer.'

Valentine didn't respond, and after several seconds Lawrence once again moved as if to stand. Valentine looked up. 'He has Alzheimer's, all right?' He finally admitted. 'He keeps wandering off, and my gran keeps calling me, terrified something's going to happen to him! What the fuck am I *supposed* to do? They *need* me!'

'You could try telling people rather than just disappearing,' Lawrence suggested, wondering why, if he was telling the truth, he hadn't.

'It's nobody else's fucking business!'

'When it's affecting the people you're working with it is.'

'I do *not* need people feeling sorry for me!' Valentine spat, plainly furious. Lawrence guessed this hatred of sympathy was what had fuelled his violent response to the newspaper article's exposure of the tragic facts of his family history. He had no doubt grown up feeling like an object of pity – whether or not he really had been – and was determined not to repeat the experience as an adult.

'So is that where you were yesterday?' Lawrence asked, hoping to catch Valentine out on the basis of time and distance if he wasn't finally telling the truth. 'Willesden?'

'Do I look like superman?' Valentine demanded, sarcastically. 'I can't fucking fly!'

'So where were you?'

Valentine rubbed his forehead with the fingers of his right hand. 'I had to make some calls.'

'To whom?'

'I was trying to organise for someone to look after them while I'm away. Getting home from Kingston or Norwich is one thing, Aberdeen and Truro are another.'

'Maybe you should consider residential care.'

'And maybe it's none of your business!' Valentine retorted. 'But even assuming it *is*, that's not my decision to make!'

Lawrence sighed. 'All right. We're going to need your grandparents' names and address so that we can confirm what you've told us, and if we can do that we'll be able to release you.'

'You're not having their address.'

Lawrence raised his eyebrows. 'I beg your pardon?'

'I'll take you there, but you can't go without me.'

'I think you're confused about who's in charge here.'

'I can't let you go alone! You'll scare the hell out of my gran! As soon as you tell her who you are she's going to think something's happened to either him or me! She's eighty-two!'

When Lawrence didn't immediately reply, Valentine continued. '*Please*,' he implored. 'We're all she *has*!'

Lawrence felt torn. He wanted to refuse the request on the grounds of Valentine's earlier behaviour, but in the circumstances that seemed callous. And, if it did mean frightening an elderly woman, cruel. At length, he nodded. 'All right.'

Valentine relaxed, clearly relieved, and even had the good grace to thank him. Whatever his faults, Lawrence guessed Valentine's concern for his grandparents was genuine. After all, when it came down to it, he wasn't just all they had. They were all *he* had.

It had taken Rebecca over an hour to get any information out of Elliot. When she first tried to return his call there was no response, and when she still hadn't managed to elicit an answer after ten minutes of repeated dialling she began to wonder whether he was playing games with her. Dismissing the idea on the grounds he was unlikely to be cognisant enough to engage in such duplicity, she continued trying. Eventually, her persistence paid off, although the victory was short-lived. When Elliot did finally answer he was confused and incoherent, and didn't seem to have any recollection of leaving the message or of why he had been calling. It wasn't long before his rather muddled train of thought went down the same road as it had in their previous exchanges that day, descending into a rambling mix of apologies, pleading and emotional blackmail.

After demonstrating a level of patience Rebecca hadn't known she possessed and issuing considerable prompting, she managed to focus his mind – as far as he was able to focus on anything – on the subject of Justin. Inebriated though he was, Rebecca knew almost immediately from the slight change in his tone that he had remembered his reason for calling. Getting him to reveal it, however, was another matter, as he spiralled down into the realms of '*I don't know what to do ... whatever I do it's going to be wrong ... doing nothing is a total betrayal ... but so is not doing nothing...'*

Rebecca pressed him carefully, mindful of the fact that the only reason he was even contemplating betraying a friend was because he was blind drunk. She reminded him two people were dead – a detail that added five minutes to the conversation, because he hadn't previously heard about Meredith's death – and leaned on his conscience with *you can't risk letting this happen to anyone else*. Then, as Rebecca began to worry his phone battery might cut out before she could draw an answer from him, he finally capitulated. Rebecca had conceived countless possible scenarios since hearing his voicemail in the pub. All of her guesses had been wrong.

Given Valentine's apparent wealth, Lawrence was surprised to find himself in a sprawling sixties brick maze for the second time that day. This time, the estate was considerably more run-down, and in Valentine's position he might have felt the need to justify himself with something along the lines of *I offered to move them but they didn't want to go*, but the young man said nothing. Immediately he was out of the car, he strode towards a ramp that led up between two buildings, and Daniel hurried to catch up with him. Lawrence followed, knowing from experience how easy it could be to lose somebody who knew their way around the labyrinth of stairwells, corridors and garages that make up many estates.

Two of the ground-level flats the young man led them past were boarded up with metal grates, and from the blackened bricks above the concealed windows of the second Lawrence surmised that it had been gutted by fire. Unlike the estate – probably less than a mile away – he had visited that morning, this one had no doors to secure the stairwells, which, at ground level, seemed to double as refuse storehouses and, if the smell was anything to go by, open-air urinals. Lawrence wondered whether Valentine had grown up in what the graffiti spray-painted on a nearby wall accurately, if illiterately, described as a *dismall fuckin hell holl*.

Turning abruptly right, Valentine led Lawrence and Daniel up two flights of stairs and along a narrow balcony with a metal gate at the far end. A couple of yards ahead of the gate, he stopped outside a front door, digging his right hand into his jeans pocket, presumably for his keys. Daniel stopped him, reaching to knock on the door. Valentine's irritation was plain to see, but he didn't voice his objection, remaining silent and thrusting his left hand into his other pocket. When, after about fifteen seconds, there was no sign of anyone answering, Daniel raised his fist to knock again. Valentine snatched his hand away, snapping, 'Give her a fucking chance!'

Sure enough, after almost as long again, the door shuddered open, and a petite, frail woman whom Lawrence could well believe to be eighty-two appeared, leaning heavily on a walking stick. On catching sight of Valentine, she raised the hand not occupied by the stick to her mouth.
'Oh pet –' she stammered, looking to Lawrence and Daniel and then back to Valentine, panic flooding her face. 'What's happened?'

'Where's Granddad?'

'I was only in the bathroom a minute – I –'

Valentine didn't wait for her to finish. Pushing a surprised Daniel aside, he took off at a sprint back along the balcony, and had all but disappeared by the time Daniel moved to follow him. Lawrence briefly considered joining the chase, but quickly concluded his time would be better spent establishing whether one was even necessary. Returning his attention to the woman in the doorway, he said, 'I've a few questions about your grandson, if you wouldn't mind.'

She regarded him anxiously. 'Who are you?'

Lawrence presented his warrant card and introduced himself before asking her name.

'Rosa. Rosa Berry.'

'Could you tell me when you last saw Valentine?'

'Wednesday evening.'

'What time?'

'Um – about six-thirty.'

'Was he here long?'

'No, he just – he brought Len home. That's my husband. Then he had to go to work.'

'Home from where?'

'I don't really know,' Rosa admitted. 'He's forgetful. Len, that is. He goes out and –' she hesitated. 'He can't always find his way back home.'

'Does that happen often?'

'It has recently.'

'Do you always call Valentine?'

She nodded.

'Even when he's miles away?'

'I know.' Tears came to her eyes. 'I know it's not fair, I know that. I just – I can't –' she broke off, swallowing hard.

'Did you call him on Monday night?'

'Yes. Why?'

'We're investigating two homicides, and nobody has been able to account for where Valentine was when the deaths occurred. And until we arrested him and threatened to detain him overnight, he wasn't forthcoming about his activities either.'

'*Arrested*?' Rosa gasped, clearly horrified. 'Oh dear God – oh – I –' she pressed her hand to her mouth again. Drawing a deep breath, she went on, 'He never talks about personal things. I don't think he really knows how.' She shook her head slightly. 'I'm so sorry, you must have so many more important things to do. You won't charge him with anything, will you?'

'No,' Lawrence reassured her. 'But this situation is clearly putting him under a lot of strain, and perhaps that needs to be addressed.'

Rosa nodded. 'Yes, I know. I'm sorry. I know.'

'Ok, well –' Lawrence began, feeling his mobile vibrate before he heard it ring. 'Excuse me,' he offered, apologetically, stepping away from the door as he slid the phone out of his pocket and checking the display before answering.

'Yes Becky?'

'Hi, where are you?' She asked, sounding breathless.

'Willesden. What's up?' He turned around to lean against the balcony, noticing as he did so that Rosa was now supporting herself with both the door handle and her walking stick. 'Hang on.' He dropped the hand holding the phone, saying, 'I don't think there's anything else. Do you need a hand back inside?'

Rosa shook her head. 'No, thank you.' She began to turn. 'And I am sorry.'

Lawrence gave what he hoped was a reassuring smile and a nod before returning his mobile to his ear. 'Becky?'

'Yes. I just spoke to Elliot, and I don't know how much truth there is in it, but there's a rumour going round that A.J. thinks Justin tipped the police off about him dealing. It may not be relevant, but I thought if you hadn't had any joy with Val then it might be worth paying him another visit.'

'Definitely,' Lawrence agreed. 'But this time I want a search warrant and a SOC team. Can you get onto that now?'

'Sure.'

'I'll be with you in half an hour.'

'So,' Lawrence began, barging uninvited into Aaron's flat the moment the door opened. 'Perhaps you'd like to tell us what you were actually doing on Monday evening when you claim to have been at home watching DVDs?'

Recovering from the initial surprise of Lawrence and Daniel's abrupt entry, Aaron responded with an unimaginative, 'What?'

Lawrence met his eyes as Daniel closed the door behind himself and leaned against it. 'You heard me.'

Aaron folded his arms, saying, irritably, 'Like I told you before, I was here.'

'So after you were released on bail you came straight home, did you?'

'Not straight home, no.'

'Where did you go, then?'

'For a drink with a mate.'

'Who?'

'Guy called Val.'

'Valentine Wright?'

'That's right.'

'What time were you with him until?'

'Um – I don't know –' Aaron paused. 'About seven, maybe?'

'And what did you do after that?'

'I stayed in the pub for a while – a couple of my other mates had come down. We had a few drinks, then I headed home.'

'Which pub?'

'The Hope and Anchor. In Highbury.'

'What time did you leave there?'

'About half ten.'

'Did you come straight home?'

'Yes.'

'So you didn't go via Justin's flat?'

Aaron's brow furrowed. 'No. Why would I?'

'At a guess, to challenge him over the fact you hold him responsible for your arrest.'

'Who the hell told you that?'

'Who did you tell might be a better question,' Lawrence returned. 'It seems to be common knowledge.'

Aaron muttered something under his breath. Lawrence wondered how many people he had shared his suspicion with, and how many had heard it second-hand.

'What happened after you left the pub?' He persisted.

'I came home,' Aaron responded, spitting his words out slowly and deliberately, as if that might make them more convincing.

'Now that's strange,' Lawrence mused, aloud. 'Because that's not what our CCTV footage suggests.'

'What?' Aaron exclaimed, this time in seemingly genuine surprise.

Lawrence sighed heavily. 'Don't make me repeat myself.'

Several seconds passed before Aaron yielded. 'Ok, ok, so I went round there. But that's *all* I did.'

'What, you didn't have it out with him?'

'He wasn't *there*,' Aaron retorted, hotly. 'Or at least, according to his girlfriend he wasn't.'

'So you did see Suki.'

'No! I didn't set foot in the fucking place! She fed me a load of lies over the intercom, then refused to answer when I tried ringing again!'

'What did she lie to you about?'

'He *was* there! I heard her talking to him when she first answered the door!'

'Did you hear his voice?'

Aaron hesitated. 'No. But who else would she have been there with?'

'What time was this?'

'Um – I don't know – elevenish, I suppose.'

'And what did you do after that?'

'I went home.'

'You didn't go looking elsewhere for Justin?'

'Why would I?' Aaron demanded, exasperated. 'I already *knew* where he was!'

'So having worked that out you decided to just drop it and go home?'

'Well I wasn't about to break the door down and spend another night in the nick, was I?'

'If that's true I don't suppose you'll mind if we take a look around.'

Aaron rested his hand on the wall, blocking the route into the flat. 'I do mind, as it goes. You're doing nothing without a warrant.'

'All right, well before we get into that, how about you fill us in on what you were doing from, say, three p.m. on Wednesday?'

Aaron frowned. 'Wednesday?'

'Wednesday,' Lawrence repeated, his tone dangerous.

'Um – not much. I was here all day.'

'Doing what?'

'Watching TV.'

'Until what time?'

'About nine. Then I went to the pub.'

'Who with?'

'Nobody. I just went to my local.'

'Can anybody confirm where you were before that?'

Aaron paused for thought before saying, 'Jake was here some of the time. I'm not sure when exactly.'

'Is she home now?'

'No.'

'Any idea when she might be back?'

'It's Friday night, she may not be back at all.'

'We'll catch up with her later, then. In the meantime we'd like that look around.'

'Not without a warrant,' Aaron enunciated, slowly, clearly riled that Lawrence didn't seem to have absorbed this the first time around.

'Oh, didn't I say?' Lawrence replied casually, reaching into his pocket. 'We already have one.' He offered the folded papers to Aaron.

'But I haven't fucking *done* anything!'

'In that case, you've nothing to worry about, have you?' Lawrence turned to Daniel without waiting for a reply. 'I'll send the SOC team in on my way out. Will you be all right to stick around to oversee this?'

'Sure,' Daniel confirmed, looking, if anything, pleased to be put in charge of the operation.

'Great. Call me if there's any news.'

'Will do,' Daniel opened the front door and stepped back to allow Lawrence to pass. Lawrence trudged up the steps, feeling torn. He would have liked to stay, although he knew the chances of the scientists unearthing anything blatantly incriminating were small. They were unlikely to have much in the way of solid answers for at least a couple of days, and his desire to stay was more the result of his reluctance to go home than any real belief he was going to miss out on much excitement. Passing the van parked outside the adjacent house, he nodded to Anton, who was heading up the team of crime scene officers. Anton gave him a thumbs up and a wave goodnight. Lawrence gave a token wave in response. He might have felt less apprehensive about going home if he'd had any idea how he was going to deal with Jimmy's behaviour – and Katie's expectations – when he got there. Supposedly, being there mattered in itself. He just wished it felt that way.

## Sixteen

'You are fucking kidding me.'

Daniel turned to find Jacqueline standing behind the police tape that spanned the doorway to the flat, arms folded beneath her breasts, which were barely contained by a skin-tight cross between a blouse and a V-necked t-shirt. Daniel fixed his eyes on her face. Jacqueline's self-assurance made him feel more than a little nervous. And aroused.

'Hi,' he offered, awkwardly. 'Sorry about –'

'Yeah yeah,' she cut him off, with a careless wave of her hand. 'What the fuck are you looking for now?'

'I'm afraid I can't answer that.'

'Can I even come in?'

'Not at the moment. Sorry'

'Fanfuckingtastic.' She sighed heavily. 'Ok, if I go to the pub on the corner can you send someone to get me when you're done? It's Friday night, you know, some of us have a life to get to.'

'If you wouldn't mind, I've a few questions before you go.'

'And if I do mind?'

'Um – well –'

She flicked her eyes momentarily heavenwards. 'Never mind. Just get on with it.'

Daniel nodded, fumbling in his pocket for a notebook and pen. 'Could you run me through what you did on Wednesday afternoon and evening, please?'

'Wednesday –' Jacqueline frowned in thought. 'I was at a pit that has the audacity to call itself a club from about two until – I dunno – four or five. Then I came home, got changed, went to a gig, stuck around for a few drinks after, then headed back.'

'How long were you home for before going out again?'

'A couple of hours, I suppose.'

'Did you see Aaron during that time?'

'Yeah, he was moping around getting in my way.'

'How did he seem to you?'

'About as pathetic as usual.'

'So you didn't notice anything unusual?'

Jacqueline shook her head. 'No.'

'And has he said anything about Justin in the last week?'

'Like what?'

'We've been led to understand that he believes Justin tipped the police off about his dealing.'

'Ah,' Jacqueline smiled wryly. 'Yeah. And Justin's supposed to be the paranoid one.'

'So you don't think Justin would have done that?'

'I don't know, but I think it's unlikely.'

'Why?'

'He's hardly a fan of the authorities. I doubt he'd want to get involved.'

'It would only take an anonymous phone call,' Daniel observed.

'Yeah, but he believes people can take his thoughts away using a microwave – or whatever – I doubt he trusts anything to be anonymous.'

'Has Aaron said anything to make you think he might seek some sort of revenge?'

'That's a pretty bold question.'

'And as this is the first time you haven't given a straight answer, I'll take that to be a yes.'

Jacqueline didn't confirm or dispute this assumption, her expression frustratingly impassive.

'What did he say?' Daniel asked.

Once again Jacqueline didn't answer directly, saying, 'He didn't kill Suki, if that's what you're after.'

Daniel persisted. 'What did he say?'

'Only that he was going to have him.'

'What do you think he meant by that?'

'Give him a good kicking, I should think. That's usually how he resolves things. But he wouldn't have taken it out on Suki. That's not his style.'

'He's looking at prison time. Do you not think he might have wanted Justin to suffer the same fate?'

'Nah. He's not that calculating. And he doesn't hold with hitting girls.'

'I'm sure publicly he doesn't.'

Jacqueline lifted one eyebrow in response to this remark, but said nothing.

'Speaking of girls, does the name Meredith Armstrong mean anything to you?' Daniel continued.

Jacqueline considered the matter before shaking her head. 'No. Sorry.'

'How about Mez?'

She shook her head again. Daniel reached into his pocket for the photograph Lawrence had distributed earlier that day. 'Do you recognise her?'

Jacqueline took the picture and scrutinised it. 'Yeah, maybe. She looks vaguely familiar, but that's all I can tell you.' She returned the image. 'So can I go to the pub now?'

'Yes. Thanks for your help.'

'You going to buy me a drink?'

'I – um –' Daniel stammered, wondering whether she was serious.

Jacqueline laughed at his obvious discomfort. 'Relax.'

'Have a good weekend,' Daniel replied, handing her his card. 'And if you think of anything else, let me know.'

Once again, Jacqueline raised a single eyebrow. 'Anything?'

He held her gaze. 'Anything.'

Jacqueline laughed again before saying something in a language he didn't recognise.

'What was that?'

Jacqueline grinned, turning to go. 'Greek.'

'And what does it mean?'

Glancing back over her shoulder as she walked away, she winked. 'Not without a Mercedes.'

'All right, mate?' Anton greeted, chirpily, as Daniel entered Lawrence's office at quarter to nine on Saturday morning.

'Missing my lie in. And you're sounding much too cheerful.'

'Ah, that's because for me it's still Friday night,' Anton responded. 'And in about fifteen minutes I get to start my weekend.'

'Bastard,' Daniel returned, light-heartedly, dropping into a chair near where Anton was lounging in front of Lawrence's desk. 'Where's Forrester?'

'No idea. But his briefcase is here, so he can't be far away.'

'How long you been here?'

Anton glanced at his watch. ''Bout ten minutes.'

Daniel nodded. 'Yeah, me too.'

'Not late, are we?'

'Technically not. Technically on time.'

'Technically?' Anton echoed, clearly intrigued.

'You must've heard this one?'

'No.'

'Oh come on, you work with Leighton for God's sake, how can you not?'

Anton still looked blank.

'Early is on time. On time is late. Late –' Daniel shook his head. 'Don't go there.'

Anton chuckled. 'Yeah, I can see Leighton would be immune to that.'

'Do you think –' Daniel broke off as Lawrence strode through the doorway, a well-stuffed envelope wallet in his hand.

'Morning guys – sorry, you been waiting long?'

Daniel left Anton to answer the question, hoping to have his own attendance assumed by proxy.

'Sorry,' Lawrence repeated in response to Anton's exaggerated, 'Ten – fifteen maybe?' Setting the wallet down in a filing tray, he turned and leaned against the desk. 'MacLennan wanted an update.'

Given that the case was still making the front pages, thanks to the public profile of several of those associated with it, Daniel wasn't surprised the Chief Super wanted to be kept abreast. That he wanted an update on a Saturday morning before the majority of the population had even finished their breakfasts made him wonder what might be in the day's headlines that he ought to know about. He opened his mouth to say something that might invite comment too late; Lawrence had already looked to Anton for his report.

'Any news?'

'Not really. We found traces of blood, but it's almost certainly unrelated.'

'Because?'

'It was spattered up the wall.'

'Suggesting it was shed in situ,' Lawrence concluded.

'Yes.'

'Well that's hardly a surprise.' Daniel remarked.

Lawrence and Anton both regarded him quizzically.

'He's been dealing smack! He's probably had people shooting up in there on a daily basis!'

'He's a total idiot if he has been,' Anton returned. 'No dealer wants an OD to be their responsibility.'

'Well for all we know he's probably using himself.'

'Don't you think I checked whether it was his blood group?' Anton snapped, irritably.

'Ok,' Lawrence held up his hands to halt the exchange. Looking to Anton, he added, 'Is that it?'

'For you. I've a couple of things for the guys in drugs, but so far I've nothing to tie him to either of your girls, and I don't think the DNA tests will be anything more than a formality to confirm that.'

'What are the chances of that happening if he had been involved?'

'Small.'

'But not non-existent?'

'Everyone knows about forensics these days. And anyone can go online and buy bodysuits and masks like the ones we wear. So for a premeditated crime people can find all sorts of ways to make our job difficult. We had a surgeon do something along those lines last year – offed his wife in scrubs, took them back to work and put them in for laundry with all the others.'

'How'd you get him?' Daniel asked.

'Confession,' Anton revealed. 'Just because you can plan a perfect crime doesn't mean you can live with it.' He stood to go. 'Although as far as your guy's concerned, I think he probably could live with it. I'm just not sure he's got the brains to plan it.'

'Morning,' Lawrence greeted in surprise on reaching the doorway of his office to find Rebecca at her desk. 'I wasn't expecting –' he stopped short. Rebecca's face looked pinched, and he guessed she had been crying, the reality of her split with Elliot no doubt beginning to hit home. Presumably she had opted to come into work despite having the weekend off in an effort to keep herself occupied. She was clearly far from it, but at that moment 'Are you all right?' was all he could think of to say.

She shrugged weakly.

'You look shattered.'

'Couldn't sleep,' she responded, her voice unsteady.

'Is there anything I can do?' Lawrence asked, at length, more for want of something further to say than anything.

Rebecca bowed her head, shaking it slightly, and raised a hand to cover her face. She remained silent, but the shaking of her shoulders betrayed the fact she was crying, and Lawrence reluctantly reached for the empty chair at Daniel's desk and sat down. Despite having spent twenty years delivering bad news to bereaved families, in situations like this one he always felt lost for words. Perhaps because he couldn't do anything that might help. Nobody was dead, and there was no justice to be dispensed for a failed relationship. In the end, he reached for the box of tissues on Rebecca's desk and offered them to her. She didn't seem to notice the gesture, and he replaced the box, feeling even more ill at ease than he had done thirty seconds previously.

'Hey, it's ok,' he said, gently, gingerly resting a hand on her shoulder.

'It's not!' Rebecca sobbed.

'No, I know right now it isn't – but – in time –' he trailed off, mentally cursing himself. He would have been better off saying nothing at all.

Rebecca gulped and drew a sharp breath before choking out, 'Elliot – took – an overdose – last night!'

Lawrence closed his eyes momentarily, wondering, even as he absorbed the news, why it had taken him by surprise. Several seconds passed before he could bring himself to ask the necessary question. 'Is he all right?'

'He's alive,' Rebecca hiccupped. 'But he's hardly all right, is he?'

Lawrence nodded mechanically, feeling immensely relieved. 'I'm sorry, Becky. I can't pretend to know how you must be feeling, but –' he hesitated, unsure how best to finish.

Rebecca solved his dilemma, interrupting with, 'It's my *fault*!'

'It's not your fault.'

'It *is*!'

'It *isn't*,' Lawrence countered, firmly. 'Becky, he suffers from severe depression and on top of that he has a serious alcohol problem. You're not to blame for any of that!'

'I *told* him to do it!'

'*What*?'

'When – when I told him it was over –' she swallowed hard. 'He was arguing with me – trying to talk me round – and he said he couldn't live without me.' She inhaled sharply. 'So – I – I told him – to – to kill himself if – if that was – what he wanted!' She returned her face to her hands.

'Everybody says things they don't mean when they're angry. Elliot knows that,' Lawrence reassured her, wondering, privately, whether he did. Lawrence suspected that, by now, Elliot had gone some way beyond rational thought.

'What if – what if he'd –' Rebecca faltered, clearly unable to say the word. What if he'd *died*.

'Don't think about that now.'

'I'm sorry!'

'It's all right.'

Rebecca sniffed and reached for a tissue. As she attempted to dry her eyes, Lawrence asked, 'Is he in hospital?'

'Yuh. At least, I assume so. He was at three o'clock this morning.'

Lawrence's eyebrows rose. 'What, did he get them to call you?'

'No – no, I don't think he was even conscious – as far as the hospital was concerned they were just calling the home number on their database.'

'Maybe that was part of his plan.'

'I did wonder about that, but –' she paused. 'The only reason he didn't –' she broke off again. 'There was a fire alarm. At his hotel. Otherwise –' she shook her head.

'Maybe he's done himself a favour,' Lawrence observed. 'From what I've gathered, I'd guess hospital's the best place for him.'

'Maybe,' Rebecca echoed. 'But he won't stay there of his own accord, and I doubt they'll go as far as sectioning him.'

'Why not? He's clearly desperately in need of help!'

'I know,' Rebecca sighed. 'But underneath it all he's also very bright, and he knows what answers people want to hear. You know as well as I do that a person's mental health can't be assessed with a blood test, and Elliot's depressed, not deranged – when he's sober he's perfectly capable of holding a normal conversation. He'll probably tell the psychiatrist he was drunk, he'd just split up with me and he did it in the heat of the moment. He'll swear he'll never do it again and then he'll probably be discharged.'

'But what on earth does he stand to gain from that?'

'He doesn't *want* to be helped.'

'Evidently. What I don't understand is why not.'

'He doesn't think he deserves to be happy.'

'Did he say as much?'

'Repeatedly.'

Lawrence didn't know how to respond to that. After a long and awkward pause he asked, 'Are you going to visit him?'

Rebecca shrugged. Several seconds passed before she spoke. 'I don't know. I'll see. But I can't do that 'til later, so I figured I might as well help you guys out in the meantime. What needs doing?'

'We could do with finding some more suspects.'

Rebecca managed a weak smile. 'I thought the idea was to narrow things down.'

'We seem to have narrowed things down to the point where we've no one left.'

'No one at all?'

'No one with any obvious motive and opportunity.'

'Well someone still needs to speak to Meredith's friend Iona – I managed to track her room in halls down through the university, but when I went round yesterday afternoon she wasn't in. I could head back over there this morning?'

'Good idea,' Lawrence agreed. 'And we should probably speak to Neil again in light of the fact we don't know where he was on Wednesday afternoon.'

'I can do that as well if you like? Seeing as I spoke to him before.'

'Not alone you won't. Why don't you take Danny with you? I've something else to take care of this morning.'

Rebecca hesitated.

'Problem?'

'No – not with Dan – it's just – I might get more out of Iona on my own.'

'Your call. He won't mind sitting in the car reading a paper while you do that. Then you can head on to visit Neil afterwards. Ok?'

Rebecca nodded.

'I'll give you a call when I'm done and we can work out what's what.'

* * * * *

'Fuck off!' Came an irate Scottish accent in response to Rebecca's second knock at the door of room 147 Walter Sickert Hall shortly after 10 a.m. She knocked again.

'Oh for fuck's sake!' Came the voice from the other side of the door. 'I fucking told you I wasn't coming to the fucking exhibition!' The door flew open abruptly and a sleepy looking girl with a bed-head bob appeared. She was still in the process of pulling her faded green towelling dressing gown shut around herself as the door crashed into the wall to her right, and narrowly avoided flashing her breasts. 'Are you comple–' she stopped short. 'Oh. Hi. Are you lost?'

'Iona Cameron?'

'Yes.'

Rebecca displayed her warrant card. 'I'm Detective Sergeant Palmer. Could I have a few minutes?'

'What's it about?'

'Can I come in?'

'Could you give me a sec?'

Guessing the girl wanted the time to throw some clothes on, Rebecca nodded, turning to lean against the wall of the corridor as Iona closed the door. Less than a minute later she heard the door reopen, and, glancing around, was surprised to find herself face to face with a sheepish-looking young man who looked to be of Hispanic origin. He had long, wavy black hair and a pierced eyebrow, and stood barefoot, his shoes and socks in his hand. 'Hey,' he muttered, meekly, as he scurried past Rebecca and on down the corridor. She smiled to herself. No wonder Iona had been so indignant at the interruption.

Shortly, she reappeared, now clad in grey tracksuit trousers and a black camisole with the bulk of her dark hair drawn into a tiny ponytail. 'Sorry 'bout that.'

'I'm sorry to have disturbed you. May I come in now?'

Iona nodded, turning back into the room and moving to sit on the unmade bed. She held out a hand to offer Rebecca the sturdy pine chair tucked beneath the broad shelf on the opposite side of the room that doubled as a desk, cluttered with text books, mugs and computer printouts, saying, 'What's going on?'

Rebecca turned the chair around and sat down before saying, 'I'm here about a friend of yours. Meredith Armstrong.'

'How come?'

'I'm very sorry, but I'm afraid she's dead.'

'Dead?' Iona echoed, weakly. 'How? When? *How?*'

'I'm afraid she was murdered.'

Iona gulped. 'Murdered? God.' She lifted her eyebrows. 'Christ. I thought – I –' she trailed off, shaking her head.

'What did you think?'

'I was supposed to see her on Wednesday – at a gig – but –' she shrugged. 'She never showed, so I figured she'd pulled some guy. She did that, sometimes – disappeared for a few days – and I've been doing exams, so –' her eyes filled with tears. 'She hasn't exactly been a priority. Christ. I barely even thought about her.'

'Nothing you could have done would have changed what happened,' Rebecca offered, hoping to ease the girl's obvious feelings of guilt.

Iona didn't reply.

'Where were you on Wednesday?'

'KoKo. At a gig.'

'Were you there alone?'

'No, I was with two friends, Collete and Laura.'

'And did you see anyone else you knew?'

Iona hesitated. 'I know quite a few people who go to see the same bands we do. Is there anyone in particular?'

'Do you know Neil Shaw?'

'Yeah.'

'How?'

'He and Merri have been – I don't know – going out, I suppose.'

'You suppose?'

'I don't think she liked him particularly,' Iona admitted. 'I think she just didn't like being alone and – he was – there.'

'And was he at the gig on Wednesday night?'

'Yes.'

'Did you speak to him?'

'Only briefly. I asked if Merri was with him, and then if he knew where she was, but he didn't.'

Rebecca nodded. 'So when did you last see Meredith?'

'Sunday.'

'Whereabouts?'

'Another gig.'

'What band?'

'Cheap Appeal. They were playing in Camden.'

'How did Meredith seem then?'

'We didn't really get a chance to chat. I was running late. I barely made it in time to see the band. And I had to head off straight after, because I had an exam on Monday morning.'

'But did she seem all right?'

'I don't know,' Iona replied, after a moment's thought. 'I mean, she seemed sad, but there was always a kind of sadness about her. Even when we were having a good time. You know?'

'Could you expand on that at all?'

Iona twisted her fingers together. 'Not really. I think maybe she had regrets, but I don't know. You only ever got so much about what was really inside with Merri. We talked about bands and blokes and that sort of thing, but she never really said how she felt about other stuff. Real stuff.'

'Do blokes not qualify as real?'

Iona smiled sadly. 'They weren't real. Not to us. Guys in bands who knew our names but not much more. She could talk about them for hours. But then there's just something about a cute guy on stage with a guitar –' she lifted her eyebrows expressively.

Unconsciously, Rebecca nodded slightly, then remembered where she was. 'So she didn't talk about Neil?'

'Not really. Occasionally she'd slag him off, but that was about it. Mostly she talked about Matt.'

'Matt Quilter?'

Iona nodded, not asking how Rebecca had known.

'How long have you known Meredith?'

'About eighteen months, I guess. We used to bump into each other at gigs after I moved down to London, and one night we got talking about a fanzine she was doing.'

'You said before that you bump into a lot of people you know at gigs. Did you know Suki Jenson?'

'Justin's Suki?'

'Yes.'

'Well, I know who she was, but I didn't know her. She never deigned to talk to the likes of me. Do you think –' she stopped. 'Are they connected? Their deaths, I mean.'

'It's possible,' Rebecca allowed. 'Do you have any idea who might have been responsible?'

Iona shook her head. 'No. We just assumed Justin – I mean – you read about schizophrenics murdering people all the time, don't you?'

Rebecca didn't comment, asking instead, 'The friends you were at Wednesday's gig with – Collette and Laura – were they friends of Meredith's as well?'

Iona shifted position uncomfortably. 'Laura was. Collette –' she hesitated. 'They called each other friends, but Collette's a two-faced bitch, she says all sorts behind people's backs.'

'But she's a friend of yours despite that?'

'No. Not really. She's someone I meet up with at gigs and in clubs. An acquaintance, I guess. But Laura's cool.'

'Could you give me her address?'

'I don't actually have the postal address, but her place is in Whitechapel. In a block called Utopia House.' She forced a smile. 'I doubt anywhere in Whitechapel has a hope in hell of living up to that name.'

'Did you and Meredith have any other friends in common?'

'Not really. A lot of acquaintances, but not much in the way of real friends. Most of my friends are here – and at home. The rock scene is fun, and I love it, but it's not my whole life.' Iona paused. 'But Merri –'

'But Merri what?' Rebecca prompted, when the girl didn't continue.

Iona sighed. 'For her I think it might've been.'

## Seventeen

Neil wasn't home when Daniel and Rebecca arrived at the Seven Sisters Road address he had provided on Thursday night, and a sleepy-looking flat mate directed them to his place of work, a small back-street record shop called *Vinyl World* in one of Camden Town's dingier quarters. The man behind the till – the only visible member of staff on duty – was serving a customer, and Daniel hung back, flicking through a rack of LPs, while Rebecca joined the queue. Shortly, he joined her, remarking, 'They've got a surprising amount of quality stuff.'

'They're big online,' Rebecca replied, glancing at her watch.

'How'd you know that?'

She met his eyes, brows raised. 'How'd you think?'

Daniel shook his head slightly. 'Sorry. Wasn't thinking.'

An awkward pause followed, which Rebecca broke with a forcibly cheerful, 'Not a vinyl man yourself, then?'

'Not really. Never had a record player.'

'Ah.'

'You?'

'I think the vinyl thing is a bit like football.'

'How so?'

'Most of the fans are male.'

Daniel smiled. She was probably right, although he guessed there wasn't much crossover between vinyl lovers and football fans. He had certainly never heard a girl champion the merits of vinyl over CD. Mind you, with the availability of instantaneous downloads and the rise of streaming, neither seemed particularly relevant any more.

The final customer in the queue lifted a carrier bag from the wooden counter and turned for the door, stuffing a handful of change into his pocket as he went. Rebecca stepped forwards, bidding the man behind the counter good morning. He was clad in a leather jacket, which seemed strange, given that the shop was far from cold and had, according to the sign on the door, been open for more than two hours already. The jacket looked worn – rather like its owner, who was, in Daniel's opinion, the wrong side of forty and in possession of considerably too little hair to be sporting a ponytail. His lower eyelids drooped slightly beneath his watery green eyes and his nose bore the puncture marks of piercings no longer worn. In response to Rebecca's request to speak to Neil, he rested his mostly beringed fingers on the counter and said, 'Who?'

'Neil Shaw,' Rebecca repeated.

'Dunno him.'

'His flat mate seemed to think he worked here.'

'Well he don't,' the leather jacket responded, shortly. 'You could try *Out On The Floor* or *Bar Vinyl* in Inverness Street.'

Rebecca sighed. 'Ok, thank you.'

'Bar Vinyl?' Daniel echoed, as he and Rebecca headed towards the door. 'Sounds more like a venue than a shop.'

'It is,' Rebecca replied. 'Well, it's both. A venue and a shop.'

'Interesting.'

'The shop's in the basement, although I don't imagine it's Neil's kind of thing. It's mostly house and garage, and he definitely isn't.'

'Doesn't sound much like your kind of thing either, but you know about it,' Daniel observed, opening the shop door and holding it for Rebecca.

'Alec DJs there sometimes.'

'Ah,' Daniel nodded, turning automatically in the direction of the street where they had left the car. 'I realised too late that –'

'We might as well walk,' Rebecca interrupted. 'It'll probably take longer to find another parking spot than to get there on foot.'

'Ok. Lead the way.'

Rebecca set off in the opposite direction. After a moment, she asked, 'What did you realise too late?'

'Huh? Oh – I was just thinking that if I had my time over again I might opt to go down the DJ route. It's got to be one of the easiest ways of making money in existence. I mean, you turn up at a club, you play a bunch of records made by other people, drink and flirt while you work, and then get paid for it.'

'You don't necessarily get paid a whole lot.'

'People make a living out of it, though. Your mate Alec can't be doing badly, his home address is only down the road from here.'

'Alec doesn't just DJ, he coordinates entire nights. If you want someone who can oversee both a gig and the club that follows it, or to provide different music in three separate rooms of a club for five or six hours straight, he can organise that. That involves a whole lot more work than changing the odd CD. You have to know your way around a sound desk for starters.'

'I bet he still gets to spend a good deal of his work time drinking, flirting and chatting, though.'

'Probably,' Rebecca agreed. 'But then he's hardly the only one, is he?'

Daniel frowned, wondering what she was getting at. 'Meaning what?' He asked, after a moment's hesitation.

Rebecca seemed surprised by his tone. 'There's no need to sound so worried.'

'I get the feeling you're making a point, but I'm not quite sure what.'

'Oh come on, where've you been?' She stopped at a pelican crossing, reaching to press the button. 'I thought you'd jump on this one.'

Daniel looked at her blankly, and Rebecca laughed. 'Have you not seen Leighton at work on a weekday afternoon?'

'He's probably not even *there*,' Jimmy protested as Lawrence drew the car up to the kerb and switched off the ignition.

'If he's not then we'll just have to come back later.'

'This is such a waste of time!'

'And graffiti isn't?' Lawrence returned, opening the car door.

'That's different.'

'Well I'm sure whoever had to clean up after you had better things to do with their time, too.'

'I doubt it,' Jimmy muttered, climbing out of the car.

Lawrence chose to ignore the remark, and, car locked, joined Jimmy on the pavement before heading for number eighteen. As he reached to open the gate, a voice greeted him hello, and, startled, Lawrence looked around. A young man with dark curly hair and smudges of soil on his nose and forehead was crouching just the other side of the wall, apparently in the process of easing an impressive dandelion plant out of the flowerbed. Hand still on the partially open gate, Lawrence bid him good morning.

'Can I help?'

'Possibly. We're looking for the vicar of St Michael's church.'

'Ah, that'd be me,' he released the dandelion and straightened up, offering a hand and then immediately retracting it on realising his skin was smothered in soil. 'Sorry. Andrew Froude. What can I do for you?'

'I'm Lawrence Forrester, this is my son Jimmy. He has something he'd like to say.' Lawrence turned to Jimmy, whose eyes were fixed on the ground. 'Jim?'

'Sorry about the graffiti,' Jimmy mumbled, not lifting his gaze.

'Look at people when you speak to them,' Lawrence directed.

Jimmy did as bid, barely refraining from rolling his eyes. 'I'm sorry,' he repeated, his expression changing abruptly. Apparently forgetting his adolescent cool, he asked, 'Are you *allowed* to wear that?'

Andrew glanced down at his Vicious Circle tour t-shirt in surprise, then nodded. 'I am,' he confirmed, looking back to Jimmy. 'So what was it about my church that particularly offended you, then?'

The boy shrugged.

'Nothing,' Andrew concluded, thoughtfully. 'Have you done that kind of thing before?'

Jimmy shook his head.

'I hope you're not planning to make a habit of it.'

'No,' Jimmy answered. 'Sorry.' Then, as an afterthought, 'Sir.'

This drew a smile from the vicar. 'Apology accepted.'

Jimmy's attention returned to the man's t-shirt. 'Did you really go to see VC?'

'I did. Did you?'

Jimmy nodded. 'Yeah. We had backstage passes and everything, it was wicked.'

'How did you come by those?'

'From someone Dad works with.'

'Ah,' Andrew looked to Lawrence. 'Do you work in the entertainment industry, then?'

'No – I –' Lawrence faltered, feeling acutely uncomfortable. That he worked in law enforcement was last thing he wanted to reveal in light of the fact his thirteen-year-old son was there to apologise for *breaking* the law. Hoping to avoid the subject, he opened his mouth to explain where the tickets had come from, but Jimmy beat him to the punch.

'Dad's a policeman,' he announced. 'But he doesn't get to drive squad cars, which would be really cool.'

'CID,' Lawrence expanded, succinctly. 'Anyway, the reason we came – other than for Jim to apologise – was to ask what he might do to make amends. I thought perhaps –'

'Do you have fish?' Jimmy interrupted, excitedly, pointing to the small ornamental pond to the left of the front door.

'Yes. Would you like to come and have a look?'

Jimmy didn't hesitate, and by the time Lawrence reached the pond his son was crouching beside it, gazing intently at something on the far side. Following his line of sight, Lawrence spotted a large frog resting on the pond's rear wall. Its retreat onto dry land was understandable given the murkiness of the water, which had rendered the resident goldfish almost invisible. Lawrence felt for the creatures. They, unlike the frog, had nowhere else to go.

As if reading his thoughts, Andrew said, 'I know, it shouldn't look like that. I think there's something wrong with the filter. I need to empty it out to take a look.'

Jimmy glanced up. 'Where are you gonna put the fish?'

'I've got some buckets. It'll only be for a few hours.'

'Are you gonna do that today?'

'That's the plan. Would you like to help?'

Clearly viewing emptying a pond as considerably more interesting than washing windows or cars – a couple of Lawrence's earlier suggestions for ways he might atone for the graffiti – Jimmy nodded enthusiastically. Lawrence sighed. The idea had been for the exercise to be punitive, not to provide a fun diversion. Although at least this way he could be confident Jimmy would undertake the task with a good grace. And, Lawrence supposed, if his son were to spend the afternoon in the company of a vicar, the chances of his getting into any further trouble were remote.

Having had no luck at either *Out On The Floor Records* or *Bar Vinyl*, Daniel and Rebecca opted to return to the car and phone around the rest of the record shops in the area, rather than traipse the length and breath of Camden. As they retraced their route, Daniel indicated a bustling cafe. 'Lunch?'

'Good call.'

'Full English?'

Rebecca shuddered theatrically. 'Ugh, no. I don't think –' she broke off, eyes on the doorway of the adjoining newsagent, from which Neil Shaw had just emerged, his attention focused on the magazine in his left hand. Holding up a hand to Daniel, she stood still, watching to see what direction Neil would take, and waiting for him to reach a safe distance for her to follow. Given its proximity, she wasn't surprised by his destination: *Vinyl World*. Bolting for the shop's front door the moment he was through it, she entered just in time to see him heading around the counter and talking to the same man who had denied knowing him less than an hour previously. By the time either of them noticed her, she was only a few feet from the till.

'I thought he didn't work here?' Rebecca opened.

'He don't,' came the leather jacket's response. 'He's just helping out.'

'So you do know him?'

'Kind of.'

'Right. Can I have your name, please?'

'What for?'

Rebecca presented her warrant card. 'Name?'

'Doug Gehry.'

'Are you the manager here?'

'Sort of. It's my shop.'

Rebecca shifted her attention to Neil, who hadn't moved since her arrival. 'You ask him to lie for you?'

'What? No!' Neil exclaimed, shaking his head for emphasis. 'I'm just covering a mate's shift so he could have the weekend off.'

'And what's your mate's name?'

'Harry.'

'Harry what?'

'Masters.'

'Address?'

'Um – I dunno – I'd have to check.'

Rebecca turned to Doug. 'I assume you have that information somewhere?'

''Course,' Doug replied, sounding less than certain.

'Great. You've got five minutes to find it.' She looked back to Neil. 'In the meantime, I want to talk to you. Outside. Now.'

Neil obediently followed Rebecca from the shop. Daniel was waiting inside the door, and remained where he was as Rebecca and Neil left the building.

'Right, first of all, can you tell me where you were between three p.m. and eight p.m. on Wednesday?' Rebecca began, once she and Neil were out of the way of the door.

'Um –' Neil hesitated, his eyes darting uneasily across the street. 'I was at home. And then on the bus to the gig.'

'Can anyone verify that?'

'I don't think so. My flat mate was working.'

'But you weren't.'

'No.'

'Do you work?'

'No.'

'Are you claiming benefits?'

'Yes,' Neil admitted, uncomfortably.

'And are you getting paid to cover for Harry today?'

'No. He said he'd buy me some beers.'

Rebecca nodded disbelievingly, wondering whether Harry even existed, and whether Neil's employment status, rather than his inability to account for his whereabouts at the time of Meredith's death, were behind Doug's denial of him.

'Ok, maybe you could tell me where you were after 10 p.m. on Monday?'

'Monday? I was at home.'

'Again. Alone again?'

'My flat mate was in – but he was in his room, so I'm not sure he can confirm that.'

'How convenient,' Rebecca remarked.

'I'm not sure it is given that you seem to be accusing me of something.'

'Really?' Rebecca lifted her eyebrows. 'What do you think that might be?'

'I don't know, I have no idea what happened on Monday night.'

Rebecca almost laughed. 'Are you kidding me? Do you live in a bubble? That's possibly the most disingenuous answer I've heard all year!'

Neil didn't respond, and Rebecca guessed he was struggling to think of a comeback.

'Did you know her?' She asked.

'Who?'

'Don't jerk me around! Suki Jenson, who else?'

'No.'

'Not at all?'

He shook his head.

'I assume you knew who she was, though? Before she died and was splashed across the papers, that is.'

Neil shrugged. 'Not really.'

'What does that mean?'

'I recognised her, and I knew she was Justin Black's girlfriend, because I'd seen them together, but that's about it.'

'Did you ever speak to her?'

'No.'

'How about Justin?'

'*No,*' Neil repeated, his voice sounding strained. 'I like the music, that doesn't make me a groupie. That was Mez's department.'

Rebecca wondered whether she was getting closer to a link between the two girls. 'On Thursday you said she didn't know him.'

'She didn't.'

'And yet she knew his friends.'

'She fawned over the ones she fancied. That's hardly knowing people, is it?'

'I guess she didn't fancy Justin, then,' Rebecca concluded, aloud, mainly to wind Neil up.

'I guess not,' he responded, tartly. 'But then I suppose there are limits to how many men a girl can chase at a time.'

'Why were you involved with Meredith if you had such a low opinion of her?'

'I've been asking myself the same thing,' Neil retorted. 'So, are we done?'

'Well that all depends, doesn't it?'

'On what?'

'Whether your boss – sorry, I mean Doug – managed to find an address for Harry.'

After leaving Jimmy with Andrew Froude, Lawrence had driven out to Enfield to pay Charlotte Jenson a visit, but failed to raise any response at her door. In the hope of salvaging what would otherwise have been a wasted journey, he decided to stop for lunch before trying again. He was just in the process of fitting a cardboard coffee cup into the car's cup holder when his mobile rang. Despite the fact he lived with the possibility of it ringing twenty-four hours a day, it made him jump, and he spilled the drink over his hand and the car's footwell. Swearing to himself, he reached into his jacket pocket with his dry hand, shaking scalding coffee from the other.

He had expected the caller to be either Daniel or Rebecca, but the words illuminated on his mobile screen read *private number*. Given the number of business cards he distributed per week, this wasn't an unusual occurrence, and he generally played a guessing game with himself as to who it might be each time an unknown or withheld number came up.

On this occasion, he guessed wrong. However, it took him a few seconds to work out who *was* at the other end of the line, because the caller was close to hysterical. Eventually, he managed to ascertain that it was Justin, but the only coherent thing he seemed to be able to say – or, more specifically, repeat over and over – was that he was scared and didn't want to die. In the end Lawrence gave up trying to extract any sense from him, and offered to come straight over. After several unsuccessful attempts to establish whether Justin was still at his mother's, he came to the conclusion it might well be quicker to go round in person. Justin could be anywhere. Harlesden was as good a place to start as any.

Rebecca entered the ward hesitantly, anticipating a confrontation with Alec, whose contact number she had given the nurse who had called in the early hours that morning. To her surprise and relief, she found Elliot propped up in bed alone, staring into nowhere. He was terribly pale and looked exhausted.

'Hey,' Rebecca greeted, stopping beside the bed.

Elliot focused on her. 'Hi.' His tone was stilted and awkward, and Rebecca guessed he didn't know what to say. She felt much the same.

'How are you feeling?'

'Like someone flushed a toilet through my bloodstream.'

'I guess that isn't entirely surprising.'

'No,' he sighed. 'Becca, I'm sorry. About calling you last night. I don't remember much about it, but I figure I was probably pretty out of order.'

'I owe you an apology as well,' Rebecca replied. 'For what I said on Thursday morning. I really didn't mean it. I'm sorry.'

Elliot nodded slightly. After a long pause, he said, 'I'm really sorry. For everything. Do you think you can forgive me?'

'I can forgive you, Elliot, but that doesn't mean we can get back together.'

'Do you think we ever could?' He asked, rather desperately.

'I don't know. If you stop drinking so much and accept you need treatment for your depression, perhaps we might. But right now we're nowhere near that stage.'

'But I need you. I don't think I can do it without you.'

'I tried very hard to help you, and it didn't make a lot of difference. You need to work this one out yourself.'

Elliot swallowed. 'So I can't come home.'

Rebecca felt heartless as she said, 'No.'

Elliot pursed his lips, struggling to control his emotions.

'I'm sorry.'

Elliot shook his head wordlessly. Rebecca wracked her mind for something banal to say to fill the increasingly uncomfortable silence between them. In the end, all she could think of was, 'Are they keeping you in for long?'

It took him a while to answer, and when he did his voice was unsteady. 'Just 'til tomorrow.'

'Will you –'

'What the *fuck* are you doing here?'

Rebecca turned to see Alec striding towards her, plainly furious.

'I just –'

'It's your fault he's in here in the fucking first place!' Alec continued. 'And if you –'

'Alec.' Elliot's voice sounded surprisingly forceful.

Alec didn't continue, although he would clearly have liked to. He walked past Rebecca, giving her an icy look as he did so, before transferring his attention to Elliot and handing him a half-litre bottle of Coke. Elliot thanked him and moved to unscrew the lid, his hands shaking. Although the bottle appeared to be full, Rebecca noticed the seal had already been broken, and as Elliot removed the lid she reached to take the bottle from him. Holding it to her nose, she could smell vodka. She looked back to Alec. 'Great idea. If he had a weight problem would you have brought him a Big Mac and fries?'

Elliot beat Alec to an answer. 'Becca, I asked him to –'

'I'm not interested in whose *idea* it was!' Rebecca interrupted. 'Figuring that out hardly takes a detective! What I want to know is why your so-called *best mate* thought it was a good one!'

'Why?' Alec demanded. 'What the fuck's it got to do with you now?'

'I still care what happens to him!'

'No you don't! You just don't want him on your conscience!'

'Well if you're going to help him drink himself to death, that'll be your problem, won't it?'

'There's not enough in there for him to drink himself any further than out of this place!'

Rebecca frowned. 'What?'

'I'm still fucking here you know!' Elliot snapped, irritably.

Alec sighed, turning towards him. 'I know, mate, I'm sorry.'

Rebecca pulled him back. 'Hold on, I'm not done. Are you seriously telling me you're feeding him vodka so the doctors don't realise he has a problem?'

Alec met her eyes. 'If he starts detoxing they will keep him here.'

Rebecca stared at him in astonishment for a moment before she managed to find her voice. 'Has it ever occurred to you – either of you –' here she looked to Elliot. 'That being here might actually be in your best interests?'

'What would you know about my best interests?' Elliot bit back. 'You have no idea what my life has been like!'

'That was your choice, Elliot, not mine,' she reminded him, setting the bottle down on the table by the bed. 'You just remember that.' She turned to leave. It took all of her strength to not look back.

Outside the ward, she leaned against the wall, trying unsuccessfully to blink back her tears. She wasn't sure why she was crying: whether it was a response to the events of the past twenty-four hours; whether it was because she felt guilty; or whether it was because she had hoped finishing with Elliot might shock him into straightening himself out. That it hadn't had that effect had already been abundantly clear, but in the aftermath of the shock that had immediately followed the news of his suicide attempt, she had allowed herself to hope that within the sober confines of the hospital he might have an opportunity to reflect on the chaotic mess his life had become. With Alec on hand to drown his sorrows before Elliot even had the chance to really feel them, that was never going to happen.

## Eighteen

Lucy Black answered the front door with a cigarette in one hand and bottle of beer in the other, looking considerably more relaxed than Lawrence had expected given the state Justin had appeared to be in less than an hour previously. The reason for this became evident almost immediately: before Lawrence could even open his mouth she said, 'Yer wasting yer time. He ain't 'ere.'

'Do you know where he is?'

'D'you really think I'd tell you?'

'I'm quite concerned about him. I spoke to him on the phone a little while ago and he seemed very upset.'

'I'm not surprised if he was talking to you,' Lucy retorted, bluntly. 'He's terrified you're gonna lock him up! How d'you expect him to be?' This was apparently a rhetorical question because, without giving Lawrence a chance to get a word in, she asked another. 'What is it you want now?'

'Actually, he contacted me.'

This revelation took Lucy by surprise, and she didn't at once reply. Recovering herself quickly, she said, 'You can't bluff your way around me.'

'I'm not trying to.'

Lucy frowned suspiciously. 'Why would he call you?'

'I don't know, that's what I'm trying to establish. But I am genuinely concerned about his welfare.'

Lucy snorted her disbelief. 'Yeah, I bet.' She shook her head slightly. 'I'm not buying it. All right?'

Lawrence ran out of patience. 'Miss Black, your son called me a short while ago hysterical, crying that he was scared and didn't want to die! Two people have already died in the past week, and I'd like to make sure Justin doesn't join them! Now *where is he*?'

Lucy paled. 'He's – he's at the hospital,' she stammered. 'At least, that's where he's supposed to be.'

'Do you want to call and check they've still got him?'

She shook her head. 'No – no, he's not a patient – he wanted to visit Floyd. I took him in a couple of hours ago, said I'd collect him when visiting was over.'

'Which hospital?'

'UCH.'

'Ok,' Lawrence pulled his mobile from his pocket and dialled Rebecca's number, realising too late that it was technically her day off. By then the phone was already ringing.

'Hey,' Rebecca answered, after four rings.

'Sorry, Becky, I meant to call Danny. You've done enough today.'

'It's ok.'

'I'll see you on Monday.'

'No, I mean I don't mind doing whatever it is you called for.' Her voice sounded strained, and Lawrence wondered whether she meant what she said.

'Are you all right?'

'I'm fine. Spill.'

'I'm trying to track Justin down,' he explained. 'The last time anyone saw him, he was at the hospital visiting Floyd, and –'

'Which one?'

'UCH.'

'I've just come from there, it'll take me five minutes to go back.'

Lawrence immediately understood why she sounded on edge: she'd been to visit Elliot. He felt he ought to say something to acknowledge the fact, but couldn't think of anything that seemed appropriate, so instead he said, 'If you're sure. I'm sorry for bothering you.'

'No worries. I'll get back to you as soon as I can.'

The seventeen minutes that followed – Lawrence counted – passed slowly and awkwardly, with Lucy chain-smoking punctuation into questions Lawrence had no way of answering, like 'Why did he call you?' and 'He'll be ok, won't he?' She didn't invite him in, and, observing the cloud of smoke drifting down the hallway over her shoulder, he opted not to invite himself. The call from Rebecca couldn't come soon enough. When it did, it wasn't the news he had been hoping for.

'Well?' Lucy demanded, the moment he hung up.

'He's not there.'

'What? But Karen was with him! She was s'posed to keep an eye on him!'

'Who's Karen?'

'Karen Newton. Floyd's mother. She knows what Justin's like! She *said* she'd look after him!'

'I'm sure she didn't mean to lose track of him,' Lawrence submitted. 'It sounds as if Floyd's in bad shape – apparently he collapsed earlier this afternoon and he's been taken to theatre for emergency surgery. I imagine Karen has a lot on her mind with all that going on.'

'Oh Christ.'

'If you give me Justin's mobile number I can have someone trace it.'

'He doesn't have one.'

'Really?' Lawrence exclaimed, thinking that extraordinary. Most people of Justin's age had owned a mobile phone before their parents had even trusted them with a set of door keys.

'He worries about the radiation.' Lucy took a long, hard pull on her cigarette. 'What about the phone he called you from? You can trace that, can't you?'

'The number was withheld, so it could take a while to get an answer on that,' Lawrence replied, apologetically. 'Where do you think he might have gone after he left the hospital? Where does he normally go when he's upset?'

Lucy's expression was rather hopeless. 'To Floyd.'

'Anywhere else?'

'Vinnie's place, maybe. But he's not there, if he was Vin would've called by now. He doesn't have much time for Just's troubles these days.'

Lawrence sighed. 'Ok, let's try Justin's flat first. Do you have a key?'

Lucy shook her head, looking close to tears.

'Vinnie does, though, doesn't he?' Lawrence recalled from the early stages of the investigation.

'Yes.'

'Can you give him a call, ask him to meet us at Justin's flat as a matter of urgency?'

'Yes,' Lucy repeated, turning back into the flat.

'And as soon as you're ready I'll drive you over there.'

'Right,' Lucy nodded, stopping briefly in the hallway. 'Right. Yes.' She exchanged the beer bottle for a handbag that lay on the shelf to the left of the door, rummaging around in it for her phone as she stepped out of the flat. She pulled the front door shut behind herself before dialling and following Lawrence along the balcony towards the stairwell, muttering, 'Come on, come on.' Eventually, the call was answered, and she said, 'It's Mum.' Pause.

Then, incredulously, '*What time is it*? For fuck's sake, Vincent, it's quarter to three in the fucking afternoon, get a fucking grip!' Another pause. 'No you can't call me back, I need you to meet me at Justin's flat with the key as soon as!' Longer pause. 'What? No! It's an emergency and you'll fucking well bring it over!' Lucy rang off without waiting for a response, and Lawrence wondered whether she often spoke to her children in such a manner. He could certainly see where Vinnie got his attitude from.

There was no sign of Vinnie when Lawrence and Lucy arrived in Mornington Terrace. Lawrence tried and then re-tried the doorbell with little expectation of success; when that failed he switched to shouting Justin's name, which elicited an eventual response only from a neighbour, who peered out of a first-floor window, presumably wondering what all the fuss was about. Conceding defeat, Lawrence stepped back onto the pavement, eyes on the windows of Justin's flat. Lucy, meanwhile, tried calling – and then pleading – to her son through the letterbox.

She was still imploring him to open the door – in between pulls on yet another cigarette – when Lawrence noticed the door of a still-moving car open as it pulled across the northern end of the one-way street. Vinnie stumbled out and sprinted straight down the middle of the road, narrowly avoiding being run over by a car heading in the opposite direction. The driver hit the horn as hard as the breaks; Vinnie flicked a finger in response. Another five seconds brought him level with Lawrence, but he didn't stop, making straight for the steps up to the front door, keys at the ready. Lawrence pulled him back. 'You're not going in.'

'What?' Vinnie blinked.

Lawrence held out a hand. 'Keys.'

'I –'

'Keys,' Lawrence repeated. '*Now*.'

'Vincent, please,' Lucy seconded.

Vinnie reluctantly relinquished the keys, turning to his mother as Lawrence took them from him. 'What the fuck is going on?'

Lawrence deftly unlocked the front door and headed straight up the stairs inside. Halfway up, he realised Vinnie was only two steps behind him, and stopped abruptly. 'Outside!' He ordered.

'What?' Vinnie exclaimed, only just managing to stop in time to prevent them colliding.

'*Out*!'

'But –'

Lawrence's expression stopped him short, and he began his retreat. Lawrence waited for him to disappear before continuing his ascent. Letting himself in the front door of the flat, he called Justin's name before identifying himself. He was greeted by silence. Moving slowly down the hallway, he looked first in through the open door to the living room. Unlike on his previous visit, nothing in there seemed to be amiss. The door across the corridor was closed, and Lawrence knocked before easing it open. Another empty, apparently undisturbed room, this one a bedroom. As there wasn't a scrap of silver foil to be seen, Lawrence surmised it to be Floyd's, and closed the door behind himself before advancing to the next one. He knocked again. 'Justin?' He tried the door. It didn't move. Glancing down, he noted that there was no lock accompanying the handle, meaning that if it had been locked, it had been done from the inside. 'Justin, can you let me in?'

No answer. Lawrence stood still for several seconds, listening for any sign of life. When none came, he decided to try his luck forcing the door. There wasn't much space in the narrow corridor, and he pushed off from the opposing wall to add some momentum. He heard the latch give, the effort apparently a success, but the door didn't move any further than the initial inch. Far from being locked, it had been barricaded shut.

Although the attempt to force the door had failed, it did succeed in drawing a response from within, and the terrified shriek that greeted the action reassured Lawrence that Justin was still very much alive. And, while evidently just as agitated as he had been on the phone some ninety minutes earlier, this time the message was clear enough. 'Get out! Get out! Get out!'

'Justin –'

'Get out!'

'I just need –'

'*Get out*!' The door slammed shut again, narrowly missing Lawrence's fingers. '*Get out*!'

'I just want to make sure you're all right,' Lawrence persisted, patiently.

This drew a different response. 'No you don't! You want to lock me up and take my thoughts and –'

'Nobody wants to lock you up.'

'You *already* locked me up!' Justin returned, accusingly.

'I'm not here to lock you up, Justin. I'm here because you called me. And –'

'I did not!'

Lawrence sighed, glancing at his watch and wondering whether Greg was on call that afternoon. The pause seemed to further unsettle Justin, who reverted to his original *get out* rant.

'I can't get out until I know you're ok,' Lawrence countered. 'Please just open the door.'

Lawrence heard a thud. He was about to try the door again when a hand on his arm stopped him. He spun around.

'I told you to wait outside!'

'I can hear him from the street,' Vinnie replied.

'I don't care! My instructions were pretty damn clear!'

'You're not going to get any sense out of him until he calms down. Give me a few minutes, yeah?'

Had he not already been running late to collect Jimmy from Andrew Froude, Lawrence might have argued the point. As it was – and given that Justin didn't seem to be in any immediate danger from anyone besides perhaps himself – he hesitated for a moment before nodding. 'Ok. I've something else to take care of this afternoon, I'll be back in an hour or so. If he goes AWOL, there will be hell to pay. Understand?'

Vinnie nodded.

Lawrence turned for the stairwell, drawing his mobile from his pocket and scrolling to Daniel's number. Vinnie might think he was being left in charge, but Lawrence wasn't going anywhere until someone else was around to keep an eye on proceedings. He just hoped Daniel could make it in double-quick time.

## Nineteen

Lawrence had been grudgingly impressed with the degree to which Vinnie had managed to settle Justin down during his absence, seemingly – given that the young man was both alert and relatively coherent – with little or no chemical help. Despite his apparent lucidity, however, Justin was unable to offer any explanation for his earlier behaviour, shaking his head, shrugging and repeating *I dunno* in response to almost every question Lawrence posed. Guessing the episode might simply have been a response to the distress caused by Floyd's collapse, and in no way relevant to the investigation, Lawrence didn't push the matter, instead instructing Vinnie to let him know if anything did come to light. Then, after asking a few questions of Vinnie and Lucy, he rejoined Daniel and set out for Enfield for the second time that day, cursing the waste of an afternoon.

Charlotte Jenson was very well dressed when she opened her front door to Lawrence and Daniel shortly before seven, and Lawrence felt surprised, thinking it unlikely she should be going out so soon after Suki's death. Taking the same seat as on their previous visit, he outlined the basic facts of the fate that had befallen Meredith before asking whether the girl's name meant anything to Charlotte. She paled.

'Merri?' She raised a hand to her mouth. 'Oh dear God –' tears came to her eyes and she fumbled in her pocket for a handkerchief. Despite her evident distress, Lawrence felt a surge of excitement at having finally made a connection between the two girls. He waited for Charlotte to recover from the initial shock before asking how she had known Meredith.

'She was a friend of Suki's. Her best friend for a long while –' Charlotte swallowed hard. 'I'm sorry,' she continued, after a pause. 'It's been a very difficult day. I've just come back from a funeral.'

Immediately understanding why she was so smartly attired, Lawrence offered to return the following day.

Charlotte shook her head. 'No, it's silly, if it weren't for –' she broke off. 'It was an old acquaintance, really. I went more on Suki's behalf than anything.'

'So it was someone Suki knew?'

'Yes,' Charlotte confirmed. Then, seeming to realise the direction the conversation might be about to take, she went on, 'It wasn't anything untoward. It was a stroke.'

'What connection did this person have with Suki?'

'It was her friend Roger's mother. I think Suki would have wanted to be there.'

'Were she and Roger close?'

'I don't know about recently – whether they were even still in touch – but they were when they were younger. He was Suki's first love.'

Lawrence nodded before turning the subject back to Meredith. As far as he was aware, Meredith's name hadn't come up once during the course of the investigation into Suki's death, so he could only assume something had happened to end – or at least seriously damage – the two girls' friendship.

'You said Meredith was Suki's best friend. When was that?'

'At secondary school. And for a while after that. They were inseparable for years.'

'Do you know why that changed?'

Charlotte sighed. 'I don't know all the details, but I know it had something to do with Justin.'

'Can you tell us any more than that?'

'I only ever heard Suki's side of the story,' Charlotte replied, her tone apologetic. 'She always maintained Merri was jealous, but I couldn't help thinking Merri might just have been looking out for her. Maybe if she'd listened –' she held her hands out rather helplessly.

'Do you have any idea whether Justin and Meredith were ever more than acquaintances?'

'I don't, I'm afraid. Suki and Merri were sharing a flat when Suki first started seeing him, so I suppose they must have had some contact, but given Merri's feelings about the relationship I doubt they spent a lot of time together.'

'How long did they share a flat for?'

'A couple of years. Before Justin came along, that is. They were making plans to move to Camden before they even left school. They had a couple of flats, then after they fell out Suki moved in with –' Charlotte's eyebrows contracted in thought. 'What was her name?' She shook her head. 'I can't remember. Finnish girl. She moved back to Helsinki towards the end of last year, and Suki moved into Sally's.'

'Do you recall Suki mentioning Meredith at all recently?'

'No. I don't think they'd spoken in months. I'm not sure they were even part of the same crowd any more.'

Lawrence suspected she was right. Keen to establish whether Suki had remained in touch with others from her past who might not be part of that crowd either, he asked whether Charlotte had an address for Roger.

'No, I'm afraid I don't, but I can give you Barbara's – that was his mother – if that would be of any use?'

'That would be a great help, thank you.'

Charlotte stood and made for a bureau that stood in the corner of the room, half obscured by a curtain. Shortly, she returned, a slip of paper in her hand. 'It's only down the road. They used to get the bus to school together.'

'Do you know the whereabouts of any of her other school friends?'

'No. The school might be able to help you, though. St Augustine's. It's in Winchmore Hill.'

'We'll get in touch with them on Monday.'

'Do you –' Charlotte hesitated. 'I know Kath – Merri's mother – moved. I don't suppose you have her address? I'd like to get in touch. If I can.'

'I'm afraid I can't give out addresses without authorisation, but if you like I can pass on your details.'

'Yes. Please. Thank you.' Charlotte nodded. 'I think the last time I saw her was at a school play. The girls loved drama.' She paused before adding, softly, 'Romeo and Juliet.' Lawrence wasn't sure whether she was talking to him or to herself. Shortly, she repeated the play's title, her expression bleak. 'No happy ending there, either, was there?'

Rebecca hesitated before knocking on the front door of the first-floor flat, hoping she wouldn't come away feeling worse than she had after visiting the hospital. When the door opened, Kaia's appearance took her by surprise: she was clad in a pink leotard, white footless tights and pointe shoes, and her long blonde hair was drawn tightly into a bun. Rebecca had known what Kaia did for a living, but had previously only ever seen her in one of two guises; stylishly, ever so slightly sexily dressed and impeccably made up, or in equally chic nightwear around the flat Elliot and Matthew had shared a couple of years earlier. Rebecca had always been under the impression Kaia was one of those girls who just don't *do* casual; in fact, she wouldn't have been surprised to learn that Kaia didn't even own a pair of trousers. To Rebecca, the mere idea of always being so perfectly turned out was exhausting.

Kaia seemed equally surprised to find Rebecca on her doorstep, and forced a smile. 'Becks. Hi.'

'Hi. I just –' Rebecca faltered. 'I'm so sorry about Suki.'

'Thanks.'

'I won't stay – you're rehearsing – I'm interrupting. I just thought – well, it's Saturday night –' she trailed off, feeling tongue-tied. 'I didn't want you to be at home alone if you didn't want to be.'

Kaia nodded before saying, 'And you?'

'Sorry?'

'I heard about you and E.'

'Oh,' Rebecca realised, aloud, wondering whose version Kaia had heard. She was caught off guard when Kaia said, genuinely, 'I'm sorry.'

Rebecca wasn't sure how to respond. In the end, she shrugged, saying, awkwardly, 'It was my choice.'

'Like he gave you one,' Kaia remarked, turning towards the kitchenette that ran along the wall inside the door. 'Would you like a drink?'

Feeling relieved Kaia didn't have the same take as Alec on her situation, but not convinced the girl really wanted her company, Rebecca offered her an out. 'Do you have time?'

Kaia looked momentarily puzzled before realising what Rebecca meant. Indicating her outfit with a wave of her hand, she said, 'I'm not doing anything important. Dancing distracts me. That's all.'

'Maybe I should take it up,' Rebecca joked, stepping inside and closing the front door behind herself.

'Matt used to call it my drug,' Kaia opened the fridge. 'I put up with him on smack for eight months. I wish I'd had the strength to walk away sooner.' She held up a bottle of white wine. 'Pinot?'

'Sounds good.'

'Nobody should have to live like that,' Kaia continued, setting to work with a corkscrew. 'You just end up with two people being miserable instead of one. Unless one of them's Alec.'

'Did he give you a hard time about Matt?'

'No,' Kaia replied, pausing to yank the cork free. 'But I'm guessing he did you. I know how he is with E.'

'So it's not just me.'

Kaia glanced around. 'What isn't?'

'Sometimes I thought maybe I was overstating his – I don't know – involvement in *everything*. It's like he thinks Elliot belongs to him or something.'

'Don't be too hard on him,' Kaia responded, setting the bottle down and reaching to take two glasses from the cupboard above her head. 'He's been through a lot, and I think he avoids facing up to his own issues by concentrating on other people.'

Rebecca shook her head slightly. 'I've heard so many excuses made for Elliot, and Alec, and Matt, and – whoever else – but it's hard to know how much their lives have been difficult, and how much they've made them that way.'

'Matt maybe,' Kaia acknowledged. 'But Alec never asked to grow up in care.'

'Care?' Rebecca echoed, feeling shaken and wondering why Elliot had never told her. She didn't ask for further details: dealing with Alec was difficult enough without the added conflict of feeling sympathy for him. Wordlessly, she moved to sit down. Kaia poured out two glasses of wine and handed one to Rebecca before perching on the edge of her bed and bending to undo her pointes. Rebecca watched her deftly untie and unwind the ribbons. As she slid her first foot out, Rebecca noticed several of her toes were bound by tape.

'Does dancing in those hurt?'

'Depends,' Kaia eased the second slipper off. 'If they don't fit right, or you don't keep your nails short. Or if you're out of practise.' She stood and made for the wardrobe.

'Do you have to wear them in?'

'Kind of. Although you have to watch wearing them in doesn't wear them out.' She drew out a floaty black skirt and slipped it on over the leotard.

'How long do they last?'

'One performance, as a rule.'

'You're kidding?'

'Nope.' Kaia collected her wine glass from the kitchen worktop before returning to the bed. 'The principals can go through two or three pairs in one night.'

'That must get expensive,' Rebecca remarked.

'Just a bit.'

'Did you always want to dance?'

'Since I can remember. It's in my blood, I think. My grandmother danced with the Kirov when she was my age.'

'Wow.'

'Yeah,' Kaia lifted her eyebrows. 'Plenty to live up to, right?'

'That must have been an incredible experience. Scary though. How did she find communist Russia?'

Kaia smiled. 'Pretty normal. She is Russian.'

Rebecca felt herself blush. 'Right.'

'How about you? Did you always want to join the police?'

'No. When I was kid I was a real tomboy. I wanted to be a mechanic. Then it was a tennis player. And after that it was an architect.'

'So what made you pick the police?'

'TV shows,' she admitted, sheepishly.

'Really?'

'Uh-huh.'

'Do you not find it hard? Dealing with death.'

'It's not always easy, but it's not as if I didn't choose this. I could've taken another route. Fraud. Vice.'

Kaia nodded. Several seconds passed before she said, hesitantly, 'Can I ask you something? About –' she faltered. 'About Suki?'

Rebecca acquiesced, wondering whether it would be something she would be able to answer.

'They let Justin go. Is that because he didn't do it, or because they couldn't prove he did?'

Rebecca sighed. 'Kaia, I can't answer that.'

'Are you allowed to tell me what *you* think?'

Rebecca felt torn. It wasn't as if her personal and professional opinions were two separate things. She decided to side-step the issue with a question of her own. 'Do you think Justin was responsible?'

Kaia shook her head slightly. 'I don't know. Sometimes. But I've seen him in a paranoid loop enough times, and he's never lashed out. His instinctive response seems to be to get away.' She ran a finger up and down the stem of her glass. 'So then I think maybe I'm just labelling him, the same as everyone else. Everyone who doesn't know him, I mean.'

'And the press.'

'Yeah. They print so much crap. It drove Matt crazy.' She paused. 'They're one thing I don't miss.'

'Do you still miss him?'

'All the time,' Kaia admitted. 'Sometimes I think I always will. You know?'

Rebecca nodded. She knew all too well.

The smell in Barbara Finnegan's hallway – a combination that included cloves and beeswax – took Lawrence back more than thirty years to his grandmother's Almshouse cottage in Exmouth. Funny, he thought, how details like that never leave you. How they prompt the recall of other memories: roasting chestnuts on an open fire; rolling marbles along uneven, sloping wooden floors; tucking into rhubarb crumble and custard. Unless, of course, you have the beginnings of Alzheimer's. Inability to recognise familiar smells was one of the first signs, or so he'd heard.

He and Daniel had been invited into the house in response to his enquiry about Roger by a slight woman of fifty-odd who introduced herself as Deborah Moore, Roger's aunt. 'I'm afraid he's not actually here,' she said, apologetically, as Daniel closed the front door behind himself.

'Do you know where we might find him?'

'No, I don't. He just said he had to go, he didn't say where. I didn't really feel I could ask, given the circumstances.'

Lawrence nodded. 'Would you mind giving us his address?'

'Not at all –' Deborah looked about herself as if the address might be lurking nearby. 'I haven't my address book with me, I'm afraid, but I'm sure Barbara had it written down somewhere. If not I'll call my husband, see if he has it in his phone.'

Lawrence wondered where her husband might be so soon after either his sister or sister-in-law's funeral, and whether he had even been around for the event. Deborah reached behind the thin curtain that partly veiled the small window at the foot of the stairs, drawing out a grubby hardback notebook decorated with faded pressed flowers. The windowsill also housed a telephone, which rested atop a copy of the Yellow Pages, a publication that seemed thoroughly superfluous in the Internet age. Besides these, the narrow hallway was completely featureless but for a garish turquoise carpet sporting a gold geometric design that looked as if it belonged in the 1970s, and a large framed photograph on the wall opposite the window.

It was a school photograph, with an oval mount, not unlike those Lawrence had at home. And, like those in his living room and study, it featured a boy and a girl, in matching uniforms. The boy, perhaps seventeen, had dark, wavy hair reminiscent of Colin Firth's in *Pride and Prejudice*, a strong jaw and a few teenage spots, and his confidence came through in his stance. The girl, a year or two younger, appeared less sure of herself. She was chubby, although he wouldn't have gone as far as *fat*, her skin splashed with freckles and her hair, a few shades lighter than her brother's, drawn neatly into a ponytail. Her smile appeared artificial, although there was no way of knowing whether that spoke of genuine unhappiness or simple discomfiture in the face of the photographer's lens.

'Is this Roger?' Lawrence indicated the picture.

Deborah glanced up. 'What? Yes. Roger and Thea.'

'Is she around?' Lawrence enquired, thinking she would perhaps be able to provide Roger's address.

'No. She's –' Deborah hesitated. 'She passed away.' She returned to flicking through the pages of what Lawrence presumed had been Barbara's address book before adding, sadly, 'She would have been twenty-two by now. Losing her broke Barbara's heart. I think that was what killed her, really.'

*Twenty-two*. The same age as Suki and Meredith.

'How did she die?' Lawrence asked, realising, as he did so, that having not explained his interest the question might seem unduly intrusive.

'Anorexia,' Deborah responded, apparently unconcerned by his enquiry. 'So sad.'

'When was this?'

'Oh, four – five years ago, now,' Deborah revealed, before seeming to realise they had wandered considerably from the original topic of conversation. Looking up again, this time with a frown, she said, 'Why do you ask? What's going on?'

'We're investigating the murders of two young women. They were the same age Thea would have been. One was an old girlfriend of Roger's.'

'Murder?' Deborah gulped.

'I don't know how close your family is, but you might remember the name Suki?'

'Suki?' Deborah exclaimed. 'Oh yes. I remember her,' she confirmed, her tone implying something more than simple recollection.

'I get the impression there's something specific to remember,' Lawrence observed.

Deborah sighed. 'Not exactly. That is, it wasn't Suki's *fault*. But she was the reason Roger moved out.'

'Would you mind telling me why?'

'Barbara wouldn't have her in the house. After Thea died.'

'Do you know why not?'

'I imagine she found it too painful. Suki was Thea's friend – that's how she and Roger got to know one another – and –' Deborah sighed again. 'I don't know. Barbara didn't cope well with losing Thea. It was a terrible shock for her. It was so sudden.'

Lawrence felt puzzled. 'I thought you said she died of anorexia?'

'She didn't exactly die *of* it – more because of it. She was taking a lot of pills – laxatives, weight-loss supplements, goodness knows what, really – and she took something that affected her heart. One afternoon she just keeled over in the kitchen. Roger got her to hospital, but by then –' Deborah trailed off, shaking her head. 'Martin – my husband – did try to help, but –' she paused, clearly struggling to word what she wanted to say. 'He's a man's man. He's not good with talking about emotions. He just gets on with things, and I don't think he really knew what to do with her.'

'So Barbara was his sister?'

'Yes. He'll be back in an hour or two, if you'd like to talk to him,' she offered, helpfully. 'He's just running our daughter back to university.'

Lawrence confirmed that he would like to do so before returning to the subject of Suki. 'You said Suki and Thea were friends. Does the name Meredith, or Merri, mean anything to you?'

Deborah's brow furrowed as she thought. 'It doesn't ring any bells, but then I don't think I heard much about many of the kids' friends – I don't suppose I'd remember Suki if she and Roger hadn't been together for so long. I'm sorry, that's not very helpful –' she hesitated, then, brightening, asked, 'Would it help to see Thea's room? Barbara hasn't changed a thing since the day she died.'

'No, that won't be necessary. Just the address.'

'Oh, yes,' Deborah remembered. Turning the open book around towards him, she indicated the third box down on the page. Lawrence glanced around at Daniel, who took the book in one hand, reaching into his pocket with the other for a notebook in which to record the information. Returning his attention to Barbara's address book, Lawrence took in the street name listed beneath Roger's name and found it oddly familiar. In fact, he recognised the whole address. It was already in his own notes.

## Twenty

'Morning. Any progress?' Rebecca asked as she entered Lawrence's office on Monday morning, a coffee in one hand and a large bubble-wrap envelope in the other.

'None whatsoever,' Lawrence sighed. 'We might as well have all taken the day off yesterday. What did you get up to?'

'Not much. I was up late on Saturday.'

Lawrence raised his eyebrows quizzically but didn't enquire further. Rebecca didn't elaborate; it wasn't as though there was much to tell. She and Kaia had sat up talking until almost five a.m., after which Rebecca had fallen asleep on Kaia's pink sofa. It had been mid-afternoon Sunday by the time she made it home. She handed Lawrence the jiffy bag.

'What's this?'

'I don't know, it was in the mail tray. Addressed to you.'

'Ah. Maybe it's that book I ordered for Kate.'

'What book's that?'

'Some fancy art compendium.' Lawrence picked at the tape that secured the package.

'Where'd you order it from?' Rebecca asked, noticing the packaging had been recycled.

'eBay.'

'Why not Amazon?'

'Out of print.' Getting nowhere with the tape, he grunted in frustration.

'Here,' Rebecca held out a hand.

Lawrence passed it back to her. Rebecca applied her fingernails and ripped the tape off in a matter of seconds.

'Nicely done,' Lawrence remarked, as she returned it. 'Thank you.' He lifted the flap and peered inside. Frowning, he tipped the contents out.

'What is it?'

Lawrence opened the hardback volume and thumbed quickly through the pages. 'Looks like a diary.'

'Is there a name in it?'

Lawrence flicked to the front. 'No,' he concluded, before leafing back the other way. 'Last entry was ... last Wednesday. And came to five pages.' He cast his eyes over the page open in front of him before coming to a sudden halt.

'Something interesting?'

'I wonder if she had time to think. If she thought about me,' he read, aloud. 'If she thought about Thea. About what we did to Thea. Whether she even cared. Maybe she didn't. Maybe Justin was her karma.' Lawrence looked up. 'On Suki's final moments, it seems.'

Rebecca frowned. 'I'm missing something.'

'Meredith,' Lawrence elaborated.

'They knew each other?'

'School friends.'

'But not friends any more?'

'Apparently they had some sort of falling out.'

'And who's Thea?'

'The sister of an ex-boyfriend of Suki's called Roger Finnegan. Who also goes by the nickname Fin.'

'Manager of the Dark Heart,' Rebecca remembered.

'That's right.'

'So what's the story there?'

'I'm not sure yet. The three girls were at school together. Suki dated Roger while they were all still there. Thea later died of an adverse reaction to a diet drug, after which Barbara – her mother – banned Suki from the house. So far, nobody's been able to tell me why.'

Rebecca opened her mouth to ask the obvious question, then answered it herself. 'And Roger's been off work because his mother died – what, the week before last? So obviously there's no chance of asking her.'

'Indeed. Danny and I spoke to her brother and sister-in-law on Saturday evening, but all they could give me was that maybe seeing Suki was too painful for her. And despite two visits to Roger's home address, we've not managed to catch up with him yet.'

Rebecca leaned to get a better look at the diary entry. 'About what we did to Thea,' she repeated, slowly. 'When I spoke to Iona, she said there was sadness about Merri. Perhaps it had something to do with Thea.'

'It must've been something serious for Meredith to think a violent death was fitting karmic retribution,' Lawrence observed, laying the diary, still open, on the desk top. 'But clearly they weren't responsible for her death, she died of – well, not natural causes, but it wasn't suspicious. Unless of course they gave or sold her the pills.'

'Do you think whatever it is might be the reason they fell out?'

'I'm thinking it might be the reason they're dead,' Lawrence replied, rising from his chair. 'I'm going to head over to her flat, see if I can find any more of those.' He nodded towards the diary. 'In the meantime, can you get someone to fingerprint the cover and the envelope, and then go through it page by page?' He reached for his car keys. 'Somebody wanted us to have that diary, and I want to know why.'

A third visit to Roger's Wembley address proved as fruitless at the first two, and Lawrence headed back to the Yard via Soho on the off-chance Roger had returned to work. The trip cost him considerably more time than he had envisaged, as a fire in Dean Street had resulted in the closure of several roads and, subsequently, traffic chaos. Eventually opting to leave his car north of Oxford Street in Rathbone Place, Lawrence walked down to the Dark Heart, bypassing cordons with a flash of his warrant card.

The bar was surprisingly busy given that it wasn't yet midday on a Monday, and Lawrence guessed the majority of the customers were there only because they had been evacuated from their places of work by the fire brigade. Although now some years older, Roger was immediately recognisable from the photograph in the hallway of his mother's house, and Lawrence leaned an elbow on the bar and waited for him to finish serving a waiting customer. Handing the man his change, Roger looked to Lawrence. 'What you having?'

'DCI Forrester,' Lawrence introduced himself. 'Might I have a word?'

Roger moistened his lips with his tongue. 'About Suki, yeah? Petra said someone came in last week.'

'That's right.'

'How can I help?'

'You can start by telling me where you were last Monday night.'

'What, you think *I* –' Roger shook his head. 'Suki meant the world to me! I could never –'

'It's a standard question, Mr Finnegan.'

'Oh,' he relaxed. 'Right. Um – Monday night – I had dinner with my aunt and uncle. He dropped me home around about ten-thirty, I think – maybe a bit before – then I watched some TV and went to bed.'

'Can anybody confirm that?'

'Not after my uncle left.'

'How about Wednesday afternoon?'

'Wednesday?' Roger's eyebrows rose in surprise. 'What happened on Wednesday?'

'Please just answer the question.'

'Wednesday,' he licked his lips again. 'I had a meeting with my mother's vicar,' he revealed, running a shaking hand through his hair. 'I was – I – about her funeral.' He lowered his eyes to the bar, drawing a deep breath.

'Take your time,' Lawrence offered, patiently. 'I realise it can't have been an easy couple of weeks for you.'

Roger nodded. 'It was bad enough – but then –' he paused. 'I saw Suki's picture – in the paper –' he stopped. 'I was on the tube – I thought –' he gave up, shrugging his shoulders.

Lawrence didn't respond, giving Roger a moment to gather himself together.

'Sorry,' he managed, at length, meeting Lawrence's eyes. 'I really cared about her.'

'When did you last see her?'

'The day before Mum passed, I think. In here.'

'I'm sorry to have to ask, but what day was that?'

'Oh – um – Wednesday. The week before last.'

'How did she seem?'

'Angry.'

'About what?'

'A customer had felt her up at work. It wasn't the first time it'd happened – with that guy, I mean – and she was pissed off he'd been allowed back into the club.'

'Did that happen often?'

'From time to time. I kept telling her she was worth more than that place, but she said she needed the money.'

'Did anything else come of the incident?'

'I've no idea. Sorry.'

Lawrence nodded. 'Does the name Meredith Armstrong mean anything to you?'

Roger's eyes narrowed slightly, and there was a pause before he answered. When he did, it was as if guessing the answer to a question. 'Merri?'

'That's right.'

'Yeah, she was a friend of my sister's. And Suki's. I didn't really know her, but I used to see her here and there.'

'When did you see her last?'

Roger conveyed his uncertainty with a facial expression before saying, 'I don't know. Four years ago? Five, maybe? I don't really remember, if I'm honest.'

'I understand Suki was friends with your sister, as well.'

'Yeah, that's how we met.'

'Your aunt mentioned that at one stage your mother stopped letting Suki into the house.'

'After Thea died.'

'Do you know why?'

'I guess she didn't want to be reminded of what Thea might've been doing if she hadn't –' he shrugged in lieu of finishing the sentence.

'So you're not aware of anything untoward having happened between Suki and Thea?'

'Like what?'

'I don't know, your mother's reaction just seems a bit extreme.'

Roger sighed. 'She wasn't – Mum, that is – good at letting go. I don't know. I suppose some people just aren't.'

Lawrence nodded his agreement, drawing his card from his pocket. 'I'm sorry to have had to put you through questioning. If anything else comes to mind, please let me know.'

'Sure,' Roger replied, with a nod.

'I'll leave you in peace then. Thank you for your time.'

'No problem.' Roger thrust his hands, still shaking, into his pockets. Lawrence turned for the door, wondering whether Roger really was ignorant of whatever it was that Meredith believed she and Suki had done to his sister. He suspected it wasn't only Thea that Barbara had been unable to let go.

*****

Rebecca closed the second of the two additional diaries that Lawrence had retrieved from Meredith's flat with a sigh. Leaving her desk, she walked the few paces to her superior's office doorway. He glanced up as she entered his peripheral vision, and took in her expression before guessing, 'Nothing?'

Rebecca wrinkled her nose. 'Thea comes up from time to time, and there's plenty alluding to her being hurt or wronged in some way, but Meredith doesn't spell out what actually happened. She's no reason to in her own diary, I suppose.'

Lawrence nodded.

'What I did get was more about what happened between Meredith and Suki. The two parted company as flat mates during the course of that volume.' She indicated the book on her desk with a jerk of her head. 'Obviously it only offers Meredith's point of view, but I get the impression she was jealous.'

'Of Suki?'

'I'm not sure. It's hard to be sure whether she was jealous of Suki – because of her relationship with Justin – or of Justin, for taking first place in Suki's life. She wasn't a particularly articulate writer, so it's hard to follow a lot of what she says.'

'That's certainly true,' Lawrence agreed. 'I had thought having diaries would help. I was thinking it was too bad all our victims don't keep them.'

'The problem is that we've got the wrong ones.'

Lawrence regarded her quizzically. 'What do you mean?'

'Oh, just that it's a shame we don't have Thea's. They'd probably be a whole lot more illuminating.'

'Did Thea keep a diary?'

'I think so. At one point Meredith wrote about Suki making fun of her when she found out Meredith kept one. Supposedly Suki likened her to Bridget Jones, then to Thea.'

Lawrence stood and reached for his car keys. 'Let's go and see what we can find, then.'

'Where?'

'Barbara's house. Her sister-in-law told me Barbara hadn't touched Thea's room since she died. If Thea kept diaries, I'm guessing that's where they'll be.'

'We're going to need a search warrant first.'

'Not necessarily,' Lawrence replied, heading towards the lifts. Rebecca hurried after him, pausing briefly at her desk to grab her mobile phone and handbag.

'So what's the plan?' She asked, as she chased him down the corridor.

'On Saturday evening Deborah – the sister-in-law – asked if we'd like to see Thea's room. At the time it didn't seem relevant. With any luck she'll still be able to let us in.'

'Technically we should be asking Roger. He's the next of kin.'

'I know, but then we'll run the risk of him saying no, and by the time we get in there it will no doubt have disappeared. Even if he had no part in the girls' deaths he probably wouldn't relish the idea of us poking around in his sister's diary. I don't know whether Carla kept one when we were younger, but if she did I don't imagine it cast me in a particularly flattering light.'

Rebecca raised her eyebrows. 'Really?'

'Lies, of course, all lies,' he replied, in mock seriousness.

'Of course.'

'Would have stood her in good stead though,' he added, as the lift arrived. 'That's what she gets paid to do these days.'

It took a moment for the penny to drop. When it did, Rebecca laughed. Carla was an estate agent.

His own daughter might only be ten, but Lawrence had seen enough teenage bedrooms during his twenty years in the Met to have some idea of the norm for a sixteen-year-old girl. Thea's bedroom didn't fall into that category. The wallpaper, curtains and carpet – which Lawrence usually ruled out of any posthumous character assessment of a minor given the potential for parental control – were relatively nondescript, and considerably more contemporary than the carpet in the downstairs hallway. But the posters that had been superimposed on the walls' subtle wisteria design were not the selection of actors, singers, art prints or antiestablishment propaganda he would have expected to see, but animal prints: dolphins, rabbits, polar bears.

Elise had already grown out of the cute furry animal phase – the latest addition to her bedroom walls had been the iconic image of Audrey Hepburn gazing in the window of Tiffany's – and Lawrence surmised that Thea had been either besotted with animals or young for her age. The plethora of ornaments and soft toys around the room lent credence to the latter. The windowsill was crammed with fairy figurines and Russian dolls, and the substantial shelf above the bed was overflowing with Beanie Babies, stacked three or four deep. Several teddies sat propped up against the cushions on the bed, one considerably more threadbare than the others.

Whilst the distribution of posters on the walls was relatively sparse, the mirrored concertina doors of the built-in wardrobe had been almost completely obscured by a patchwork of post cards, animal pictures, wrapping paper and magazine pages. There wasn't another mirror visible anywhere in the room, and Lawrence wondered whether Thea's illness had culminated in an aversion to her own reflection.

Leaving Rebecca to search through the books on the shelves by the bed, he sat at the pinewood desk and reached to open the top drawer. Not unlike that in his study at home, this held a myriad of stationery essentials: stapler, hole punch, paper clips, rubber bands, glue, highlighter pens, erasers. The items had been neatly – one might even say neurotically – arranged in sections, and in boxes within sections, in a desk-tidy tray. The tray didn't perfectly fit the drawer, and the space that ran alongside it was filled with sticky fixers, Blu tack, hole reinforcers and the like, all carefully stored in their original packaging. There was nothing concealed beneath the tray, and Lawrence moved on to the next drawer down.

Like the first, this was immaculately arranged, and contained two piles of notebooks of decreasing size, one stacked at the front, against the drawer's left side, the other, left of centre, against the back. None of these turned out to be a diary, but, to Lawrence's surprise, every single one in the rear pile was an address book. There were seven in total, all brand new. In the nearer pile were notebooks; some ruled, some hardback, one with a faint reproduction of the cover illustration on every page. They all had one thing in common. Like the address books, they were unused.

'Strange.'

'What's that?' Rebecca asked, glancing up from where she was kneeling on the floor.

'She had a drawer full of address books and notebooks that she never used.'

'I used to collect stuff like that too,' Rebecca responded, casually. 'Although I tended to use things and then regret spoiling them.' She returned a book she had been holding to the bookshelf. 'I spent years in the pursuit of perfect handwriting.'

'Did you ever get there?'

'You've seen my writing, what do you reckon?'

Lawrence smiled. As he returned his attention to the drawer, another thought occurred to him.

'You must have kept your addresses somewhere.'

'Yeah, I used to update from one book to another from time to time, and spend hours agonising over the process.' Rebecca flicked through a book. 'But I'd have thought these days kids would keep that kind of information electronically.'

'Perhaps that's why Thea's are all completely untouched.'

'Maybe,' Rebecca concurred. 'Or else she was too much of a perfectionist to risk spoiling them. A lot of anorexics are perfectionists. That's probably one of the reasons they can stick to such a formidable regime.' She rearranged herself so that she was sitting cross-legged. 'She clearly cared about aesthetics. The clothes in the wardrobe are arranged by colour, as are the ring binders over here.'

'What's in those?' Lawrence asked, supposing a diary might not take the traditional form of the hardback book. 'The folders, I mean.'

'School work, by the looks of things. I've not checked them yet, but they're all labelled with different subject names. Do you know whether she had a computer?'

'No,' Lawrence realised, aloud, making a mental note to follow that up as he opened the third desk drawer. At a glance, this appeared to be full of writing paper and notelets – something else he doubted young people had much call for in the digital age. He was about to check between the sealed packets when an exclamation of disgust from Rebecca diverted his attention.

'What?'

She let out a loud sigh that sounded like relief. 'Nothing. I just opened a book and some dried flowers fell out. I thought for a second it was a spider.'

'What sort of flowers?'

'I don't know. Dead ones.'

Given where they were, Lawrence tried to stifle a laugh. 'Well if they've been inside a book for five years plus they'd be hard pressed to still be alive, wouldn't they?'

Rebecca flicked her eyes heavenwards in response to the pun, then held up three delicate, conjoined stalks, each of which supported a head of translucent, overlapping yellow-orange petals. 'Recognise them?'

Lawrence didn't, although that could well have been because they had long since lost their natural form and colour. Pressed flowers struck him as being the botanical equivalent of the Egyptian mummies. Desiccated and shrivelled, a poor replica of their former selves, trapped somewhere between death and decay. Yet, through anthropological association, one had creepy connotations, while the other was viewed as an art form. Yet another example, he supposed, of the egocentric nature of the human condition. According to biologists, all life on Earth descended from a single common ancestor. Lawrence wondered at what evolutionary juncture man had come to believe himself to be superior. In terms of many of the behaviours Lawrence came across in the course of his work, humans compared unfavourably with creatures most considered primitive. Ants and bees looked after their own. People didn't always follow suit.

## Twenty-one

Lawrence was about to switch off his laptop and head home when a knock came at his open office door. He glanced up to see Leighton standing in the doorway.

'Hey,' the pathologist greeted. 'Mikey said you were still about. Figured I might as well drop this off in person.' He waved an envelope file before reaching for one of the chairs scattered about the office and pulling it up to Lawrence's desk so that they were sitting opposite one another. Lawrence spent the few seconds that this activity took trying to place a Mikey, or Michael, with whom he had worked at the Yard. He drew a blank.

'Mikey?'

'Postie.'

'Right,' Lawrence nodded, wondering whether there was anyone in the building Leighton *didn't* know. Probably not. Leighton was definitely one of life's chatters. How much that was down to his sociable nature, and how much it just served as a displacement activity from working, Lawrence wasn't sure. Either way, the end result was much the same.

'Oooh, did I miss out on a field trip?' Leighton asked, reaching for the small evidence bag containing the pressed flowers Rebecca had unearthed that afternoon. He inspected them closely before announcing, '*Prunus serrulata*.'

'What?'

'Japanese cherry.' He returned the bag to the desk. 'Over here it tends to be grafted, so it doesn't bear fruit.'

As a keen gardener – admittedly mostly in his imagination of late, having had little time for the genuine article – Lawrence felt both impressed and put out that Leighton had managed to identify something he hadn't. He had to ask. 'How do you know that?'

'My job. Plants have their part to play in forensics.'

'I know, but usually it's the job of specialist botanists to actually identify things.'

'Ah, I like to go the extra mile,' Leighton replied. Then, obviously sensing Lawrence's scepticism, he laughed, and admitted, 'My Masters' thesis was on forensic botany.'

'Really?'

'Yep.'

'I'll remember that.' Lawrence sat back in his chair. 'So. What's in the folder?'

'A bunch of largely useless DNA profiles – at this stage, anyway – and a fingerprint hit, although I'm not sure whether it's a relevant one.'

'Oh?'

'Does the name Barbara Finnegan mean anything to you?'

Lawrence's eyebrows shot up. 'Barbara Finnegan?'

'Yep.'

'Is she on the database?'

'Yep. DUI.'

'Her prints were on the *diary*?'

'No, the bubble wrap lining the envelope.'

'Ah.'

'Why would that be such a surprise?' Leighton enquired, clearly intrigued.

'She's been dead almost a fortnight. The latest entry in the diary was made last Wednesday.'

'Dead?' Leighton echoed, eyebrows rising, clearly anticipating unnatural causes.

'Not in a relevant way. Stroke.'

'Who is she? Was she, rather.'

'The mother of one of Suki's ex-boyfriends, and of a girl called Thea, who was at school with Suki and Meredith.'

'Interesting,' Leighton responded, tossing the folder into Lawrence's in tray, leaning forwards and resting his forearms along the edge of the desk. 'Which one you gonna start with?'

'Well the girl's dead, so that narrows things down.'

Repetition of the word 'dead' elicited a repeat reaction from Leighton. As he opened his mouth to speak, Lawrence pre-empted him.

'No, no, she wasn't murdered. But Meredith's diaries indicate she and Suki did something to her detriment. The question is whether it was something that might have led her brother to kill.'

'Anyone alive you can ask?'

Lawrence shook his head slightly and held out his hands to express his uncertainty.

'Any other diaries?'

'Thus far we've been through several others and drawn a blank. Supposedly Thea also kept one, but we've had no luck tracking that down.'

'What's the betting whoever sent you that one has it as well?'

Leighton was right. And they now had grounds for arrest, and, by extension, grounds to execute a search. Lawrence reached for the phone.

Roger seemed more surprised than concerned to see Lawrence again so soon. Leaning against the frame of his front door and linking his thumbs through the belt loops of his jeans, he asked how he could help. When Lawrence informed him that he was under arrest on suspicion of Suki's and Meredith's murders, Roger stared at him in what appeared to be genuine shock.

'Merri? What happened to her?'

'You tell me. You were there, weren't you?'

'What?' Roger exclaimed. 'How? How could I possibly have been? I don't even know where she *lived*!'

'We'll discuss that later. In the meantime, DS Palmer will escort you to Scotland Yard. Do you have any objection to our searching your flat?'

'Yes I bloody do! You'll have to get a search warrant before you go poking around in my stuff!'

'Given the circumstances, I don't actually need one.'

'You what?' Roger responded, incredulously. 'You can't just go bursting into people's homes!'

'Actually, we can,' Lawrence responded, levelly. 'And this will be a lot easier if you do as you're told.'

'For who, me or you?'

'Well, I get paid either way, so you work it out.'

Roger looked incensed.

'Ok,' Lawrence concluded, aloud, when the young man didn't immediately reply, standing aside and gesturing for Roger to step out of the flat. Glowering, he complied. Rebecca took his arm and led him up the steps from the basement flat, towards the unmarked police car waiting at the kerb. Lawrence watched until they were safely in the car, then turned to Leighton, who was shaking out a bodysuit.

'Right, your turn. I'll be out here.'

'You'll have a long wait,' Leighton remarked, stepping into the suit. 'You might as well head back to grill the guy. I'll get you what I can by morning.'

'I was hoping we might be able to get our hands on Thea's diary sooner than that.'

'Assuming I find it, I'll need to check it over before you do.'

Lawrence sighed. 'All right. But call me if you do find it. Or anything else.'

''Course.'

'You don't look convinced.'

'He seemed pretty stunned by the news about Meredith,' Leighton observed.

'I don't buy that.'

'Because you know something I don't, or because you don't want to?'

'I beg your pardon?'

'As far as I'm aware, all we have to connect him to Meredith is three fingerprints belonging to his mother, which don't come with a date stamp,' Leighton pointed out, thrusting an arm into a paper sleeve. 'Given that his sister used to be friends with both the girls concerned, and that Roger dated one of them, it's not inconceivable that, over time, the envelope passed from Barbara to one of her kids, and from there to Meredith or Suki. A lot of people recycle that kind of thing.'

'Given the time period concerned that's rather a stretch, isn't it?' Lawrence responded, neglecting the fact that Suki and Roger had remained in touch until just days before her death.

'Maybe, but that's hardly going to stand up in court,' Leighton answered, zipping up the bodysuit.

'Obviously not. That's why we're here,' Lawrence returned, shortly. 'Now, if you're done second-guessing my job, perhaps you could get on with your own?'

'I'm sorry, I thought offering advice on the basis of evidence I'd examined *was* my job,' Leighton responded, curtly, before bending to retrieve his bag. 'Just because you don't like what I have to say doesn't make me wrong.' He stepped into the flat and, without another word, closed the door behind himself.

Lawrence bit back an expletive, turning to climb the steps to the street. He was accustomed to interactions with Leighton winding him up – usually on account of the young man's laid-back attitude to his work – but he wasn't used to feeling that way because Leighton was *right*. The evidence against Roger was tenuous at best. And, in the absence of any other obvious suspects, Lawrence had to admit he probably had been guilty of building it up to be more than it was. All the same, it wasn't Leighton's place to challenge him on that. With a sigh, he headed for his car. He would clear the air with the pathologist later. Right now he wanted some answers from Roger. Starting with the one he had conveniently avoided answering earlier that day: what he had been doing for the duration of Wednesday afternoon.

Roger hadn't spoken on the journey from Wembley to Scotland Yard, his eyes tracing the ever-changing view from the car window. Rebecca had kept half an eye on him from the passenger seat while making small talk with the uniformed police constable at the wheel. Name, Kevin; age, 27; ambition, to follow Rebecca's footsteps into CID and the serious crime unit. Like so many others. Rebecca had lost count of the number of times she'd been asked for advice on how to get there, lost count of the number of times she'd disappointed people by telling them that, at least in her experience, it had been more a matter of luck than judgement. Of being in the right place when a short-handed DCI needed assistance. It almost made her feel as if she should apologise for her own success.

On arrival at the Yard, Roger muttered the bare minimum in response to the custody sergeant's questions and, once booked in, followed Rebecca to an interview room in silence. She fetched him a cup of tea, and herself a coffee, and was on her way back to the room when she saw Lawrence heading down the corridor towards her.

'That was quick.'

'Leighton's going to get back to us first thing tomorrow. So we'll go through what we can now and then adjourn.'

The news came as a relief. It was already after ten, and Rebecca was tired; the idea of waiting hours for more information wasn't appealing.

'Ready?'

She nodded.

Lawrence opened the door to the interview room and held it for her. Inside, she set the plastic cups in her hands down before taking a seat. Lawrence joined her as she pushed the tea towards Roger, who mumbled his thanks, eyes on the table. He looked close to tears and Rebecca felt for him. Whatever he might or might not have done didn't change the fact he had just lost his mother. She hadn't a clue how she would cope with losing hers.

'Right,' Lawrence began. 'Could you start by running through what you did on Monday evening again?'

'I had dinner with my aunt and uncle. He drove me home. I got back about half ten. After that, I watched some TV and went to bed.' Roger didn't raise his gaze from the table, his hands clasped tightly in his lap.

'Alone?'

'Yes.'

'And Wednesday afternoon?'

'I met with the vicar at my mother's church, then went home.'

'What time was the meeting?'

'Half one.'

'Until?'

'Um – I dunno – three, three-fifteen.'

'And you went straight home from there?'

'Yes.'

'Can anybody substantiate that?'

'No.' By this time Roger's voice was almost a whisper. 'I didn't *do* anything,' he added, weakly, his voice trembling. He looked up, his eyes wet. 'I don't understand why you think I did.'

'We'll come onto that later.'

'I still cared for her!' He protested. 'She was my best friend! I don't – I don't even –' he shook his head, bowing his head.

'Who?' Lawrence enquired. 'Suki?'

Roger nodded.

'Did you see a lot of her?'

'Yuh. She came in – most days – when she was working.' He sniffed.

'When did you last see her?'

'Um –' he frowned in thought. 'Wednesday, I think. Two weeks ago.'

'Did you hear from her after that?'

'No.'

'She didn't get in touch to see how you were after your mother died?'

He shook his head.

'I thought you said she was your best friend.'

'She was, but –' Roger shrugged. 'She didn't – what with –' he paused, drawing a deep, unsteady breath. 'She couldn't always get away. Her boyfriend was – he –he had problems. I knew that, so –' he trailed off with another shrug.

Rebecca wondered whether this was a prelude to his trying to lay responsibility for Suki's death at Justin's door. She stole a glance at her superior, eyebrows raised. He met her eyes, and nodded an answer to her unspoken question.

Rebecca rested her forearms on the table. 'Did she talk about him much?'

'Yes.'

'What did she say?'

'That she was scared, and that she couldn't risk leaving him – in case –' he faltered. 'I guess you know he's ill. Mentally, I mean.'

'Yes,' Rebecca confirmed. 'Are you saying she wanted to leave him?'

Roger shrugged. 'I think she might've been a bit overwhelmed. It's a lot to cope with, and by all accounts he was pretty unpredictable.'

'Do you think she was scared of him?'

Roger blinked. 'I didn't – I'm not suggesting that he – I didn't mean –' he stammered. 'I don't know what went on between them, just that she worried about him a lot. Outside of work she never seemed to have time for anything else.'

Rebecca added two and two. Given what Petra had told them a few days earlier, she suspected Suki had used Justin as an excuse to avoid committing to social arrangements with Roger. Anything she had told him could therefore be taken with the proverbial pinch of salt. Whether Roger had any idea of the reality of the situation, they might never know. But Rebecca suspected that, whether or not he had been responsible for Suki's death, he, like many others, saw Justin as an easy target onto whom to shift the blame. Then again, she reflected, maybe the obvious scapegoat wasn't a scapegoat at all. Thus far, they had very little evidence either way.

## Twenty-two

Lawrence entered his office shortly after eight on Tuesday morning to find Leighton reclining so far back in an adjustable chair that he was closer to horizontal than vertical. He had his feet up on Lawrence's desk, and was leafing through a magazine that rested in his lap.

'Morning,' Lawrence greeted, cordially, hoping his arrival would prompt Leighton to move his feet. It didn't.

'Howdy,' Leighton muttered, focus still on the magazine.

'Something interesting?'

'Nah, don't think so.' He looked up. 'I was just trying to join some dots.' He indicated the timelines, crime-scene photographs, names and other data mounted on the wall.

'Meaning what?' Lawrence asked, setting his laptop bag on the desk and sitting down. 'You've got nothing else for me?'

'Yes and no. I found your diary, but thus far I've nothing else. No conveniently bloodstained clothes or crime-scene trophies.'

'Ah, to be in a TV drama.'

Leighton smiled. 'I've sent a bunch of samples to the lab, so I might have something for you by the end of the week.' He reached down into the bag beneath his chair and brought out a hardback A4 book in a clear plastic bag. 'In the meantime, you guys can get busy reading.' He slid it onto the desk.

'Thanks. I'll ask Becky to do that. I've a meeting with the AC at nine.'

'Lucky you,' Leighton remarked, sarcastically, returning his attention to the wall. After a moment his eyes narrowed slightly.

'What?'

The pathologist looked down at the magazine with a frown, flicking back a few pages. 'Am I right in thinking Justin's brother is a member of Quarkonia?'

'That's right.'

'They were playing at KoKo last Wednesday,' he held up the magazine to display an advert for the event. 'That's only a matter of minutes from Meredith's flat.'

'I know, I spoke to him on Saturday evening. He was with his band all afternoon, sound checking and giving magazine and fanzine interviews. After that, they all went to get something to eat and had a few drinks in a local pub ahead of the show.'

'Are you sure he was with them *all* afternoon?'

'As far as I can reasonably ascertain. He says so, and so do his band mates. I tracked a couple of them down on Sunday.' Lawrence turned his chair to face the wall of information. 'And they weren't the only ones in the area, most of our suspects were at the gig that evening. Alec even *lives* between Somers Town and KoKo, and he has no alibi for most of Wednesday afternoon – supposedly he was alone at home – but what motive he might have for killing either girl I don't know. I also chased up the other members of Justin's band. The bass player and the drummer claim they were together at the time – whether or not that's true is anybody's guess. And we've still no idea of Floyd's whereabouts.'

Leighton nodded thoughtfully.

'That reminds me, did you get an ID on those pills from his bedroom?'

Leighton's eyebrows pulled into a frown. 'Was that not included in the bundle of stuff I left for you on Friday afternoon?'

'It may well have been,' Lawrence admitted. 'What were they?'

'Morphine. Not a brand available on prescription in this country, so presumably purchased online or from – how shall we say – a well-connected friend. Although given that he had an astrocytoma the size of a golf ball I can't say I blame him.'

'A golf ball?' Lawrence exclaimed.

'They can get a lot bigger.'

'Well I suppose given the circumstances we can overlook the fact he was in possession of a controlled drug.'

'And I wouldn't spend too much time worrying about where he was on Wednesday afternoon, either. If the state he was in last Tuesday morning was anything to go by, I think he's unlikely to have been running around killing people.'

Lawrence felt inclined to agree. He regarded the information on the wall for a moment before asking, 'Could it have been a woman?'

'Depends on the woman. The degree of damage to Meredith's mouth and jaw would've taken a lot of strength,' Leighton said, before observing, 'Theirs seems to be a very small world. Did her boyfriend know Suki?'

'Not more than in passing, as far as we've been able to establish. Otherwise he'd be high on my list – he hasn't had much good to say about Meredith.'

'Then why waste time being with her? Surely nobody's *that* good in bed?'

'And there's my cue,' Rebecca quipped as she entered the office, armed with her usual morning coffee. Leighton tipped his head back to bid her good morning and lost his balance, nearly falling out of the chair. Lawrence stifled a laugh; Rebecca managed to contain herself only long enough to put the coffee down on Lawrence's desk, dissolving into giggles immediately thereafter. Leighton carefully righted himself before getting to his feet, looking mildly abashed but no less cheerful.

'That concludes my part in this morning's entertainment, so I'll be getting off.' He retrieved the magazine from where it had fallen on the floor and held it out to Rebecca, saying, 'Yours, I believe?' before reaching to reclaim his bag and making for the door. Then he stopped abruptly and turned back. 'Call me, won't you? If you manage to make two and two make four?'

The design on the hardback book in Rebecca's hands reminded her of the stained glass designs of Louis Comfort Tiffany. The turquoise background was criss-crossed haphazardly with uneven black and sliver lines, and splashed irregularly with embossed silver and blue flowers. The black margins down the cover's edges were matched by one through the centre, as if to divide the image into panes. Rebecca loved Tiffany's work, especially the windows, and Elliot had once promised to take her to see the collection at New York's Metropolitan Museum. He'd even gone to the trouble of tracking down a copy of an out-of-print poster of her favourite design. With a sigh, she turned the book over. Perhaps unsurprisingly, the words 'Tiffany Magnolia' were printed beneath the manufacturer's name.

Turning back to the front cover, she released the magnetic clasp holding the book shut and flicked through its faintly lined pages. The paper had yellowed slightly with age, and bore the worn, grimy look of incessant handling. She wondered how many people before her had leafed through it, and how Thea might have felt about the fact.

Besides a few brief attempts as a teenager, Rebecca herself hadn't kept a diary since childhood. Her parents had encouraged her to do so to document her early summer holidays, and had allowed her to select postcards to accompany her brief reports of trips to museums, monuments and parks. Re-reading them years later, they had contained precious little detail about the main subjects, the focus leaning towards the peculiar miscellany that had seemed important to her at the time: the favourite toy her father had had to rescue from a stream after she dropped it into a weir on a nature reserve; the chocolate cake with the marzipan motif in a museum café; the brightly coloured lizard on a London street that had turned out to be a discarded Haribo sweet. Looking back, she suspected her parents had come up with the idea more to keep her and Angela quiet for half an hour every evening – or perhaps to improve their writing skills – than out of any real belief it might preserve worthwhile memories for posterity.

Rebecca wouldn't have minded others having access to either those writings or the few she had penned since, because none of what she had committed to paper had documented her thoughts or feelings in any real sense. She wasn't sure she would know how to begin. In fact, she was fairly sure she wouldn't. On the handful of occasions she had considered keeping a journal – calling it a diary had seemed too much of a cliché – during her adolescent Che Guevara phase, she had never made it past a few lines describing the day's events. Maybe she just wasn't much of a writer. Maybe her thoughts hadn't seemed profound or insightful enough to be worth chronicling. Or maybe she just hadn't felt the need to write down what was going on in her head when she could talk about it with her sister or her friends.

And perhaps therein lay the answer. Could it be that personal diaries – as opposed to those of a historical or political nature – were kept by those who had nobody to talk *to*? Maybe they weren't so much a record of a life lived as a testament of loneliness.

'Any joy?' Lawrence asked as he returned to the office shortly after eleven.

Rebecca nodded. 'From what I've read it sounds as though neither Suki nor Meredith was much of a friend to Thea. Or, if you do call them friends, they were the sort that render enemies redundant.'

'Ah.'

'Yep. Either Thea was a fantasist or they were grade-A bitches. I'm not surprised she started taking diet pills with some of the comments documented in here.'

'Is that what she attributed it to?'

'Pretty much.' Rebecca brushed a hair out of her eye. 'How'd the meeting go?'

'Fine. Are you ready, or do you want some more time?'

'I'm good to go.'

'Sure?'

'Yep.' She moved to stand, reaching for the diary, which was now annotated with Post-it notes.

'Let's go.'

Rebecca completed the necessary formalities before giving Roger her undivided attention. He looked tired, his expression sullen, eyes on the interview room table. Rebecca stood Thea's diary on end, cover facing him. 'I'm guessing you had some idea of what you were going to find in here before you actually opened it,' she began. 'I can't imagine you were oblivious to what was going on at the time, just that it was convenient to ignore it.' She opened the diary at the first Post-it.

'Maybe you could join us,' she read, aloud. 'I'd love to see you in a cocktail dress. If you met a blind man you might even pull. Blow jobs are only three calories, you know. And at least you wouldn't have the dilemma of spit or swallow – it'd be a natural reflex.' She returned her attention to Roger. 'Shall I go on? Remind you of some of the other vicious things your first love had to say to your little sister?'

Roger didn't move.

'Did you wonder how many times your mother had read and re-read those pages over the years?' Rebecca continued. 'How she felt? Whether she blamed you?' She raised her eyebrows. 'Or did you already know the answer to that one?'

Lawrence watched Roger keenly. His expression was set, every muscle in his face pulled taught.

'Not that it makes any difference now,' Rebecca went on. 'It's too late for apologies. Too late for your mother. Too late for Thea.' She sat back in her chair. 'I imagine that makes the guilt even worse. Did it help to know Meredith felt the same?'

'How would I know how Merri felt?' Roger asked, his voice strained.

'Well you read her diary, didn't you? Before you posted it in to us.'

'What?'

'Your mother's fingerprints were all over the envelope.'

'My mother's fingerprints?' Roger exclaimed. 'That's ludicrous! How would you even *have* her fingerprints?'

'She didn't tell you she got done for drink driving, then,' Rebecca concluded. 'I suppose that's not surprising, she was probably embarrassed. Mortified, even.'

Roger's expression confirmed the first of these assumptions.

'So. Did it help?'

'What?'

'Knowing how Meredith felt about the way she and Suki behaved.'

'Why would it? It wasn't going to change anything.'

'And killing them did?'

Roger opened his mouth to protest, but Rebecca cut him short. 'And don't waste my time denying it, we have a witness statement that puts you in Mornington Terrace the night Suki died.'

The latter wasn't strictly true; all they actually had was Aaron's account that *somebody* had been in the flat with Suki at a time when both Justin and Floyd were elsewhere. That it had been Roger seemed like the bet with the best odds.

'Just because I was there doesn't mean I killed her!'

'Oh, so you *were* there now?' Rebecca queried. 'Last night you hadn't seen her since before your mother died.'

'I was scared you'd think it was me that –' he stopped. 'I didn't hurt her, I just went over to talk. I –' he hesitated. 'I just wanted to know she was sorry.'

'Suki? Was *sorry* even in her vocabulary?'

Roger flinched and Lawrence guessed Rebecca had hit a nerve.

'Well?' She pushed, when Roger didn't reply.

'I didn't kill her,' he asserted.

'I'm sure you didn't *intend* to kill her,' Rebecca returned. 'I can believe you just wanted to talk, wanted an apology. But you didn't get one, did you? So what then?'

No response.

'What then?'

Roger shrugged.

'You were angry and upset, so in the heat of the moment you lashed out. I can understand that. I think most people would.'

Eyes cast down, he shook his head.

'What about Meredith? I know she was sorry, that much is clear from her diaries. Was that not enough?'

Roger shook his head again, rather desperately this time. 'I didn't –' he began, his voice shaking.

'What, she just let you rummage through her belongings and walk off with her diary?'

'No! I took it after that. When she was – when she was – already dead.'

Rebecca's expression was incredulous. 'You're telling me you turned up, found a body on the floor, didn't bother to notify anybody but stuck around long enough to find the diary? Seriously?'

'Of course not! After that!'

'After what?'

'After she'd – you know – gone.'

'Gone where? The morgue?'

Roger winced. 'Yes.'

'Well you must be the invisible man.'

His brow furrowed. 'What?'

'The flat was under surveillance,' Rebecca informed him. 'Yet you somehow managed to get in, help yourself to Meredith's belongings and get out without anyone seeing you. MI6 will be wanting a word.'

Roger swallowed hard but didn't offer any kind of defence.

'She guessed, didn't she? As soon as she saw you, she knew exactly what had happened to Suki. I'm sure she promised to keep it to herself, pleaded for your forgiveness, begged for her life. It must have been satisfying to hear that from the girl who once deliberately misquoted Coco Chanel.' Rebecca flicked to another page in the diary. 'Dress shabbily and they'll remember you're fat. Dress impeccably and they'll remember you're ugly.'

She closed the book. 'Then again, she was clearly just following Suki's lead, so –'

'Her choice, though, wasn't it?' Roger cut in.

'And yours,' Rebecca replied. 'You chose Suki too. You betrayed Thea.'

'I didn't *know*,' he protested, his voice breaking.

'You didn't look.'

Roger drew a long, shaky breath. 'She was like two different people,' he said, brokenly. 'I only knew the other one.'

'Until last Monday.'

'She laughed,' he admitted. 'When I asked if – if she was sorry. She *laughed*!'

'Your best friend.'

'I thought it was her boyfriend who was supposed to have the split personality, but she was – she was –' he shook his head. 'I didn't even *recognise* her! She consoled me after Thea died! She held my hand at her funeral! After she'd made Thea's life a living hell! And she didn't even *care*!'

'So you hit her.'

Wordlessly, he nodded, his eyes wet with tears.

Rebecca didn't respond, no doubt waiting to see what he might add given the opportunity.

Roger sniffed. 'I didn't mean to,' he whispered. 'I didn't really know – it all happened so fast – I just –' he stopped. 'It didn't seem like me. It was like I was watching. From a distance.' He rubbed the tears from his eyes. 'I didn't know what to do!'

Rebecca passed him a packet of tissues. He mumbled his thanks, fumbling with the plastic wrapper, hands shaking, eventually managing to pull one out.

'What about Meredith?' Rebecca asked, after some thirty seconds had ticked by.

Roger shook his head slightly. 'I don't know. I didn't mean –' he sighed. 'I had to see her. I just *had* to. I don't know why. I wouldn't have –' he paused. 'It sounds ridiculous, but I just didn't think. I didn't think she'd realise.' He sniffed again. 'She got hysterical. I couldn't shut her up, and I just – lost it with her.' He twisted the tissue between his fingers. 'I took the diary because I never got a chance to ask.'

'About Thea?'

'Yes.'

'But why post it to us?'

'I thought someone might realise it was missing. And I wasn't named in there. Other people were.'

Rebecca nodded.

'I didn't mean it,' Roger asserted. 'I didn't. I just –' he shrugged, rather hopelessly. Several seconds passed before he looked up. 'What's going to happen to me?'

'I don't know. That'll be up to the courts.'

'Funny how justice doesn't cut both ways,' Roger observed, bitterly. 'Those bitches killed my sister and they didn't have to worry about so much as a caution.'

'They didn't actually kill her.'

'Well it's their fault she's dead. Comes to the same thing, really, doesn't it?'

Good question, Lawrence thought, the old school-yard rhyme about sticks and stones coming to mind. He wondered how many people a year words did kill. What percentage of those deaths might arguably be considered manslaughter. There would undoubtedly be those who believed Roger's recent actions had secured justice – somewhat belatedly – for his sister. Lawrence disagreed. Retribution was not equal to justice. But the fact remained that, according to the laws of the land, Suki and Meredith would never have been held accountable for their behaviour, making Thea a silent statistic. How many more were out there?

## A note from Sadie

Thank you for choosing to read my third book. If you have enjoyed *Sticks and Stones,* I would be very grateful if you would consider rating it, or even writing a review – just a few words can make a difference in helping to persuade others to give my books a try!

Made in the USA
Monee, IL
12 May 2023

33599855R00152